P9-EFI-909

FLIGHT
RISK

FLIGHT RISK

A NOVEL

JENNIFER FENN

ROARING BROOK PRESS · NEW YORK

Published by Roaring Brook Press
Roaring Brook Press is a division of Holtzbrinck Publishing
Holdings Limited Partnership
175 Fifth Avenue, New York, NY 10010

fiercereads.com

Library of Congress Cataloging-in-Publication Data

Names: Fenn, Jennifer, author.
Title: Flight risk : a novel / Jennifer Fenn.
Description: First edition. | New York : Roaring Brook Press, 2017. | Summary: Having
    grown up in a trailer park with an overworked mother and attention-deficit disorder,
    Robert Kelley, now eighteen, steals—and crashes—three airplanes before being caught.
Identifiers: LCCN 2017018482 (print) | LCCN 2016038432 (ebook) |
    ISBN 9781626727601 (hardback) | ISBN 9781626727595 (ebook)
Subjects: | CYAC: Stealing—Fiction. | Airplanes—Fiction. | Single-parent families—
    Fiction. | Attention-deficit hyperactivity disorder—Fiction. | Runaways—Fiction. |
    BISAC: YOUNG ADULT FICTION / Action & Adventure / General. | YOUNG
    ADULT FICTION / Social Themes / Runaways.
Classification: LCC PZ7.1.F48 Fli 2017 (ebook) | LCC PZ7.1.F48 (print) |
    DDC [Fic]—dc23
LC record available at https://lccn.loc.gov/2017018482

Our books may be purchased in bulk for promotional, educational, or business use. Please
contact your local bookseller or the Macmillan Corporate and Premium Sales Department at
(800) 221-7945 ext. 5442 or by e-mail at MacmillanSpecialMarkets@macmillan.com.

First edition, 2017
Book design by Andrew Arnold
Printed in the United States of America

1 3 5 7 9 10 8 6 4 2

For Brian and Zadie

Life is locomotion. If you're not moving, you're not living.
—THE FLASH
The Flash (New 52, Vol. 1, #1)

For once you have tasted flight you will walk the
earth with your eyes turned skywards, for there you
have been and there you will long to return.
—LEONARDO DA VINCI

PROLOGUE

From *The Beginning Pilot's Flight Guide* (p. 14):

ATTITUDE + POWER = PERFORMANCE

Robert Jackson Kelley stole his last plane on a cloudy night, the moon casting hazy light through the gray-gauze sky. He crouched in the trees, his legs cramped, pausing only to be sure the cops hadn't beaten him to the hangar. This time he had to move fast. No rummaging for food. No thumbing through the manuals or pacing around the planes, admiring their gleaming wings and sleek bodies like diamond rings in a jeweler's case. Asking to be smashed and grabbed. All he needed was to pick a plane. Get into the air.

He had to stay focused.

He bolted for the building, arms pumping, sharp pain puncturing his ribs—probably bruised or cracked from his prior botched airborne escape. The cold numbed his stiff fingers. The screwdriver he'd pocketed the last time he broke into Tomkins Airstrip thumped against his leg as he ran.

He was eighteen years old.

Nowhere to go but up.

Yellow police tape fluttered across the door he'd jangled, bullied, and finally kicked in three nights before, when he'd stolen his second plane from this very airstrip. The door hadn't been replaced, the splintered wood still gaping like he'd left it.

Perhaps they were preserving evidence, but it felt to Robert like they were welcoming him in.

He stepped over the tape, but he knew he hadn't crossed the finish line just yet.

He scrambled for the hangar door and pulled it up, rattling on its track. Cold air rushed by him into the cavernous room, chilling his clammy skin.

The Cirrus SR22 wasn't what he'd flown before, but it was close enough. Its Garmin system was just as simple. The plane's nose was tipped in sea-green paint. And the cockpit was unlocked, a sign that this plane was his as sure as if his name had been printed on its keys. He slid into the pilot's seat, shut the door behind him.

Robert had already decided on Canada for his final destination, but he had sudden second thoughts. What about somewhere warmer, where he could surf year-round? This plane could fly him to Puerto Rico. Jamaica. The Bahamas. He didn't really care, as long as he made it to a new island. Anywhere but Yannatok. He'd torched his bridges in Washington.

He rapped on the plane's control panel, drumming a rhythm as fast as his heartbeat. He knew how important it was for him to hurry, but his churning stomach stalled him. His fingers slipped over the screwdriver's cold tip.

He thought he'd seen on TV that Puerto Rico had white sands and Bermuda had pink. Maybe he'd see the difference from 10,000 feet. When he got there, he could land this last flight on the beach and leave it behind, waves lapping at the wings.

Then he changed his mind. He'd stick to his plan. Canada was the way to go. Only fifty miles north. Safer. Landlocked. He'd had enough of islands. He jimmied the screwdriver into the ignition.

Two days before, the world had learned the name of the kid who could not be caught. The sheriff had released his soon-to-be-notorious mug shot, and an ambitious graffiti artist had emblazoned the Yannatok Bridge with tall red letters, spindly stalks stretching skyward: *WWRF*. Robert's mother drove past it on her way to the 911 dispatch center; Robert saw it from the vacation home he'd broken into. *WWRF.* Lots of environmentalists on the West Coast. *World Wildlife something something?* Some riff on *WTF?* The sheriff delegated the cleanup to his deputy, and eventually someone from the Parks Department power-washed the letters away, dripping crimson into the bay. None of them figured it out. None of them knew how every time the tagger had paused, the wind blowing red flecks back into his hair, he'd gazed at the sky, looking for a star that moved.

Where would Robert fly?

Robert Jackson Kelley's Facebook page—which wasn't his, and was in fact created and maintained by Scott Adams of Levittown, New Jersey, after the second stolen plane made the news—boasted the mug shot that ran in the *Seattle Times*, photos of planes Robert had never flown, and 100,961 friends. Goth kids, frat boys, preps, tattooed bikers, the odd soccer mom, from South Africa and Amsterdam and every US state. Kids from Yannatok High whom Robert had sat next to in study hall and never talked to. Scott Adams himself was a high school sophomore and his own Facebook page hadn't been updated in months, its stale *Family Guy* memes reaching only forty-eight friends. On the night Robert stole his last plane, he had no idea that his Facebook status was a flippant "See ya, suckers!"

Robert Jackson Kelley had 100,961 virtual friends. But when he was on the run from the police, crouching in a vacant house or in the woods, plotting his next migration, the only person he had wished he could call was his mom.

* * *

This last plane flight, Robert knew as he huddled inside the aircraft like a cave-dwelling bear, might not work out like the others had. He knew the basics of landing from searching the Internet, and the simulators had been preparation enough: slow down, extend flaps, turn downwind, power back, level off. No tower to approve his nonexistent flight plan. Googling *Cessna* back when his only flights had been the simulated kind had yielded all kinds of useful diagrams, along with shots of six-year-olds at the controls, playing pilot. But in his gut he knew that twice he had not landed but crashed, and another crash could take him out. Or even worse: a crash could crack his spine, sever his legs. Even just breaking them would leave him helpless and bleeding in a field, or crawling through the spruce trees. Or stuck in the wreckage like an animal with a snared limb.

From the pilot's seat of this last plane, he smiled despite the pain in his neck, his chest, the rash of seat belt burn. Then Robert tweaked the screwdriver until the engine fired.

He'd land this one.

Or die trying.

ACT I

PREPARE FOR DEPARTURE

From *The Beginning Pilot's Flight Guide* **(p. 13):**

Perhaps the most important influence on a student pilot's safety is the flying habits of his flight instructor, both during instruction and as observed by students when conducting flight lessons and procedures. Students consider their flight instructor to be a model of skill whose habits they consciously or unconsciously emulate.

"No, wait. Here's what happened.

"He left a Dum Dum at each crash. Root beer a lot of the time, sometimes sour apple, sometimes cherry.

"Oh my God, it was hilarious—those cops, the sheriff, their guts flopping over their belts, chunks of wrecked plane smoking all over the place, the metal all twisted. Robert Jackson Kelley long gone. And the cops stuck with those Dum Dums and no clue how to find him."

When Robert was six, he decided sleep was a big, boring waste of time and to do as little of it as possible. He didn't have a bedtime, though sometimes his mother invented one. *Eight o'clock. In five minutes. Next commercial.* Deb would tuck him into bed before leaving for the late shift. Robert would wait until her car had clattered away, then he'd slide out the screen door, quiet as a cat burglar. The Kelleys' trailer hunkered down between two others on a sparsely green lot. The trailer had been Deb's inheritance, a double-wide streaked mossy green and moldy gray, a metal stub where the hitch used to be. Behind their patchy yard, dense Douglas firs and cedars hid bears and raccoons. They had a rusting mailbox, a bannerless flagpole to tie his dog Hulk's leash to, and a porch with cinder-block steps. They weren't going anywhere.

Hulk knew not to bark as they ran circles around the

small lot in the dark. Robert was Spider-Man, web-slinging up the flagpole. He was Batman, the front step his racing Batmobile. He'd aim an imaginary gun at the full moon and dive for cover from enemy fire. He never stuck with one character for very long. He and Hulk skirted the edge of the firs, but stopped short of the thick brambles. He would poke a stick through the branches, fearing and hoping that some creature would latch on.

He put himself to bed when he decided.

When Deb worked nights, she'd pull in just as the school bus was shuddering up to the trailer park, and he'd pretend not to see her wave hello and goodbye. A dozen new mosquito bites would be the only evidence of his stolen playtime. On weekends, he'd bound from his bed and back outside, while Deb slept off eight hours at the Lower Coastal Counties Emergency Response Center. Robert would built ramps out of old two-by-fours and send battered Tonka trucks flying into the dirt. He chased Hulk in tight loops between his trailer and his neighbor's. The Pacific Northwest's constant fog cooled his skin and dampened his hair. On weekends Deb emerged sometime after ten, phone pressed between her ear and her shoulder, juggling her first coffee and cigarette.

She never caught him.

One Sunday morning Robert was throwing Hulk a graying tennis ball when a police cruiser pulled in. Gravel bounced off the flagpole. Robert hastily retrieved the ball and knelt down to scratch behind the dog's twitching ears. An officer ambled out of the car. Robert inspected the dirt; even though he couldn't think of his crime, he for some reason felt guilty.

"Good morning. I'm Officer Holt." The man bent down and stuck out his hand. Robert tentatively shook it, his scrawny arm flapping like an unhinged gate. Morning light winked off the officer's badge. "That's a fine-looking dog you got there. A beagle?"

"He's a mutt. I picked him from the pound."

Holt patted Hulk's head. The officer had dark eyes, a clean-shaven face, and closely cut hair. A coffee and pine smell. "I bet he's part beagle."

"He's real fast. His name's Hulk," Robert said. He'd christened Hulk himself, though the dog didn't weigh more than twenty-five pounds and hightailed away from squirrels.

"I have a dog, too. Name's Copper," Holt offered.

Robert's mother ducked her head out the screen door. She coughed and rasped, "Everything all right?"

"Got a report of a bear back here," the officer called. He straightened up. "Getting a little brave around the trailers."

Deb shrugged. Her hair had been hastily rubber-banded back. She fished a cigarette from her sweatshirt pocket and stepped onto the porch. The door rattled shut. "Haven't seen anything." Then she added, as she always did to people in uniform, his teachers, anyone important, "I work for dispatch."

"Do you?" Officer Holt said. "Then we're practically co-workers." Holt glanced toward the thick spruces, the wall of Douglas firs. "I'm glad he's not in your trash cans, making a mess. We're going to try to get him out of here before he does."

"How will you catch him?" Robert asked. He hoped they wouldn't shoot the bear. He imagined Officer Holt emerging from the woods with a net slung over his shoulder, the bear glowering through the diamond-shaped gaps.

"We're going to lure him into a trap," the cop announced. "And then sedate him and drive him into the mountains, where he won't bother anybody. I'm going to set the trap today."

Robert had no idea what *sedate* meant. He pictured Holt and the bear wrestling, crashing and rolling through the trees.

Deb shrugged again. "Not bothering me." She lit her cigarette, cupping the flame with her long fingers. Robert wondered how much older than Officer Holt his mother was. They'd had dinner at Red Lobster to celebrate her birthday last year, but Robert had only eaten the cheesy biscuits, and his mom had gotten a doggie bag for his fish

15

sticks. And any time he asked his mom how old she was, she shushed his question away.

"They're happier in the mountains anyway. Here"— Officer Holt gestured at the trailers—"there's too much trouble to get into." He retrieved a bulky sack from the backseat and saluted Robert. Robert quickly reimagined the animal's capture, this time with himself tagging along. Maybe Holt would need him to wriggle into a hollow log or narrow cave.

"Can I come?" Robert asked. He raised his hand, like he was in school instead of his own backyard.

Holt didn't laugh. He seemed to actually consider Robert's question before replying. "Thanks, but I think this is a one-man job. But you give me a call if you see that bear, young man. And take good care of that dog."

Robert nodded and returned the salute. Officer Holt stomped into the woods. Robert lingered in the yard until Deb called him in to take a bath. He scrubbed quickly, then ran back to the yard, hair still wet, but the police car was gone.

The woods spooked Holt.

Every rustle, every snapping twig sent his head swiveling. His fingers brushed habitually against his gun. Drawing it in his frazzled state would be a mistake; he might end up

16

pointing it at a hunter, a camper, a kid. Not the best way for a rookie officer to make friends.

He was used to drunks, speeding tickets, noise complaints. The occasional break-in or fight. Tourist season was picking up and so were arrests, and he'd spent the night babysitting the drunk tank. A particularly obnoxious guy had been rounded up, his face tomato red, reeking of beer and sweat.

"Say good night, Rob," Sheriff O'Shay had ordered, pushing the drunk into the holding cell and slamming the door. He locked the cell, then warned Holt. "Rob here really likes to talk. Do not encourage him."

O'Shay then went back out on patrol. Rob, a bulky guy in a flannel shirt and a Mariners cap, slouched against the wall for a moment with his eyes closed. He groaned, head lolling to the side. Holt wondered if the guy would throw up. He certainly didn't want to smell the contents of this drunk's stomach all night.

"Hey," Holt said. "You gonna puke? Toilet's two feet to your right."

Rob opened one eye, unleashed a bullfrog belch, and grinned. Then he beat a fist against his chest. "I'm a former marine. Iron stomach."

Holt nodded and tried to busy himself with paperwork.

Rob closed his eyes again, rapped his hands randomly against the floor. He was quiet for a few minutes, and Holt thought he heard faint snores. Then Rob abruptly opened his eyes and belted the chorus of "Bad Moon Rising."

"You like CCR?" Holt asked. Rob had slightly botched the lyrics.

"What do you know about CCR? What do you know about *anything*?" Rob's eyes narrowed. Then he pointed, his finger aiming for the opening between the cell bars. "I'm gonna tell you something. I seen a bear tonight, right back there behind the tavern, big enough to eat a horse. Bet he's got a few hikers in his belly already."

"Did you, now." Holt kept his voice flat, even, unimpressed.

Rob rocked forward, his fingertip steady in Holt's direction. His wolfish grin revealed surprisingly straight white teeth. "About fifteen years ago, when I was still up at the elementary school, bear did eat a man. An officer of the law like yourself, I believe. He tore that poor bastard to shreds. Threw his bones all over the woods. I bet it's that same bear. And I bet you, Sheriff, are going to have to go out there and tangle with him before he makes a tourist his dinner."

"I'm not the sheriff," Holt replied.

Rob sang one last time about bad moons, blowing hurricanes, and overflowing rivers before passing out, head on the bare mattress of the cell's lone bunk.

Holt laughed, shook his head, and flicked on the station's television. He tried to distract himself with a baseball game,

18

but when O'Shay finally returned to relieve him at two a.m., he had to force himself to stride slowly to his car instead of breaking into a run.

And then Kent Yardley from the Parks Department had called, elevating Rob's ramblings to a prophecy.

"Just lay the trap," Kent said, claiming a crippling stomach bug, the result of potluck macaroni salad left too long in the sun. "I'll owe you. I've got some lady up on Dunes Road on my ass, saying she's afraid a bear's gonna eat her Pomeranian. Did you see the *Tide*?"

Holt squinted against the sun, rays piercing through some cloud cover outside his window. He cleared his throat, tried to shake off the drunk's tall tales. Of course he'd read the *Tide*. Copies of the local newspaper were always around the station. "I read it."

The article's title had been "A Bear of a Problem." Holt bit his tongue and didn't mention how the reporter had detailed the futility of the Parks Department's relocation attempts. As a newbie, Holt didn't want to state what the paper already had: relocation was a bad idea. Relocated animals often struggle to survive in their new homes, and introduce new diseases and parasites to the area. The only truly effective way to alleviate conflicts between man and beast is to eliminate whatever lured the animals out of the woods in the first place. Instead, Holt asked, "What should I do if I see it?"

"You mean what should you do if it sees you? Throw your hands over your head. Hold still. Whatever you do, don't try to run. But you're not going to see it. Just lay the trap."

Holt fervently hoped the beast had skipped town of its own accord. How long did wild bears live? Ten years? Twenty?

"No Pomeranians will be eaten on my watch, sir," Holt said. He'd hung up the phone and headed for the woods.

A bird fluttered past him, perching high in the trees. Holt craned his neck. The dense branches blocked so much light that ten a.m. looked more like dusk.

Why hadn't he brought Copper? His canine chum would be welcome company. Holt crept through the brush until he came upon a clearing large enough to lay the trap. He bent down, unzipping the bag.

A branch snapped like gunfire. Holt jumped. He drew his pistol, aimed it at the trees. The branches a few yards to his left thrummed, leaves bungeeing. Holt quickly replaced his gun. Hadn't that article said that hikers should clap their hands, make noise, if they encountered a bear? That it was best not to sneak up on the animal, make it feel trapped?

Holt continued unzipping the bag. He sang as loud as he could about bad moons.

He made it through the song three times before the trap was set, and he hustled out of the woods, blinking at the sun.

Interview with Mira Wohl, Willamette University cafeteria, October 2, 2010

From *Flight Risk: The Robert Jackson Kelley Story*

"Listen, I know firsthand what happened. I knew him. I mean, it's a small island. We went to elementary school together. Half of what people are saying now is totally made up.

"You gotta picture this. The plane's crashing through the trees. Branches breaking, birds flapping away. Rattling like the wings are gonna tear off. Robert's about to eat pine. His life's flashing before his eyes like in the movies. He's wondering what God will look like.

"Bam! The plane hits the ground. It's a steaming hunk of scrap metal.

"And he just walks away.

"They found pieces of the plane for miles. I know somebody selling them on the Internet now. Robert was just an annoying kid from the trailer park, and now everything he ever broke is for sale."

JULY 1998

---

911 dispatchers didn't make a lot of money, but they had to "keep their heads," as Deb always said. That she could stay calm on the phone while people were bleeding to death and clutching their chests and pleading with her to help amazed Robert. Particularly when she was freaking out about the dishes not being done and the trash over-flowing in pungent heaps, or screaming at him to slow down and *focus*. Think about what he was doing, for Christ's sake.

Robert imagined her talking to Officer Holt, giving him directions to the bank robbery or the four-alarm blaze. *Ten-four*, he'd say. *Over and out*, Robert's mom would reply.

The operators shared their strangest calls, and Deb came home with plenty of warnings.

"I ever catch you fooling with a BB gun, I'll break it in half," she'd say. Or, "Don't let any idiot kid talk you into a stupid stunt like cannonballing off a roof into somebody's pool."

She didn't seem to realize she was giving him ideas.

Two Sundays a month his mother worked a second job, mucking out stables and exercising a wealthy couple's horse. His mother was a horse person. She didn't do the job for the money, which was menial, but for the chance to ride. She had some friends who were horse people, too, and Robert noticed that a lot of horse lovers resembled their prized animals in some way: the prominent teeth, the knobby limbs. His mother's blond ponytail. As if they wanted to be horses.

If Robert could be any animal, he'd be lazy, happy, tail-wagging Hulk.

Or a bird.

Those Sundays Deb would try to get Robert's father to come by and watch him. Robert Senior almost always said no, and Deb would slam the door behind her. In that case, Deb just left him with Hulk.

Robert had only met his dad seven times. The first three times, they played checkers and ate potato chips at the trailer while Deb mucked the stables. The fourth time, Robert Senior took his son to the Pine Tavern and let him wing darts at the black-and-red board. The fifth time was only for a few minutes, until Deb kicked Robert Senior out of the trailer, screaming and red-faced for reasons Robert didn't know. During the sixth visit, Robert discovered his father was a war hero.

"Operation Desert Storm! Stormin' Norman!" his dad crowed. "You ever hear of him?"

Robert shook his head. They were ensconced in the elder Robert's pickup, slurping down thick milkshakes and munching on salty Arby's fries, staring into a night sky that skimmed the beach like a drawn stage curtain. Deb had slammed through the front door earlier that evening and been confronted with a pile of Hulk's shit curling on the carpet. She had noticed the mess in time not to step in it, but instead had mashed a tender foot onto one of the five hundred or so Legos Robert had dumped out of his plastic tub to build the world's tallest tower. She had hobbled to the phone and demanded Robert Senior come get his son right this goddamn minute. And surprisingly his truck had rattled up, and he'd hoisted Robert onto the front seat.

"Stormin' Norman Schwarzkopf," his dad repeated, nodding his head reverentially. "Shoulda run for president."

Robert still didn't know who Schwarzkopf was, so he pictured Shaquille O'Neal. Robert Senior was just about as big and could lift Robert Junior over his head with one hand, his tree-trunk arms bulging. He'd drop his son back on the ground, the boy red-faced and out of breath.

"I've never told you about Desert Storm?"

Robert shook his head. He didn't think so, but

sometimes, even when he thought he was listening, he didn't remember what teachers or his mom said. A forgotten homework assignment, a skipped chore, a missing shoe or key or pencil: each lapse ambushed him anew. Maybe his dad had told him about Desert Storm and he just didn't remember.

Robert Senior gulped his milkshake, his cheeks ruddy beneath the brim of his camouflage cap. "I was fresh out of basic, rarin' to go. Head shaved! Still in my twenties! Can you picture that?"

Robert grinned and shook his head. He got his own head buzzed every June, but his dad always had a mess of shaggy blond hair.

"I got sent right to Kuwait. You know where Kuwait is?"

Robert looked out the window. White tents dotted the beach. Someone must have been having a party. Must be rich people. At every party Robert had gone to, they just ate brownies the kid's mom made from a mix and chased each other around the yard. Or played video games, if the kid had them. Robert shook his head again.

"You know where Egypt is?"

Robert nodded, even though he didn't.

"You're so quiet! Whose boy are you?" Robert Senior elbowed him in the ribs. "Say 'Yes, sir.'"

His side smarted. "Yes, sir."

"Anyway, the USA gets there and we're prepped for a

long fight, but the Kuwaitis treated us like heroes," Robert Senior continued. "Miles of desert and surrendering Kuwaitis. They'd give their guns right over, smilin' away. You'd bring some lollipops and pencils for the kids. They'd hug your legs." He slurped his milkshake. "So the Iraqis had gotten a prisoner. Daniel McQuaid. Sweet-lookin' kid with a wife and a baby, and while the Iraqis are getting their asses handed to them, they're broadcasting video of Danny McQuaid, saying America is the great devil and praise to Allah and all that garbage. You can tell looking at the tapes that Danny McQuaid hasn't had a wink of sleep in weeks. He's got two shiners and they've probably got electrodes hooked up to his balls."

Robert Senior used the end of his straw to shovel the thickest parts of his shake, so Robert Junior did, too.

"One day we're sailing through the desert, waving to the Kuwaitis, when we come upon this cave. And lo and behold! It's Danny McQuaid," Robert Senior said. "He's surrounded by Iraqis, but me and my guys open fire. McQuaid was so weak I swung him over my shoulder and carried him, like I used to carry you to bed. Guns were blazin' behind me. We get out of the cave and there's sand blowin' in my eyes. Can't see anything, but I get old Danny to the chopper and back to the USA."

Robert couldn't recall his father ever tucking him in,

but that must have been because he'd been too young to remember.

"They don't release the soldiers' identities in cases like that. Some people don't want all the press. I know I didn't. McQuaid got all the attention. After the war I just wanted to come home and live with your mom, but you know how that turned out." Robert Senior shrugged. Robert had only ever seen his parents argue. They'd gone to high school together, but the trailer was so definitively Deb's—her sweaters and jeans strewn about, her boots slouched by the door, her Bud and Diet Coke cans littering the kitchen, her Marlboro Menthols and fluorescent pink lighter stashed with her keys on the windowsill over the sink, her horse wall calendar, her grandmother's hand-crocheted afghans slung over the secondhand sofa, *Oprah* and *Law & Order* blaring on the television. Robert couldn't imagine his dad ever living there.

"I did meet the president, though. George Bush. Shook my hand, thanked me for serving my country with such bravery." Robert Senior nudged his son. "That's what you should do. Enlist."

Robert's milkshake was just about gone, a melting mound of chocolate. "I want to be a policeman."

Robert Senior laughed and shook his head. "A cop? Uh-uh. Not you."

Why not? Robert didn't ask. Maybe his dad just didn't like cops.

When he was a bit older, Robert realized that was the longest conversation he and his father had ever had.

Then came that seventh time. The last time.

"When you're a kid, everyone's always asking, 'What do you want to be when you grow up?' I usually said actress. Sometimes singer. When I got a little older, my dad kept trying to convince me I wanted to be a news anchor. I even went through a phase where I thought I wanted to be president. But I always knew I wanted to be famous. I wanted crowds and lights and cameras and autographs and couture dresses and magazine covers and all of it.

"But for now anyway, Robert's the most famous person I know. And he got that way by running away. By hiding. He disappeared and so we could decide he was whatever we wanted him to be. And what we wanted was for him to never get caught."

AUGUST 1998

Rapping on his window woke Robert up. Robert Senior peered in. Robert tossed his blankets aside and scrambled out of bed. He struggled with the window, his race car–covered pajama top riding up his tummy as he tugged, but finally he got the frame pulled about a quarter of the way up. Cold night air rushed into his closet-sized bedroom.

A thin rivulet of blood ran down the bridge of Robert Senior's swollen nose. His knuckles were scraped raw. Sweat and liquor pinched Robert's nostrils.

Robert Senior looked hurriedly over his shoulder. "The cops are looking for me. I borrowed one of their cars. You should have seen the sheriff's face! Got them good." He chuckled and swung a thumb behind his shoulder. "Left it a ways back there. Think I hit a deer."

Bright lights flashed over both of them, illuminating Robert Senior's swollen, rubber Halloween mask face.

"They're coming for me, boy!" His eyes lit up. His face flushed. He drummed on the windowsill, chuckling again. "I'm gonna have to make a run for it!"

"Run, Dad!" Robert yelled.

Robert Senior grinned at his son. He reached out and ruffled the boy's hair with a sweaty palm.

Then he crashed into the woods, and Robert never saw him again. He never told Deb he'd spoken to his father that night. And when Deb said a few weeks later that Robert Senior was in jail in Seattle, the maximum-security prison this time, Robert decided she was wrong. Robert Senior was camping in the woods, where there was less trouble to get into.

Holt and O'Shay recovered the sheriff's cruiser at the edge of the trees, its door flung open. Glass from a smashed headlight littered the asphalt. Scratches clawed the driver's-side door. Holt reached inside to turn off the lights, still splashing blue and red over the trees.

A boot, Rob Kelley's own dirt-crusted Timberland, lay on the cruiser floor. Like Rob had gnawed it off to free himself from a trap. Holt took a slim digital camera from his holster and began snapping photos. A long shot of the boot, tipped over, laces still tied. Close-up of the tread, to compare with any footprints they might find.

31

"Oh, *shit*," O'Shay swore. Holt hustled over to the front of the cruiser, where O'Shay had been surveying the damage.

A body was splayed near the middle of the road.

Holt's peripheral vision shrank. An arm, snapped and bent. A wrinkled hand, fingers stretching toward the car's front right wheel. The head turned away from him, mercifully, so that all he could see was white hair sprouting beneath a ball cap.

Something gleaming in the road, a white island in a sea of maroon. A tooth.

Holt lunged backward and hung his head over the grass. He gagged and heaved, and finally spat bile into the dirt. O'Shay called for an ambulance, though they both knew it was far too late. Then he took the camera from Holt. When he was done taking pictures, O'Shay covered the body with a blanket from the cruiser's trunk.

"Do you know who it is?" Holt asked.

"No. Could be a vagrant. No ID." O'Shay pointed at the trees. "Rob's that way. I just know it."

"He told me he was a marine," Holt said. A sour taste oozed down his throat. He peered into the woods. Broken pine boughs marked where Rob must have dived into the forest. Holt ran a hand down his own stubbled cheeks. Those needles must have torn up Rob's face, his bare arms. Holt turned back to O'Shay. "Maybe he has survival training."

"That's bastard's no marine!" O'Shay yelled. "He's a drunk with a kid he doesn't support. I've been hauling him in since he was fifteen years old. He disappeared in Seattle for a few years, probably making a complete pain in the ass of himself there, too. But he tells all kinds of stories about what he was up to. He's a war vet. He's a middle-weight boxer. He's been crab fishing up in Alaska. I used to think I could help him. Don't ever make that mistake. People like him just drag you down with them." O'Shay spat toward the trees. "At least now he'll have a true story to tell in jail."

O'Shay returned to the car and popped the trunk. Holt took a few steps toward the trees. The curtain of needles could certainly hide a man. After all, it still held the bear that Holt had failed to trap.

He tried to forget this second fugitive lurking in the forest as O'Shay tossed him a thick jacket and a pair of gloves, and they parted the trees.

Interview with Brad O'Shay,
Pine Tavern, October 9, 2010

From Flight Risk: The Robert Jackson Kelley Story

"Before that night, Rob Kelley was a drunk, an obnoxious one who'd get himself fired from shitty job after shitty job and try to tell you he was Batman after he'd had a few. But he was harmless. There were about a dozen other guys on this island just like him, warming seats in this tavern every night. I never thought that son of a bitch would cost me my job. Cost somebody his life. You talk to James Holt about any of this?

"He won't talk? Doesn't really surprise me.

"That night, Rob's practically falling off his stool, and he starts talking about the Gulf War. Barely making any sense. Going on and on. I'm off duty, technically, but around here the sheriff's shift never really ends. I have the cruiser. Usually do. I try to shut Rob up. Tell him to go home, get some sleep. Eat something. Of course he doesn't listen. Never did.

"Gets to be the time of night that Rob retires to the drunk tank. But he doesn't want to go quietly this time. We scuffle a little bit. Nothing major. He can't hit the broad side of a barn at this point, but he's nothing if not persistent. So we tangle. But my keys are sitting by my beer, and damn if he doesn't grab them. He's grinnin', ornery, so pleased with himself. He runs off and hops in my cruiser. There are people who'd say I should have shot him right then. But that's not how the law works. I gotta call in for backup. By the time they show up, Rob Kelley is *gone*.

"Took all my men, plus SWAT from Seattle, to finally get him. Snipers were leaning out the windows of the high school gym. After all, the man was a wanted murderer.

"After three days in those woods, his fingertips were black. Broken nose, too. I heard he lost two toes. And still he tried to run. But we were ready for him. Tased him.

"Can't run forever. Like father, like son."

NOVEMBER 1998

Robert liked first grade. He liked the busy hallways, teeming with other kids like darting fish. He liked the cafeteria's warm, crunchy tater tots and cold milk cartons. He liked the library with its shelves and shelves of books, liked to pull one free, flip through it, put it back, grab another. He liked his teacher, Ms. Milhauser. He liked her tiny silver earrings, the way she let the kids shout along when she read *Green Eggs and Ham*, and how she let them take as long as they liked at the water fountain. He liked her even when she moved his seat away from the window, even when she tapped his paper and quietly said, "Focus." He liked gym, how the kids' sneakers squeaked across the shiny floor. He was always the fastest, and he never got tired.

* * *

At home, Robert found a dirt-streaked beer bottle near the mailbox, its Coors label peeling and flaking like sunburned skin. Coors, he vaguely remembered, or perhaps decided, was what his father always drank.

The bottle winked against the mailbox's stake. Robert bent the label's corner, picked at it like an itchy scab. He almost expected to find a letter scrawled on the back. Instead the paper crumbled between his fingers.

Two days later, he spotted a plume of smoke dancing over the trees like a charmed snake.

Could his dad be hiding in those trees? Was the bottle a sign? He'd seen TV shows with castaways hurling bottles with rolled-up messages into the sea, hoping they'd wash up on the shore. Of course, the bottle he'd found had been empty. But still. Maybe his father just didn't have a pencil and was counting on Robert understanding anyway.

Robert watched the twisting gray trail of smoke until it fused with a few threatening thunderheads and the storm drove him inside. The trailer's roof had started springing leaks. Water plinked onto the kitchen floor, smearing bright streaks of yellow linoleum through the room's coat of grime. Robert stood beneath the biggest hole and tried to catch drops on his tongue. Hulk's paws slipped, and his feet slid out from under him. A damp chill invaded the rooms.

Deb finally recruited a neighbor, a man, to climb up onto the roof and secure a blue tarp over the trailer. He covered the part over Robert's bedroom, too, which was lucky, because new gaps poked through the ceiling soon enough.

On nights when Deb was home, when Robert couldn't sleep and couldn't escape into the yard, he piled on blankets and studied the holes and thought about the signals his father sent from the woods. He tried to fit them together, decipher his dad's coded messages.

When Hulk barked at night, Robert knew his dog could see Robert Senior, too.

Sometimes, as his eyelids finally fell, the blue pinpoints melted into falling, streaking stars. Sometimes, he wished that he could stretch his arms high enough to push away the tarp and peel the trailer's roof away like the top of a tin can, and let in the sky.

Officer Holt visited Yannatok Elementary one Wednesday afternoon. He brought two obedient German shepherds, whose ears pricked with attention as Officer Holt talked about stranger danger and saying no to drugs.

Robert sat up straight and tried to ignore the whispering classmates around him. He wondered if Officer Holt recognized him. He wondered if he'd be able to ask him if he'd caught the bear.

The kids behind him were talking in hushed tones about

a video game Robert didn't have, one where the player pretended to steal cars and lead the cops on a wild chase down a crowded highway.

"Half the time, you crash," one kid said.

"Not me," bragged the other.

Robert turned around, caught himself, and swiveled forward again before the teachers noticed.

"I made it to the city level," the kid replied. "You get to jump the car onto the sidewalk in that one."

They swapped tips and dubious tales of video game glory, and Robert found himself picking at his shoelace, jiggling his knees, and sneaking glances over his shoulder until he caught a teacher in the aisle glaring at him. He straightened and tried to pin his stare to the front of the auditorium.

When Officer Holt started passing out pamphlets and lollipops, Robert suddenly realized the assembly was over. He reddened, embarrassed he'd missed important crime-solving tips and a possible update on the wild bears behind his house.

"Hi there, young man," Officer Holt said when he got to Robert. He shook Robert's hand. Officer Holt's jaw was pink and freshly shaven. His brow furrowed for just a moment, and he kept hold of Robert's hand when he asked, "Is your last name Kelley?"

"Yeah," Robert replied, grinning. Officer Holt remembered him. He scrambled to stand up, pumping Officer

Holt's arm. He hoped all his classmates were paying attention.

Holt nodded slowly. Robert felt like he'd been called on and for once answered a question correctly. Holt released his hand and asked, "How's that dog of yours?"

"Good," Robert answered. "Did you catch the bear?"

Officer Holt chuckled. "You know, we never did. He ate donuts right out of my trap and ran off." He handed Robert a sour apple Dum Dum. "But don't worry. We'll get 'im."

Interview with Joey Kovach, Gold's Gym, Seattle, October 10, 2010

From *Flight Risk: The Robert Jackson Kelley Story*

"He was in my class in second grade, I think. At least that's what I remember. One day, early on in the year, it was pouring outside and we had indoor recess, which everybody knows is the worst. But Kelley especially couldn't handle it. He was like a fly stuck indoors, buzzing around, crashing into the windows, trying to get free. Meanwhile, I'd been bothering everybody, knocking down blocks, interrupting card games, messing with the girls. Finally, the teacher plunks us both down in the corner and gets out Risk. You know, that old board game that takes like five days to play? Teacher says, 'Play this. Don't get up until somebody wins.'

"Well, that game had about ten too many rules for us to deal with, so we just made up our own games. We would set up armies and then just roll the dice at them, try to knock them over. Or we'd set up all the armies, real precise, and then we'd yell, 'Earthquake!' and just shake the shit out of the board. Or we'd set it up on the floor and pretend to stomp all over the world. Kept us busy, anyway. That teacher was cool. He let us play that game sometimes on regular recess days, too, when the rest of the boys were playing basketball or football and we were just standing around, not getting picked.

"Risk. We never did learn to play that game the right way."

SEPTEMBER 2001

On September 11, Robert hunched in a desk with the rest of the fourth graders and watched the second plane hit the second tower on the small television in the classroom's corner. As it dawned on both the teacher and the news anchors that something more sinister than an aviation accident was in progress, the teacher directed the kids to open their readers and scrambled to turn off the broadcast.

All the kids on Yannatok grew up around planes, as much a part of the scenery as the ocean and the forests. Every day Robert's school bus lurched past Yannatok County Airport, one of the island's two airfields. Tomkins, a few miles beyond the bus route, catered to tourists looking for private island tours and tandem sky diving. Commuters and locals made up most of Yannatok County Airport's traffic. A private plane could shorten the commute to Seattle from a three-hour ferry ride to a twenty-minute blue-sky jaunt, skipping over the spiraling, tourist-filled lines. The island was full of amateur airmen, retirees whose private planes were like an old dude's convertible. Geese waddled on the runways in the weak morning light, honking and pecking. Anxious pilots fired their rifles into the air to scare them off, the shots booming and echoing while Robert was at the bus stop, the frantic Vs scissoring above him.

As his teacher whispered into her classroom phone, Robert read and reread the same paragraph in his reader, words scattering like those startled birds. Before he'd ever heard of terrorists and radical Islam and jihad, all Robert could think was, *How stupid do you have to be to crash a plane into a giant skyscraper?*

On September 11, Sheriff Holt met with a frantic coast guard and visited the island's airstrips. In his three years as sheriff, he'd never had a busier day. He spoke with the owners about security and ID checks. The importance of reporting anything amiss, no matter how minor. Yes, he admitted, the terrorists in this horrible case were swarthy and dark, but danger could come in any guise. A white tourist, he had to go so far as to say while stopping at Tomkins Airstrip, should be treated with the same scrutiny as one who looked Middle Eastern.

He flew the flag outside the sheriff's department at half-mast for the rest of the month.

At one a.m., after an endless, grueling day, he drove to the beach, took off his shoes, and let the waves wash against the cuffs of his pants. He watched the sky.

When he was eleven, Robert tired of his patch of grass and dirt outside the trailer and decided he would learn to surf. Yannatok Island's small but pretty beach was only a few minutes away. Vacation homes sprouting decks and grills and umbrellas hugged the shore. All summer Deb dropped him off on her way to the dispatch center and picked him up when the sun's last rays sparkled on the water. He wore his only pair of swim trunks, ragged ones with a ripped lining, printed with a salt-faded, hinge-jawed shark.

Deb gave him five bucks to rent a board. *Island's cheapest babysitter,* she'd chuckle. Hulk tagged along, barking at the waves and licking salt off Robert's feet. Robert staked out a patch of sand away from the castle-building kids and the tanning teenage girls and laid out his towel and T-shirt. The current tugged and sucked at his ankles; the sand and sun and the ocean's brine toughened his skin. Robert paddled out on a chewed-up board and let the waves toss him like a piece of beach glass. Time and again he fell under the churning water and washed up after his board. He'd scramble to catch it, give Hulk a quick scratch behind the ears, and run back into the waves.

Jeeploads of teenagers tumbled onto the sand mid-afternoon, the girls in bikini tops and cutoff shorts and the boys carrying gleaming boards. When he saw them with their boards tethered to their wrists, Robert realized the rental boards were missing leashes. The older guys didn't waste the time board-chasing that Robert did.

All day they tracked between the shore houses and their towels, dripping six-packs dangling from their fingers. He knew none of them had a sticker fixed to their school ID to let the lunch ladies know they qualified for free lunch. He knew that if their boards got shredded on rough sands, they'd buy new ones.

They ignored Robert, but, sitting on his board, he sometimes took a breather and watched them. The guys sailed to the sand on wave after wave. They'd still be there when orange streaked the sky and Deb pulled up and honked, engine running. The summer sun didn't set until nine o'clock, and even when she wasn't working, Deb let him stay out until then.

July and its bright heat had arrived before Robert managed to ride a wave straight to shore. The ocean was whirling and gray green, and he liked standing above it, as if he were its master, as if at any moment he could take off and skim its glassy surface, soaring and dipping like a gull. He landed on the shore, coasting to a sandy stop, and he and Hulk danced and whooped on the beach.

This kid is unstoppable! Ladies and gentlemen, the legendary surf champion!

The water never warmed past sixty degrees, even on the hottest summer days. Robert tried swimming with his T-shirt on, but he shivered in the thin material. Goose bumps prickled over his skin. Robert was still flailing through his victory dance when someone tapped him on the shoulder. One of the teenage boys held out a ratty rash guard, the stitching loose around the edge of its long sleeves.

"You're gonna freeze to death," the older boy said. "Take it."

Robert slipped the rash guard over his head, the collar hanging loose like a secondhand turtleneck. He struck scrawny muscle poses and kicked up sand. The teenagers laughed. Then he splashed back into the surf.

Sometimes while he waited for a wave, paddling on his board and staring out over the horizon at the glittering water, he spotted a plane, getting ready to land at one of the island's two runways. And he would imagine Robert Senior's tour in Iraq, and he eventually decided that the most likely place for his dad to be by now was Canada. He'd have hiked his way through the forests all the way up to the border. He would have grown a thick, furry beard and crossed Canada's invisible line under the cover of night, crawling on his belly, calling on his stealth military training. From there he could have worked all kinds of odd jobs: fixing engines, painting houses, cutting down trees. But Robert figured his father had probably chosen to keep hiding out. Hunting. Drinking and fishing from the clear, crisp streams, maybe even grabbing trout with his bare hands.

One of the best parts of Holt's job was helping out the local kids. When he was elected sheriff, shortly after Brad O'Shay resigned in disgrace after pictures of his stolen cruiser appeared on the front of the *Tide*, Holt had aimed his first public initiative at the island's youth. As far as Holt could see, Yannatok parents had two major concerns: drugs and water safety. The two were often connected. Boredom led to drinking and drugs; drinking and getting high near the beach led to unsafe swimming. So Holt had worked with the Parks Department to sponsor low-cost surfing and swimming lessons. At least one lesson each session addressed emergency first aid basics and the dangers of participating in water activities while intoxicated. Holt had ridden out to the beach during the first day of lessons, and though he was instantly sweating in his full uniform, hat and all, seeing the smaller kids splash around and the older ones wobble to a stand atop their surfboards had put a smile on his face. He had squinted at the water, lucky to have been entrusted with these kids' safety. He had been as proud as a father.

Once he'd returned his board to the rental shack and headed home, Robert spent his evenings engrossed in his other new hobby: flight simulators.

Zonked from the sun and the waves, Robert zoned out in front of the computer. Deb had made a big deal out of the Internet being for school only, something she hoped he'd use to raise his increasingly mediocre grades. "No excuses now," she crowed. "Don't have to rely on the library."

Deb talked about installing blocks and monitoring his searches, but she never got around to it. She set up the computer, a refurbished Dell, in the cramped living room, where she could peek over her son's shoulder. Robert clicked away, hopping from one page to the next. TV had never kept him entertained, but the computer could follow his every twitching, scattered thought. Videos of heinous surf wipeouts! Pictures of the inside of a shark's stomach, a surfer's hand buried in the gleaming pink guts! A gnarly toothy shark tattooed on a guy's arm! The world's most tattooed man, his skin a grimy blue gray, inked over every inch.

Other kids he knew liked Myspace and shooting games and even videos of people having sex. He watched some sex videos, too, ferreting out the free ones, the ones with two girls, the ones with two girls and one man. Joey, for example, had a list of the free sites folded into the back pocket of his bookbag, for easy reference when his mom thought he was using their computer for homework.

One evening, one click led to another to another, and on a page filled with diagrams of WWII fighter jets, a link promised a "historical flight simulator." Robert tried to download it and gave up several error messages later. But then he found and downloaded another free flight simulator, billed as "the most realistic free flight sim on the web!" His screen transformed into a plane's dashboard. He'd later come to recognize the Cessna's round meters and long, rectangular center panel. He pounded the space bar, tapped at the arrows, and for flight after imaginary flight didn't make it into the air at all before veering off the runway or petering to a disappointing stop. The simulator offered another point of view: from outside the plane, like a passing bird. He tried the alternate perspective, then switched back to cockpit mode. Easier to concentrate that way.

As he played, the trailer and his mother fell away; he shed them like a snake sloughing off skin. Deb complained that the game's noise—engines revving and firing, static bursting with control tower inquiries—bothered her, and she brought home a busted pair of headphones from the dispatch center. The set was mended with a cocoon of Scotch tape, wound over the left earpiece, but Robert didn't care. Now his focus was impenetrable, a force field against the outside he'd never experienced before. He didn't take his eyes off the screen until he flopped into bed, Hulk curled up at his feet, waves and sky dancing on his eyelids.

For his twelfth birthday, Deb bought him a refurbished surfboard. She'd stuck a ribbon on its chewed-up tip and propped it against the kitchen table, where it was waiting when Robert emerged from his bedroom in his boxers and a T-shirt.

"It's secondhand," she said, puffing on a cigarette, "but they waxed it up for you. I got a great deal buying off season."

Robert ran his hand over the board's smooth white surface. Three bold yellow stripes raced across the board's deck. Its nose was pocked like aged skin, but otherwise the board could have been new.

Deb stuck a candle in a chocolate chip–speckled Eggo, and they sang "Happy Birthday." Hulk howled along.

The February water was frigid, so he would have to wait a few months before he could try it out, but in the meantime he stood atop the board on the porch, cresting imaginary waves. Robert couldn't remember a better birthday.

Winter chugged by, and Robert got antsier and antsier. School had gotten so boring. Instead of going from activity to activity like he had in first and even third grade, he was crammed into his desk, his knees bumping against its metal bar. He lost his third library book and wasn't allowed to check out any more until Deb paid for all three. He crumpled up the fine notice and never gave it to her. His teachers moved his seat again and again: away from the window, away from Joey Kovach, away from the girls, into the front row, closest to the teachers' desks. His work grew sloppier and less accurate no matter where he was stuck. Suddenly the bottom of his backpack was a nest of papers marked with red Fs and orders to *See me*.

The short days left him with precious little time before dark. He logged on to his flight simulator every night and only reluctantly left the computer to slump at the dinner table, squinting, his vision fuzzy, pixelated.

"Are you smoking pot?" his mother asked him.

Half his simulator runs still ended in flameouts. He always seemed to neglect part of the necessary procedures for a successful flight. Too little throttle. Nose too low or too high. Brake still on and engine stalled.

As the weather warmed, the school suffocated him, as if he were a wilting hothouse plant. After a day spent running down the halls and fidgeting in his seat, his chin bumped against his chest through last period, his eyes heavy with boredom.

On the last day of school, he flew from the building like a bird released from its cage.

With his new board, Robert's confidence surged and he got good, fast. He rode wave after wave straight to the shore, coasting in on bursts of salty spray. He stayed in the water until his skin puckered and his nails were tinged blue. He tanned until he was caramel. He wore his donated rash guard daily; on rainy days Deb would snatch it up and wash away the sea smell. Gradually, he inched his ratty towel closer to where the high school kids made camp. The guys were all lean muscle, with pounds and inches over Robert. They guzzled foaming beers between waves, water dripping from their sleek wet suits. The waves seemed to be bigger over here, smashing against the starfish-dotted rocks that hulked close by. The tide sucked more insistently at his feet. Dungeness crabs occasionally scuttled by on their forbidding claws, hiding in the eel grass.

He paddled out and tried to catch a swell. The board slid

out from under his feet and careened to the beach. He sputtered through a mouthful of salt water and scrambled after it. His wet hair and limbs flung droplets on a trio of tanning girls, who shrieked and clutched at their towels.

"Sorry!" Robert shouted over his shoulder. He retrieved his board just in time to see the older guys glide in. He kicked the sand and bounded back into the water.

He decided he'd match them wave for wave.

One evening, when the sun had melted to a red sliver, one of the high school guys strolled over, holding a tattered piece of paper. Robert had ridden in his last wave and started toweling off Hulk. Deb had complained that her car stank like wet dog.

"You're getting pretty good," the older guy said.

"Thanks," Robert mumbled. He toed the sand, studied the grains.

"There's a contest here in a few weeks," he continued. His blue wet suit gleamed. He looked like a costumed superhero. "Competition won't be that bad in the kiddie division. Hell, you might be the only entrant."

The yellow paper was creased into quarters and spattered with salt water. Yannatok's only surf contest had six divisions and a cash prize for each.

"Keep it." He shook water from his ear. "I'm entered already."

Robert folded the flyer back up and trotted to the

parking lot to wait for his mother. He shivered in his T-shirt and tugged his towel around his shoulders as the temperature dropped. He handed the flyer to Deb as soon as she pulled up.

"Fifty dollars?" Deb's brow wrinkled at the entry fee. "I mean, Robert, you probably won't win any money."

"I don't want to win any money," Robert said. But why did he want to do it, then? If the point wasn't winning, what was? He couldn't explain; he just knew that crumpled paper had been his ticket to something bigger than a surf competition, and if his mother wouldn't sign him up, it'd be just one more place other kids could go that he never would. Kids who'd flown on *real* planes, taken real vacations. Kids who crossed that bridge and left Yannatok more than once a year. Kids who didn't have to beg for the money to keep doing something they were good at.

His mother left the flyer folded up in the car's cup holder. Robert grabbed it on his way into the trailer and marched into the living room. Deb was shaking her foot out of one boot while balancing on the other, a hand pressed to the small of her back.

Robert held up the flyer. "Did you even read it?"

"Enough, Robert." Deb flopped onto the couch and trained the remote on the TV. "Please. You're giving me a migraine."

Robert stood in front of the television. He imagined he

could feel the remote's rays hitting his chest and crashing to the floor, like arrows hitting armor. "Mom, is it really that much money? What if I did win it? Wouldn't that be an investment?" He was pleased with the maturity of his argument.

"How much does gas cost? How much does food cost? How much does *dog food* cost?" Deb said pointedly. Then she shooed him away from the TV. "You have no idea. Get away from the television."

"How much do cigarettes cost?"

Deb flung a pointed finger toward the door. "Get your smart mouth out of this room before I kick you out."

Robert stomped to the computer and tugged his headset over his ears so roughly that the skinny plastic band snapped. He flung it to the floor and stormed to the kitchen, pulling open drawer after drawer in a fruitless hunt for tape.

"We don't even have any tape!" he screamed over *Law & Order*'s credits.

He played the simulator without his headphones and crashed over and over, like invisible walls were keeping even his avatar from escaping. He scrolled down the simulator's destination menu. *New York. Los Angeles. Paris. Rome. Tokyo.* Each sounded as unlikely as landing the plane on the moon. As far-fetched as a beach house, a Disney vacation, or a college education.

Before he went to bed, he tucked the flyer into her purse, next to her cigarettes.

Soon, the days shortened and the water grew icier and Robert stopped going to the beach. He stayed inside and played with his flight simulator instead. He crashed the planes over and over again, flying too fast and rocketing into mountains and trees and the air control tower. He'd watch the dashboard burst into flames and reload the program.

Lyrics from "Ballad of the Lollipop Kid"

Written by Ellis Atkins, music by Gull Trouble, 2010

Verse 1:
Robert Kelley
Was tired of treadin' water.
Robert Kelley
Was tired of standin' still.
The keys were there
So he took to the air,
Now he's waving at us below.

Chorus:
Look up in the sky!
It's a bird, it's a plane!
It's Robert Kelley!
The kid can't be contained!
Look up in the sky!
It's a bird, it's a plane!

It's Robert Kelley!
The kid must be insane!

Verse 2:
He didn't care
About latitude and altitude.
He didn't care
About the cops in hot pursuit.
Robert Kelley has nine lives,
But once he's caught, he's screwed.

Bridge: (drumroll, horns clatter and fade)
We represent the Lollipop Kid!
The Lollipop Kid!
The Lollipop Kid!
And in the name of the Lollipop Kiiiiiiiiiddddd!

Chorus:
Look up in the sky!
It's a bird, it's a plane!
It's Robert Kelley!
The kid can't be contained!
Look up in the sky!
It's a bird, it's a plane!
It's Robert Kelley!
The kid must be insane!

SEPTEMBER 2005

School. Was. So. Slow.

Eighth grade was a torture that began at 7:15 when the bus belched its way to the trailer park, chugging down the road and slumping in front of his mailbox. Robert climbed aboard and the bus plodded on, past the Sunoco and the kayak rental place, the marina, and Shipley's Market. Orange globes strung on the high-voltage lines like gaudy Christmas ornaments marked off the miles and warned away low-flying planes.

Classes ended—any class, every class—and Robert careened down the corridor, pinballed around his classmates, lingering in the hall between bells for as long as he could. Each room was a box that he couldn't wait to spring from. He slapped the lockers, loving the hollow metallic banging. He fist-bumped Joey Kovach. Sometimes they pretended to fight. Robert had taught Joey a great trick. Joey would aim at his face with an open palm, a faux strike across the cheek, and at the last second, Robert would raise his own hand to his face, as if shielding it from Joey's blow. Their palms would hit, the sound of a slap, and Robert would fall backward, sometimes sprawling on the floor, cupping his jaw. He'd wait for gasps or the chants of "Fight! Fight! Fight!" before leaping up and high-fiving Kovach.

Joey never wanted to switch roles and end up on the floor, though.

Then Robert would burst into his next classroom, plop down in his seat, and unleash a tornado of pencil-smeared papers, a crumpled-worksheet tsunami. His stubby pencils and leaky pens rolled across the tiles, and he bounded out from behind his desk to retrieve them.

Study hall was the worst part of Robert's day. He traipsed back to Mr. Wharton's homeroom with marching orders to start homework or read a book, which he never had. He couldn't even go to the library to get one. The librarian had banned him for running through the stacks. Sometimes Wharton tried to make him read the dictionary.

When he got really bored, he tore chunks off his eraser and flung them at his classmates. Then he'd pivot and examine the bulletin board over his shoulder. *You got the wrong guy.*

He knew that his teachers sent him on "errands" just to get rid of him. Once, Ms. Conrad had given him a note to deliver to the office, a folded slip of notebook paper. He strutted down the hall, flashing his yellow hall pass like he was backstage at a rock show. A few doors away from the social studies classroom, Robert had gingerly opened it, only to find a penciled smiley face and *Thanks for five minutes of quiet!*

He tapped his pencils, clicked his pens, and jiggled his knee, like an earthquake trembled under only his desk. And that was when he was actually trying to listen.

"Ten!" he called out in English class, his hand fluttering over his head.

"Metaphor!" he yelled in algebra.

The class laughed the first few times.

He scribbled down his homework, and the paper ended up buried in an avalanche of worksheets, cascading out of his locker. He patted down his jeans for a phantom writing utensil and then borrowed one from the teacher and by his next class it had disappeared, vaporized, vanished.

The school psychologist insisted Robert call him by his first name and gave out half-melted lollipops each time he met with a student. Barry's office was plastered with posters of gleaming Harleys. He sat behind his desk with a copy of Robert's most recent grades.

"So." Barry punctuated the lone syllable with a drumroll

on his desk. "Lot of Ds and Fs here." He sighed. "How do you end up with a D in art?"

Robert knew how. His locker was a graveyard of unfinished art projects: a Sunny Delight–stained charcoal sketch of Hulk he'd tried to finish at lunch, a watercolor of the beach he'd smudged and smeared, the hardened lump of a handleless clay pot. Whatever Robert touched seemed to smudge or tear or crack.

He shrugged. Barry was sitting directly under one of his motorcycle posters, so that the handlebars sprouted from his head.

"Would a tutor help?" Barry asked. "We have a free tutoring program."

"For art?"

"For everything."

"Barry, I don't want a tutor," Robert said.

"Anything going on at home?"

Robert shook his head.

"Well, the situation is that if you don't pull these up, you're going to end up in summer school at best, repeating eighth grade at worst. You don't want that, right?" Barry wrote something down. "I'm going to go ahead and give your mom a call, and I'm thinking we'll get her okay to have you in for some testing. See if we can get a handle on just what's going on here."

His schoolwork was so easy that Robert couldn't believe

what he was hearing. He nodded. Summer school? They might as well lock him in jail. He had to ace whatever tests Barry was going to give him. Robert pointed at the gleaming motorcycle. "Do you have one of those?"

Barry shook his head.

He met with Barry a week later for the testing. It was supposed to take two hours, but Robert was finished in forty-five minutes. Barry kept telling him to slow down, focus, concentrate, but Robert was sure he crushed it. If he could only keep it together for the rest of the year, he'd dodge summer school, no problem.

JANUARY 2006

His pediatrician, a middle-aged guy Robert had seen since he was a baby, prescribed him extended-release Adderall after Robert's flaming disaster of a first-quarter report card and Barry's dismal findings. While Robert's IQ was well above average—"in the gifted range," Barry had reported—his reading comprehension level was equivalent to a fourth grader's. His math computation skills were two years below grade level.

"Gaps," Barry had told Robert, "that seem to represent a lack of attention, not a lack of ability."

These results, coupled with his teachers' evaluations, compiling Robert's every fidget, every blown assignment, every detention, had Dr. Rishni reaching for the prescription pad within minutes.

They were supposed to schedule a follow-up appointment with a child psychiatrist, who could monitor

Robert's symptoms and medication dosage. The business card disappeared in the depths of Deb's purse.

The pills were round and baby blue, and they slid easily down his throat. He gulped them down without water, though his mother covered her eyes and told him not to. His knees ceased their hyperactive jig. He could sit still, could read for fifteen minutes at a time. He remembered more of what people said. He passed eighth grade, and at home his digital aviation abilities improved dramatically. His takeoffs smoothed out and his landings steadied, and he thought about the fighter pilots who'd jetted over Iraq. With his newfound concentration, could Robert make it in the air force?

His surfboard stayed in Deb's car.

First Deb started taking away the bottle on the weekends, once ninth grade started and Robert returned to school as pale as the digital clouds he'd spent all summer navigating through. "You're a kid. It's not natural for you to be on pills all the time." She tapped the bottle against her palm. "Go outside, for Christ's sake."

So he would ricochet around on the weekends, chasing Hulk, not doing his chores or his homework, and his mother would yell at him like always.

When Christmas break rolled around, Deb decided he wouldn't take them that whole week either. He ate a dozen candy canes in one sitting, crunching them between his teeth while his mother cringed. He woke up with tight hamstrings, and eventually realized the soreness was the result of his knees' constant tremor.

For his fourteenth Christmas, Robert's mother bought him a computer joystick and a startlingly realistic flight simulator with graphics much sharper than those in the free program he'd downloaded; the scenarios took torque and slipstream into account. The controls mirrored a commercial jet's. The program was his only gift, but it was a good one. For his mom, Robert had smoothed out his beach watercolor from art class, finished it up with some muddled but usable Crayola paints, puddled and forgotten in a drawer, and signed his name with a flourish.

Robert played his new simulator standing up, letting the room grow dark around him as day faded to night. He soared past the pyramids, looped around the Leaning Tower of Pisa, zoomed over Niagara Falls.

"You want to go to the stables?" Deb asked once. Her thick, high boots clomped across the trailer. In three days he'd return to school, for the long slog until spring break. "There's a horse you can try out."

Robert barely looked up. He pulled up on the throttle and the digital runway narrowed. "Nah."

She never asked again.

The vacation ended and he still didn't resume taking the Adderall. His mother rumpled his hair and kissed the top of his head. "That's not you on that medicine. I want my son."

Really, Robert hadn't minded the way the pills made him feel. He didn't feel woozy or slow, like when he had to take Benadryl. Before long, he was a walking crash site again, spreading a debris field of lost assignments, tattered textbooks, and unsigned detention slips.

"I think Robert's off his medication," said Mira Wohl, a red-haired girl in his homeroom, one day in January. He'd been at the front of the room while the teacher was in the hall talking to the principal, showing off his break-dancing skills. He had, in fact, been trying to impress Mira, and knowing next to nothing about girls, assumed her eye roll meant she was properly awed.

"Didn't work on me," he said, and winked.

"I mean, honestly, we all thought he was annoying. He was the kid behind you bouncing his feet on your seat, dropping his pencil six million times, trying to look off your paper. Asking you for the homework every homeroom. Teachers would assign partners for labs or projects, and if you got him, you knew you were stuck doing all the work. And you felt bad for him, too, because sometimes he would try, but you knew if you turned in what he did you'd get a shit grade, so you just did it yourself.

"But, seriously, he had to be some kind of secret genius. Teaching himself to fly a plane. It's not like that's easy. And lots of geniuses get shit grades. Look at Einstein.

"And now everybody says he had to have an accomplice, a friend, who was feeding him, helping him cover his tracks, putting him up at night. Somebody who taught him to fly in the first place, took him up in their own plane. But everyone knows he barely had any friends. And forget about a girlfriend! That's hilarious! He was just Clyde, no Bonnie.

"I mean, we had no idea he was gonna turn around and do what he did. I don't think he did either."

JULY 2009

Deb decided to get her real estate license; she was hoping to supplement her dispatcher salary by getting in on vacation home sales.

"Laura Roth's a Realtor," she said, referring to one of her horse pals. "Look at all she's got."

Robert had been to the Roths' a few years ago, for Amber Roth's birthday party. Deb, Laura, and a few other moms had hung out in the kitchen, picking at a fruit tray and listening to the kids splashing around in the pool. Robert had fun, even though he knew he'd only been invited because his mom and Amber's were friends. And he thought it was kind of weird that he could see the ocean from the cement around the pool. The chlorine burned his eyes, and he'd wondered why they didn't just hop into the salty waves.

The classes met at the high school two nights a week. Or so his mother said. Robert didn't really believe her until Deb starting falling asleep in front of a real estate law book instead of *Law & Order*.

KELLEY, ROBERT J.

Guardian: MacPherson, Debra

Date of incident: 09/25/2009

Location: Library

Reported by: Mike Wharton

Incident: Robert's class was completing a web quest requiring them to locate photographs and first-person sources from the Great Depression. A classmate pointed at a picture of itinerant workers and loudly announced, "Robert's ancestors." Robert pushed classmate out of his chair and struck him.

Action taken: 2 days ISS. Attempt to contact Ms. MacPherson unsuccessful.

Reviewed: Principal Lorraine Simena

In twelfth grade, Robert was the oldest student on a school bus crowded with elementary kids swinging their lunch boxes and middle school creeps carving their names into the seats and throwing paper. The driver pulled over at least once a week and screamed at his passengers to sit down and shut up before he swerved off the road and got them all killed. The high schoolers who could afford cars zoomed around in Jeeps and Civics. Mira Wohl, arguably the school's most popular girl, drove a hand-me-down BMW everyone knew she'd nicknamed Stella. Mira gave her three best friends and her boyfriend, Alex Winters, a ride every day. They all jeered and gave the bus the finger. Robert couldn't help but feel that those digits were raised at him.

Robert ambled off the bus and met Joey Kovach crouching by the bike rack, locking up his rickety dirt bike, a secondhand one not likely to tempt any thief. Joey was a squat kid, a foot shorter than Robert at least, a stumpy bull-dog to Robert's slim greyhound. They were always in the slow classes together, but unlike Robert, Joey never knew the answer to anything.

"Man." Joey sighed and stood up. They slapped hands, gripped hard, slapped again. "Can't believe it's Monday."

"What? We have school today?" Robert cracked.

They wandered into the building. Yannatok High School held only about 375 students, nearly all of whom had attended classes together since kindergarten. Even though Robert and Joey had been friends since elementary school, Robert hadn't ever invited Joey out to the trailer. He'd never seen Joey's place, either, so Robert guessed that was just how guys were sometimes.

They shared their first two classes, through which Joey mostly slept and Robert doodled on his shoes. Then Joey had Strategic Reading and Robert had Scientific Concepts. The slow-kid classes. The ones where you almost have to try to fail. And in a school as small as Yannatok High, if you failed, odds were you would have the same teacher again next year. Often, Robert's teachers didn't want to punish themselves with another year with him, so they bent over backward to pass him: inventing extra-credit assignments fit for a third grader, taking work months late, scratching out requirements, and just plain ignoring his mistakes and missing work. Finding that magic point to bump his F to a D– and shuffle him off to their next unfortunate colleague.

Joey and Robert reunited for the early lunch, at a ludicrous ten fifteen. Still, they both shoveled in all the french fries a free lunch ticket could buy and slurped down chocolate milk.

"Did you read the article for Ms. Tell's class?" Robert asked.

"Naw, man."

"Me neither, but we talked about it today," Robert told him. Several times Robert had flung his hand into the air to ask a question, until Ms. Tell had finally told him that many of the answers could be found in the article. Might he want to read it? He'd gone back to drawing Martians on his shoe's white rubber edge. "It's about living on Mars. People could go to Mars, set up colonies, but never come back. Ever."

Joey's brow furrowed. "If you could get there, why couldn't you get back?"

"Take too long. You'd die on the way," Robert explained. "And you'd have to find some way to make fuel on Mars, 'cause you couldn't transport it. Weighs too much."

Joey grunted noncommittally. Robert continued. "So she has you write about whether or not you'd do it."

"Naw. Food probably sucks. And it's hot as balls."

Robert looked out over the cafeteria, at the guys wadding up straw wrappers and winging them at each other, the girls crowded around someone's pink cell phone. "I don't know. If I could take my dog, I might seriously consider it."

"You would. I'm gonna start lifting," Joey said. He flexed and his T-shirt sleeve barely shifted, a flag signaling surrender on a windless day. "Get big."

"I should, too," Robert said, reluctantly abandoning thoughts of a hypothetical Martian colony. "Get ready for the army."

"I've got a busted-up bench at home." Joey spun his milk cap like a coin. It tottered and fell. "A jump rope, too."

"You can use water bottles for weights," Robert offered. His mom sometimes pumped water-filled sixteen-ounce Diet Coke bottles while she watched TV. Had to be able to rein in those feisty horses. Somehow this seemed embarrassing, even though Joey wouldn't have had a clue, so he added, "I saw it on TV."

Mira Wohl drifted in. The crush of girls around the phone parted to make her its new center. What was the word? He'd heard it in science, every year since seventh grade. Nucleus. Making everyone else protons or something. What if Robert just went over there and talked to her? Asked her if she would, theoretically, ever go to Mars?

Mira piled her hair, strawberry-hued like Mary Jane

Watson in *Spider-Man*, on top of her head and then let it fall again, like a red wave.

"Good call." Joey flicked his milk cap again. Robert tried to set his spinning, too, but it only wobbled once and fell to the table. Joey returned his tray, and Robert sat alone for the last few minutes of lunch. He glanced at Mira. Now all he could see of her was a swatch of that glossy hair. He could answer his own question. Mira Wohl would never want to go to Mars.

After a few more tries, he twisted his wrist in just the right way, and the milk cap spun like a top, like a propeller.

That afternoon, they had an assembly about taking the SATs. Barry took to the stage and explained registration dates and test centers and score reports. Robert hid in the back. He jiggled his knees and wondered if Barry was still riding motorcycles. The district was so small that he had an office in both the middle and the high school; Robert couldn't seem to escape the guy.

Barry said, "Everyone should take the test at least once, no matter what you think your post-graduation plans are. Just to see what happens."

No way was Robert going to come to school on a Saturday and bubble in a Scantron for three hours just to see what happened. He knew what would happen. He'd bomb the test and then his mother would be pissed she'd wasted the registration money.

Post-graduation plans. What the hell would be left for him on Yannatok when he was finally unleashed from this box of a building? He usually couldn't think one hour into the future, let alone years. Would graduation roll around, and after a few photos in his dorky cap and gown and dinner at Red Lobster, he'd just go back to the trailer with his mother and play on the computer? Where could he possibly get a job? Bagging groceries at Shipley's? Would he walk there every day, dodging tourists snaking down the no-shoulder roads, stocking shelves in a fluorescent-lit cavern? Deb had inherited the trailer. Would he be willed it, too, one day? Was his life sentence already in the making?

His knees shook. He clamped a palm over each one. Why hadn't he thought of any of this before?

After the assembly, Joey sidled up beside Robert at his locker. Robert started to take a step away—why had Joey gotten so close?—but then he realized that Joey was showing him something that was just nudging out of his pants pocket. The childproof top of an amber pill bottle. "Check it out, man."

"Cool," Robert replied. He didn't know what else to say or what Joey's point was. Joey smoked weed, but drugs barely interested Robert. He was too poor to afford anything that would get him high. He shoved the SAT papers into his locker.

Joey leaned in again. "Adderall, dude. You got some

more, right? Give them to me and I'll cut you in. I'm selling mine for two bucks a pill."

So that was why Joey's schoolwork had been even worse than usual.

"You need to be popping those yourself, bro," Robert said. Joey rolled his eyes and Robert tried to joke. "You're getting dumber every day!"

"Whatever. I'll find somebody else who wants to make money."

"Hold up, man," Robert said. At least one nearly full bottle haunted a kitchen cabinet, behind a family-sized bottle of Aleve and some expired antibiotics.

He needed that money. If he put every penny toward a car, then he could get off this island and away from that trailer, looming like one of those aboveground crypts.

After school, he hunted in the kitchen cabinets for his old bottle of Adderall. All that turned up was miscellaneous junk: rubber bands, safety pins, dead batteries, loose change. Robert pocketed the nickels and dimes and wound a thick rubber band around his wrist. He continued with his quest, snapping it against his skin as he wandered the trailer, Hulk fast at his heels.

He wondered if Deb had hidden the pills to prevent him from the very scheme he was trying to pull off.

Robert didn't make a habit of going through his mom's stuff. Her possessions were either boring or horrifying. They already lived with the mutual indignity of a shared indoor clothesline, leaving his boxers and Deb's bras to stretch across the living room, a banner of embarrassment he had to duck under to reach the computer. Her closet floor was littered with battered Sue Grafton paperbacks and mismatched shoes. Sparkly, strappy clothes she never wore. Zero interest to him.

But when he opened the bottom drawer of her narrow nightstand, he hit the jackpot. Instead of the one bottle he expected, three rattled around the drawer, soldiers alive and well, all prescribed to him. Some had only a handful of pills filled at the Ready Drug, way back when he was in middle school. Robert shook a bottle like a maraca. The blue circles were tinted sea-green through the amber plastic.

Why was his mom collecting Addies the way other mothers collected Tupperware?

Maybe she kept them at the ready, in case of an eighth-grade-level academic code red.

But that didn't seem like Deb, who'd been so insistent that Robert stay unmedicated back in middle school, when his grades had been at their most dire. And hadn't quite a few do-or-die, hanging-off-the academic-ledge-by-a-curled-pinkie situations already come to pass, without any suggestion of pharmaceutical intervention by his mother?

Maybe she had plans to sell them herself.

Maybe she'd looked at the prescription and seen the cash to buy a horse, a new truck, a shiny new pair of boots.

He thought about flushing the pills down the toilet and leaving her to discover the empty bottles. Put her in a pretty bad spot, since to accuse him of taking her secret stash she'd have to cop to having had it in the first place.

Robert took out a pill, rolled it between his fingers. The tablet left the faintest chalky residue in the whorls of his fingerprints. His hands must be sweating.

But who would his mom even sell to? The other ladies at dispatch? Seemed unlikely. Her horse buddies? Robert had heard that Addies killed your appetite, and that was why girls bought them.

Was Deb taking them herself to try to lose a few pounds? His mom was already pretty thin. And she was so insistent that Robert not be a "druggie." But then he thought about her late nights on the phones and her long days at the stables.

Pain had begun to radiate from the center of his forehead. He returned the loose pill to its bottle and pocketed it. Then he slammed the drawer shut.

He slipped the pills to Joey at the bike rack the next morning.

KELLEY, ROBERT J.

Guardian: MacPherson, Debra
Date of incident: 10/21/2009
Location: Gym
Reported by: Oscar Austen
Incident: Mr. Austen reports that Robert is displaying a pattern of intentional disruption in gym class. His recent actions include interrupting directions, purposely disrupting game play by scoring points against his own team, splashing classmates with water from the water fountain, and refusing to return from the girls' side of the gym. Robert has also been removed from class after multiple incidents of horseplay.
Action taken: 2 days' detention. Ms. MacPherson expressed frustration with Robert's behavior and said

she was "out of ideas." She also expressed concern that Robert lacks a positive male role model. Ms. MacPherson was referred to Barry Lancaster for recommendations.

Reviewed: Principal Lorraine Simena

OCTOBER 2009

---

*The army recruiters were stationed at a folding table out-*side the cafeteria. They'd Scotch-taped posters of diving fighter jets to the wall, peeking out between olive and gold balloons. A matching banner festooned the table. A blond girl and a guy with a crew cut hung out behind racks of brochures and clipboards.

Be Strong. Army Strong.

Robert lingered around the booth, avoiding the cafeteria and watching other kids pick up fliers. Some took them as a joke. One kid snickered out of the recruiters' earshot. "I enlisted Connor. He'll look great with a shaved head."

Robert finally walked over and scrawled his name and phone number on the sign-up sheet. He was only the fourth student to do so, not counting Connor's involuntary drafting.

"Have you guys gotten to go places?" Robert asked them. "Do you train kinda far away?"

The girl straightened. "I served in Afghanistan for a year. I'll go back in four months."

"I was in Germany," the guy quickly added. "Before that I spent time in the Philippines. And now we go all over the country for recruitment. So being in the army definitely takes you places."

"What makes you want to join the army?" the blonde asked.

"I want to join the air force. Be a pilot."

"Do you have good eyesight?"

"Perfect." Robert was guessing. "Bionic."

The recruiters laughed. Crew Cut said, "Well, that's one requirement down. You'll get a call in the next couple of weeks."

Robert saluted, and pocketed a pamphlet and a free sticker. That night, he practiced simulated flights over Afghanistan.

KELLEY, ROBERT J.

Guardian: MacPherson, Debra

Date of incident: 10/30/2009

Location: Science classroom

Reported by: Marissa Tell

Incident: Robert's class was beginning a crayfish dissection lab. Robert loudly stated, "I don't wanna do this. Little f***ers have eyes." A classmate responded, "You're such a p***y." Robert left seat and shoved classmate.

Action taken: 3 days ISS. Spoke with Ms. MacPherson on phone and she agreed with consequence, though she did express concern that the other student be disciplined as well.

Reviewed: Principal Lorraine Simena

Interview with Joey Kovach, Gold's Gym, Seattle, October 10, 2010

From *Flight Risk: The Robert Jackson Kelley Story*

"I got a rep at school for being a snitch. A liar. But it was the other way around. Kelley turned on me. My older brother knew all the junior tweakers, the burnouts who'd be snorting meth in a year but would gobble up all the pills we could sell them in the meantime. Adam Neff, Ryan Marling, Caden Marsh. I had a connect in Seattle who wanted five hundred Addies for a party. So I was hoarding what Robert gave me, working some other sources, and just making smaller deals off my own stash. We were set to make some money. All the kids there knew where they could get Addies if they wanted, for parties or to cram. We were playing a long game, and Robert never understood that. He could only see one move ahead.

"But toward the end, some people were trippin' 'bout even talking to me, and the connect fell through. They were worried about Robert's big mouth. Like he thought he was a real thug or something. Didn't surprise me when he snitched."

The morning his class sharpened their number two pencils and filed into the high school to bubble in their SATs, Robert finally navigated a virtual fighter jet between the Twin Towers. One of the simulator's tougher tricks, and one that wouldn't be included in future versions, he was sure. He usually crashed into the right tower, flames filling his windshield, flickering over his screen-reflected face. But this time he tilted the plane just so, sliding neatly between the two. The view through his windshield sloped as he skimmed the cloned buildings, brushing past them.

He lifted Hulk's paw for a high five and kept flying.

The cafeteria buzzed with students, but since no one cared what Robert and Joey talked about, they could discuss their burgeoning drug empire openly, over Joey's greasy, bubbled pizza slice and Robert's crushed package of peanut butter crackers.

"You got any more?"

"More what?"

"You know."

"Yeah, I got some more." Robert retrieved a folded piece of paper from his pocket. "Listen. You tell me: Am I reading a list of new animals discovered this year from my current event for Ms. Tell's class, or the name of the deathcore band I'm going to start?" Robert held up his hand. "Number one: tyrant leech king."

"Band. You gonna bring them in?"

"Wrong. Number two: dragonfish."

"Animal," Joey guessed. "Are they all animals?"

"Ding, ding, ding! Correct!" Robert laughed and shook his head. "This one, he's gnarly lookin'. Number three: blue fang skeleton tarantula."

"Dumbass, you gave it away. Animal, obviously."

"Oh yeah." Robert crumpled up the paper. "And 'bald parrot' would be a very lame band."

"Are you gonna bring 'em in or what, man?"

"Yeah, I'll do it. When am I gonna see some money?"

"All in due time." Joey took a swig of milk. His mouth was rimmed with white, like a clown who'd been interrupted in the makeup chair.

"You're disgusting."

"Thank you." Joey grinned.

"I mean it about the money. I'm going to have to go mob on you soon."

Joey snickered. "'Go mob' on me?"

"Like, break your fingers." Robert wished he could sound more menacing, but even his threats sounded like jokes. "Joey Kovach sleeps with the fishes."

"Dude, I am not going to rip you off, all right?" Joey spread his hands. "Quit acting like it."

"All right," Robert said.

Joey was his only friend. If he couldn't trust Joey, who could he trust?

The first Adderall had fizzed in her blood, firecrackered in her brain.

Deb had been a daydreamer when she younger, her grades always solidly mediocre. In elementary school, the fantasies revolved around wearing brand-new white breeches and shining black riding boots and jumping her own Thoroughbred, which would be chocolate brown and named Abracadabra. By high school, diversions took the form of boys. Later, one boy, who'd knocked her up and kept her from going to even community college. But she'd grown out of her inattentiveness. Or so she thought.

Now she was just exhausted.

When she'd signed up for Real Estate Fundamentals in July, Deb had been picturing her face on ads at the bus station, in the *Tide*. Smiling, bathed in soft light, confident. A local celebrity, really, like Laura Roth. *Trust Deb MacPherson*, the posters would advise, *to find your dream home.*

The dispatch center was a windowless cave. When she stepped out for her smoke breaks, she squinted like she was coming out of hibernation. She talked to dozens of people a day, sometimes while they were experiencing the worst moments of their lives, and she never saw a single one of their faces. If she were a Realtor, she'd have a reason to dress up. She'd shake people's hands. They'd know her name.

And the money, even if she just sold a house or two a month, would give her a cushion. She could save to enroll Robert in something, somewhere, once he graduated. She didn't delude herself that he was still college-bound, not with the grades he'd been getting, but she would be able to pay for vocational training. Her son was certainly smart enough to be an electrician, an EMT, a graphic designer.

And maybe, eventually, she could buy her own horse.

The class met at Robert's high school. Something about being in that school's stuffy, boxy rooms melted her focus. A pre-class Diet Coke failed to perk her up. When she'd seen those posters with Laura Roth's carefully straightened hair, her snappy red suit, she'd had no idea that the course itself would be so boring.

During her third class, somewhere between joint tenancy and community tenancy, her chin crashed into her chest as she nodded off.

The state of Washington required ninety classroom hours to obtain a real estate license. She hadn't made it through two and a half.

She slipped from the classroom as quietly as possible and walked down the dim, empty hallway, hoping that a little movement would rouse her. She snuck out for a quick cigarette, but back in the classroom, she still felt one step behind, struggling to finish taking notes while her classmates were already opening their textbooks. She didn't hear what page she was supposed to turn to, and by the time she found it, everyone was closing their books again.

On her way out of the class, she passed Barry Lancaster's office. His name on that closed door, right over its frosted glass pane, was what reminded her of the Adderall. She could practically hear his voice again, reassuring her over the phone that Adderall was a safe drug, one that could help her son reach his potential, smooth out his discipline problems, pave a path for his future.

She'd filled one bottle for Robert as soon as Dr. Rishni had prescribed it, on their way home from the appointment, in fact. And then Robert hadn't finished it, and somewhere along the way she'd misplaced it. Wasn't in the medicine cabinet. Wasn't on the kitchen counter. Had she mislaid it cleaning, somehow? She'd dumped Robert's book bag and rifled through his things, making sure he hadn't gotten any dumb ideas about selling the stuff. Deb had driven herself crazy looking for the missing bottle, but it had never turned up. So she'd told herself she'd made up her mind that Robert wasn't going to keep taking the pills anyway, so what did it matter if they'd accidentally gotten tossed in the garbage? Then about a month later, Deb had gotten another call from Lancaster, asking her how she thought the meds were working, expressing concern about Robert's still-dismal grades. And so she'd called Rishni's office and gotten the prescription refilled. So committed had she been to straightening her son out once and for all that she'd asked Ready Drug to fill it automatically, and so a month later another bottle had been ready for her, surprising her when she'd only run in for lipstick and cigarettes. Despite the fact that she'd once again changed her mind and decided that rather than medication, what her son truly needed was a solid kick in the ass, she'd paid for the pills and stuffed them in her night-stand next to the other bottle Robert had never finished.

Two hours before class the next week, she swallowed one with a swig of soda in the dispatch center parking lot on her break.

After the initial jitters, the drug careened through her like a roller coaster, and she found even real estate taxes incredibly interesting. Her notes were a masterpiece of acronyms and highlighting, her capital letters marching across page after page. She did the week's homework as soon as she got back to the trailer, and had it completed in less than an hour.

The next day she felt a little foggy. A headache pulsed behind her eyes. But if one pill had made her this productive, this sharp, why not two next time? She popped them before her next class and waited for the rush to fade like an outgoing tide.

But the motivation and focus never returned. Her hands shook. Her feet tapped a nervous rhythm on the classroom floor. Her thoughts galloped, and though she fiddled with her pencil like a twirler leading a parade, she didn't take a single note. Two pills was clearly one too many, the fine line between medicated and high as a jet plane breached.

This must be what my son feels like all the time, she realized.

After class she didn't sleep. Instead, she cleaned the trailer. She dusted and then scooped out the corners of the windowsills with a Q-tip. She scrubbed the toilet, shook out the rugs. She organized her socks by color.

Or so she thought. The next morning she'd find she was so distracted she'd thrown clean clothes into the hamper with dirty ones, completely misplaced her own hairbrush, and left every kitchen appliance unplugged.

But now, armed with a bottle of Windex, she sprayed and

wiped, sprayed and wiped, sprayed and wiped each window until it seemed she'd polished the glass into night-black oblivion. Like she could climb through the empty window frame and fly out of the trailer.

Instead, she studied her own reflection, imposed over the dark spruces at the edge of the yard, and remembered the night, over ten years ago, that Robert Senior had tried to disappear.

After he'd hit and killed a man, Robert's father had ended up back at their trailer, this time tottering up the front steps and knocking on the door. Deb had answered and, moved by the thick tears of a man she had once thought she'd marry, had allowed Rob to wait crouching on the porch while she packed him a bag: a granola bar, an apple, a bath towel, a can of Diet Coke, and five cigarettes rationed from her own pack. She'd pressed the cigarettes into his hot, slick palm and bundled the rest into a trash bag, knotting it closed. He'd asked for money; she'd refused, and then shut the door. She'd watched out the window as he stumbled across the yard, rounding the trailer's back corner, where he'd pass right under his sleeping son's bedroom window before bounding into the forest. She'd turned away before she had to watch him disappear.

At the time, she'd thought she was helping her son's father. She kept silent during the manhunt, when Sheriff O'Shay came to the trailer and asked if she knew where Rob might run to. But now she wondered if Rob would have been better off if she'd turned him in. She could have stalled him, said she was going to get some money, while she quietly called in the tip. Even later, she could have pointed the posse searching for him in the right direction.

Rob might have gotten a lighter sentence if he hadn't made Sheriff O'Shay look like such a fool. If the search for him hadn't dragged on for days, while the *Tide* slammed the Sheriff's Department and island residents railed against their incompetence. If Rob hadn't given the sheriff a black eye when they finally dragged him out of the woods, if Deb had made the call before Rob could even part those pine branches, he might not have gotten the maximum sentence for his crime: eighteen years. The difference was what kept Rob Kelley behind bars today.

Branches pogoed. Her heart hopped like a startled rabbit. She half expected Rob to step out of the woods with a caveman beard and the towel she'd given him knotted to a stick, roaring about how he'd survived by trapping critters and munching on crickets.

Finally, he'd have a true story to tell.

An animal, a blur of fur with twin flashlight eyes, darted across the yard and under her neighbor's porch.

She wiped away Rob's memory like just another smudge, and shut all of the trailer's blinds.

She was cleaning her own room, peering under the bed,

when she spotted an amber cylinder lying on its side. She stretched and grasped until she could grab it. That original bottle of pills, the one that had seemed to walk away. It'd been here all along. She hid it in her nightstand drawer with the others.

She'd been right not to keep Robert on this medication, and she was going to stop taking it herself. She'd keep the bottles around, just in case, until she had finished her ninety hours of classwork. Then she'd flush every last little blue tab down the toilet.

Interview with Barry Lancaster, Yannatok
High School guidance office, October 4, 2010

From Flight Risk: The Robert Jackson Kelley Story

"He wasn't a bad kid. Not mouthy, not disrespectful. Would wave to me when we passed in the hall. He was one of those kids you wanted to help out, but there was just no follow-through at home. And everyone knew his father was in jail, but the mother never took him to any kind of counseling to process it. How does a kid deal with that? I think he was just in denial, avoiding the whole thing. Stuffing down all that emotion. Kids like that explode eventually. Should I have called Children and Youth, gotten a social worker involved? I didn't think so. There wasn't abuse. Truancy was never an issue. It was like he couldn't wait to get to school, actually, so he could run around with Joey Kovach. Like he was lonely, really. I was hoping I could just help him get through without too much damage, run out the clock, basically, and get a diploma. After that, well, everybody's got to grow up and take responsibility sometime, right?"

———————

The barking started in sixth period. Robert was doodling through algebra; he'd failed it last year and was only doing slightly better this year. He needed the math credit to graduate, so he made an attempt at the homework during homeroom most days, scribbling equations through the pledge and morning announcements. Mrs. Main looked at him pointedly when she caught him drawing, but the scribbling busied his hands enough that he could listen to some of what she said.

The barking grew louder, punctuated by heavy footsteps. Robert's hand shot up. "Can I go to the bathroom?"

"Not now," Mrs. Main replied without looking away from the board. "You can see here that the variable—"

"Mrs. Main, I really gotta go," Robert interrupted.

"You cannot go while the dogs are out there," Mrs. Main snapped. "Am I making myself clear?"

Robert slumped in his seat. The dogs passed the slim, rectangular classroom window a few minutes later. German shepherds with alert ears and dark eyes, exclamation-point tails, hungrily sniffing the lockers.

His stomach dropped. Drug dogs. What else could they have been? If Mrs. Main would let him go to the bathroom, he could warn Joey.

They called Robert to the office just before study hall. Vice Principal Diederman escorted Robert there.

"What's up?" Robert asked. He ran his palms down the rows of lockers. He usually enjoyed the clanging, but all he could think was how he should have ignored Mrs. Main. He should have bounced out of the room and through the school's double doors and kept going until he hit the beach, the woods, the highway to Seattle.

"Don't touch those lockers," Diederman said. "You good friends with Joey Kovach?"

"Yeah." He kept his hands in his pockets for the rest of the walk.

How dumb was Joey to keep the pills in his locker for days on end? Still, Robert felt sorry for his friend. If the school made him do community service, he'd probably have to pick soggy, stinking trash off the beach.

Diederman led him right into Principal Simena's office. Simena was flanked by two cops, both at least a foot taller than she was. A walkie-talkie crackled. Joey slumped in front of Simena's desk. He sniffled and didn't look at Robert. Was he seriously crying?

"Yo, Joey." Robert tried to get his attention. "You need a Kleenex, bro? It won't be that bad. A few weekends and you'll be done."

"Take a seat, son." The first cop nodded at the empty chair next to Joey. Robert recognized Holt immediately. His hair had grown in, but Robert was sure it was him. "Holt!"

The man didn't smile. "*Sheriff* Holt. 'Sir' will do fine."

"Sheriff Holt, sir. Listen, I was wondering—"

Robert wanted to ask about the bear, if it had finally been lured out and set free in the mountains.

Simena interrupted him as she rifled through a file. "Robert, does your mother have alternate contact information? Another phone number? You don't have an emergency contact."

Robert slouched into the chair. Joey still wasn't looking at him. He gnawed on an already raw fingernail. "She's at work."

"We'll try her again," Holt said.

"I'm going to call down Barry Lancaster," Simena mused.

Holt showed Robert a baggie with three amber bottles inside. "Do these belong to you, son?"

"My name's on them," Robert sighed. *And my mom filled them.*

Holt squinted at the label's print. He looked at Robert. "So you're Robert Jackson Kelley?"

Robert sat up. Holt did remember him. "That's me."

Holt studied him. "Do you live in a trailer out on Cove Lane? Near the woods?"

"Yeah," Robert answered. "Listen, I think there are still bears out there. You guys should get some more traps and—"

Principal Simena interrupted. "Should Robert answer questions without an attorney present?"

"I'm simply ascertaining the boy's residency, ma'am," Holt said. He cleared his throat. "Do you know how these pills ended up in Mr. Kovach's locker?"

No. He must have stolen them. A lie that would have been difficult to disprove. But then Joey took a tattered tissue from his pocket and blew his nose. Simena reached across her desk to hand him another, and Joey swiped at his red-rimmed eyes.

Robert's heart leaped like it would take off. *I will not be a snitch.* "I gave them to Mr. Kovach. Sir."

"And why did you do that?"

Robert paused. "Mr. Kovach told me he would sell them and I could have some of the money."

Joey kicked Simena's desk. Robert jumped at the hollow thud. Simena stood and leaned over her desk. "Do that again and we'll add destruction of property to this report! Do you understand me?"

Joey nodded miserably. Robert quickly added, "But I'm pretty sure Joey here is a terrible salesman. Because I haven't gotten paid, and I don't think Joey's sold any."

"I appreciate your honesty, son," Sheriff Holt replied. Robert felt strangely proud. He'd probably saved Joey from getting in a lot more trouble. How can you be a dealer if you haven't sold anything?

Joey's mom came right away. Her curses and crying penetrated the office door. She yanked Joey up by his collar and dragged him out to her car. Robert didn't get to talk to his friend before he left.

Robert was stranded in the office for a slow hour before they relocated him to the ISS room. He studied the graffiti-covered desk. His fingers itched to add his own contribution to the initials and doodles. He drummed instead, palms slapping the faux wood. He wondered how long he'd be suspended. Joey would surely get a stiffer punishment than he would; even though Robert had done everything he could to help his friend out, they'd found the pills in Joey's locker.

Three thirty came and went without Deb answering her phone.

The longer Robert waited, the more anger roiled his stomach. He smacked the desk until his palms stung. Deb, too busy to talk to the sheriff, but with plenty of time for a pharmacy run.

Eventually, Holt drove to the dispatch center to deliver

the news while Robert waited. Deb would be sitting with her headset on, or sneaking a smoke break, when Holt told her what had gone down. Would she stomp out her cigarette, spitting curses? Throw her Diet Coke against the wall?

Maybe Holt would ask her why they had all those prescription bottles in the house in the first place. Just who had filled them all and then left them lying around, nobody paying enough attention to miss them?

Robert wished he could hear *that* interrogation.

Holt returned alone. He stood in the ISS room doorway. "Your mother is declining to leave work to pick you up. She says she has a night-school class, and that you'd benefit from a night in custody anyway."

"In custody?"

"In a jail cell."

Robert laughed. "Seriously? She wants me to spend the night in jail?"

"I don't think there's anything funny about this."

"I don't, either, man," Robert said, though he laughed again.

He'd call her bluff.

They passed soccer practice, guys' and girls', on their way to Holt's car. Robert got ready to wave, or bow, something smart-ass to show that none of this mattered, but the kids didn't look up from their shooting drills and wind sprints.

Holt pointed to the backseat. Robert ducked and slid in.

He leaned forward to get a better look at the dashboard computer. The center console, lodged between the two front seats, bloomed with red switches and knobs. Still, the whole operation must not be that hard to figure out. His father had done it. Drunk.

Holt climbed in, started the car, and Seattle's classic rock station burst from the speakers. Holt lunged to turn the song down, but not before Robert recognized it. The one about the bad moon, the guy warning everybody to stay home.

They passed the airfields. No one was landing or taking off, so Robert watched Holt drive, disappointed that he didn't make use of the console gadgets.

"What do you have to do to be a cop?" Robert asked.

Holt raised his eyebrows. "You want to be a police officer?"

Robert shrugged. "Maybe. Or join the army. The air force."

"The biggest thing for you is to keep a *very* clean record from here on out." Holt glanced at him in the mirror. "*Exceptionally* clean, in your case. Do more community service than the school requires. Get very good grades."

"Well, getting suspended is going to screw me there."

"I spent some time in the army, myself," Holt continued. "You know, I got into a bit of trouble when I was your age, too. I grew up in a small town. Not the most exciting place to be, just like here, and bored kids get up to all kinds of things. Military straightened me right out. The structure can be good for a guy like you."

Robert fiddled with the silver door lock, imagined himself combat-rolling onto the road. The door wouldn't budge. "Were you in Desert Storm?"

Holt shook his head. "I didn't see combat."

They rode without speaking. Static burst over the radio.

Robert turned from the window, bored. Same view he saw from the bus every morning. He asked, "Do you have kids?"

"No. A few nieces and nephews." Holt paused. "You've made a big mistake here, young man, but you can still get back on the right path. You're young. You don't have to repeat another person's mistakes. You start making the right choices and sky's the limit for a kid like you."

Robert nodded, but didn't speak again. *Another person's mistakes.* His mom's, obviously. Holt seemed to get it.

Ten minutes later, they pulled into the station. Robin's-egg-blue paint peeled off the cinder-block walls. The shining linoleum floor reflected back the cell bars' grid. A bed topped with a thin mattress and flattened pillow stretched across the far wall. Toilet paper unspooled next to the stainless steel toilet.

Holt read Robert his rights and recorded his prints,

staining his fingers an inky black. Then Holt posed Robert in front of a white wall to snap his mug shot.

"What do I do?" Robert asked. He thought of his school pictures, how the photographers would line him up on the red X and have him tilt his head just so. Deb hadn't bought a package since elementary school, so Robert usually crossed his eyes or stuck out his tongue.

"Just stand there," Holt answered. Robert grinned broadly. The camera's flash momentarily blinded him. Then Holt steered him by the elbow to the precinct's holding cell.

"You're lucky it's empty." Holt jingled a heavy key ring. "Wouldn't want a roommate."

The cell door clattered. Holt locked it and walked away.

Robert paced the length of the cell, then the width, his heels tracking his toes. About six by eight. He looped the perimeter a second time to check his measurements.

He drummed on the bars, tried slipping an arm outside. He poked his elbow through the lattice. He stuck his foot out, tapped the floor outside, stepped back into the cell.

"And that's what it's all about," Robert sang, and laughed with no one. He plopped down on the bed and studied the dark whorls of his fingerprints.

A fly buzzed into the cell, flitted around his head, flew out and down the corridor. Robert took a dime from his pocket and flung it through the bars. It hit the floor and spun, colliding with the wall and finally falling. He wished he'd tried to skip it like a stone across a creek and wanted the coin back so intensely for a moment he thought he might cry.

He tried to hurry the minutes with a nap. He'd wake up and it'd be time to go. But the bars tattooed the backs of his eyelids, a million repeating squares. The matrix dizzied him; he anchored one foot on the floor and still his stomach didn't settle.

Robert imagined his father lumbering around a cell this small. Bumping into the walls, his feet hanging over the bed's edge. His voice booming down the corridor, bouncing back to him. The old man had to have been six two? Maybe even six three, six four. Robert knew it was childish, but he couldn't help but picture his dad like Paul Bunyan, arms wide as redwoods bursting from a flannel shirt. Robert Senior would have hated being caged like this even more than his son did.

Good thing they'd never caught him.

How had Robert Senior gotten away? He must have outrun those cops, and the cops gave up, simple as that. By now, he could have a whole new name, a whole new life set up for himself. Maybe his dad was like a spy with a briefcase full of disguises.

Robert should knot some toilet paper around his neck

and scare the shit out of his mother when she showed up. Robert could hold his breath long enough to mottle his face, let his tongue loll out.

He rolled from the bed and stood on tiptoe to see out the slim window. Sky sliced by more bars.

Outside, an engine backfired. A dog barked, endlessly.

Suddenly Robert leaped back from the window. He wrapped his hands around the cell bars and shook them. He could swear the cell was shrinking, that if he were to pace around it again, he'd count five steps where he'd just measured six. His clammy hands left damp blotches on the iron.

He couldn't spend the night here. He'd lose it.

He walked the perimeter of the cell again. Still six by eight. Of course. He did it three more times, counting like the numbers were a protective spell.

He realized his bedroom wasn't actually much bigger than a jail cell. That the trailer was pretty much four or five holding cells that had stretched a few feet, like the walls couldn't wait to get away from each other, and sprouted closets and a bathroom like tumors.

Sometime after the iron-slashed sun had slid down the sky and disappeared into the trees, Deb came to spring him. Already swathed in her post-work leggings, hoodie, and ponytail, makeup scrubbed off, she looked perhaps more like his sister than his mother. A notebook stuck out of her purse.

Holt accompanied her to the cell.

Robert pretended his legs were as leaden as bars and refrained from charging toward the door. "I thought you were going to make me stay."

"Maybe I should."

"Maybe I want to."

"Get up *now*."

Robert took his time, stretching his arms above his head and strolling intentionally out of the cell. He scooped up his escapee dime and pocketed it.

He waited while his mom and the sheriff reviewed some paperwork. Deb signed page after page, quickly enough that Robert knew she wasn't reading the fine print. He wouldn't have, either. When they were finished, Robert stood and saluted Holt. "Till we meet again."

"Hopefully we won't," Holt answered.

Robert laughed. "It's a small island. A small, boring island."

"Let's go," Deb snapped.

In the car, she said, "The school's going to expel you. The principal says you're done there. You realize that, don't you? You and that Kovach kid. Whose mother blames *me* for this, by the way. I've had to deal with her all afternoon, too. With all these people calling me at dispatch, you're lucky I didn't get *fired*."

Expel *him*? His mom had filled the prescriptions, and

Joey had been the one trying to sell the drugs. The translucent bottles had been in his possession for less than twenty-four hours, and now *he* was going to get kicked out of school?

"This is such *bullshit*," Robert said bitterly.

"You know what's bullshit, Robert? Working my ass off every day to try to give you some kind of future, and you throwing it away. Like it's nothing." Deb shook her head. "Unbelievable."

"Why did you have them? Were you going to sell them?" Robert meant to yell it, to shake the truck windows with the truth. Instead he mumbled his questions, strangled the words as they croaked from his throat.

Deb snorted. "Yeah, I was going to sell them. We chop them up and snort them at dispatch. It's a hell of a time."

"Why'd you have them, then?"

Her answer was quick. "I filled them each month for a little while, whether you were taking them or not, in case we lost our insurance, and then suddenly, you needed them."

He practically whispered. "Are you telling the truth?"

Deb drove through two lights in silence. Finally she sighed. "Yes. I'm telling the truth."

He watched her white knuckles as she turned onto their street, trembling at the edge of her sweatshirt's cuff, and knew she wasn't. Not completely, anyway.

They didn't speak for the next two days.

* * *

Of course she'd lied to her son. If Deb had copped to taking Robert's Adderall, wouldn't that basically grant him permission to foul up his brain with any pill or powder or potion he could scrounge up?

She'd been the one to answer the calls of a dozen other mothers whose kids had sniffed gasoline or slurped bottles of NyQuil. Once Deb had even sent an ambulance to a house where three kids were puking their guts out after smoking nutmeg.

She would not give Robert an excuse for acting like a fool.

Interview with Mira Wohl, Willamette University cafeteria, October 2, 2010

From *Flight Risk: The Robert Jackson Kelley Story*

"I saw a picture of his mom in my uncle's yearbook, and she was, like, really pretty when she went here, had all kinds of boyfriends, but you see her now, she just looks old. Tired, like she's always hungover. If you go by the dispatch center, you'll see all those women huddled together on their cigarette breaks, puffin' as quick as they can. She's the blonde, the short one, always bundled up, arms wrapped around herself like she's freezin' cold. You see her at the supermarket, the gas station, the bank, but she doesn't give more than a quick nod, if that. I swear, it's like she hates us for being young and not being stuck here.

"She didn't need to put up that Beware of Dog sign. Her face said it all."

NOVEMBER 2009

————————————

At the expulsion hearing, his mother cried like they were at a wake. Sobs tore from her throat and wracked her body. She coughed thickly. Members of the school board whispered to each other, then tried not to look, as she honked her nose into a thin, holey tissue. Robert left a seat between them, more angry than embarrassed. What did she have to be so distraught about? He was the one on trial. He tried to capture his shaking knee in his palm and refused to look at her.

Principal Simena wore a skirt and blazer. She patted Deb on the shoulder. She leaned down so that their foreheads almost touched, and she whispered and Robert's mother nodded, and then they stood up and walked out, Simena's arm around Deb's jean jacket–clad shoulders. Great. Maybe they'd become best friends and ride horses together.

The principal could probably smell beer on Deb's breath.

She'd gulped several before they'd left for the meeting, while she tore through Robert's closet, searching for a collared shirt. She'd found one balled up on the floor and then burned her fingertip on the steaming iron.

"Get off the goddamn game!" Deb had howled, kicking a loose sneaker across the trailer, her finger wrapped in a wet paper towel. The tattered shoe sailed over Robert's head. He'd been standing at the computer, maneuvering his plane through crowded Atlantic airspace.

"Mom, you're going to make me crash," Robert complained.

"Get dressed!"

"You've been saying for days that I'm getting expelled! What does it matter what I wear? Why are we even going?"

"That's it!" Deb stomped to the computer and yanked the plug from the wall. The screen flickered and darkened. "You're done with this game! You need to go out and get yourself a job! Or I'm going to make you work at the stables. Shovel horse shit all day long and you'll see how easy you really have it." She wrestled the cord free from the computer, wound it up, and stomped away again.

He ended up wearing the collared shirt, wrinkled.

And that was *before* the board voted to expel him, unanimously.

Joey Kovach's mom wore a blazer, too, and black pants. And Joey's collared shirt was straight and spotless. And he

119

got expelled, too, right after Robert. Robert was surprised by how quickly it all went down; he'd expected more of a courtroom scenario, with questions and arguing and maybe even a chance to talk himself. Instead his name was called and they didn't even mention what he'd done, just that Simena and Barry were recommending him for "placement" until the beginning of the next school year, whatever that meant. He caught one important word: "residential." After that, he couldn't listen; he was too busy picturing the county holding cell and himself locked inside it, clad in a striped jumpsuit.

Not that Deb was in the room to hear the verdict. Robert sat by himself for another hour, as the board tackled the budgets and building reports, until Simena tapped him on the shoulder and told him to meet his mother in the lobby.

He passed two older people, concerned citizens, no doubt, and a science teacher he'd had in middle school, and was almost out the door when he saw Holt sitting in the back row, in uniform.

"Hey!" Robert said. He saluted sharply. The science teacher turned. Robert lowered his voice. "Hey. You got any other clothes?"

He wondered if Holt attended all the school board meetings, to keep up on the local scene, or if he'd specifically wanted to see what would happen with Robert. The sheriff didn't lift his eyes from the board member, ignoring

Robert as determinedly as Robert had been stonewalling his mother.

"Let's go," Simena whispered, hurrying him along.

"Till we meet again!" Robert crowed.

Deb wasn't in the lobby, either; she'd already gone to the car. Robert didn't tell his mom about Joey's clothes and how little it all mattered. And he didn't ask for the computer cord.

Robert signed a diversion agreement, whatever that meant, to dodge a drug charge. He pretended to read through the document, but he focused on one stipulation only: he'd be unable to take his driver's test for another year. He hadn't been able to take drivers' ed; his mother thought it was a waste of money, since she always had the truck and Robert would rarely be able to practice. Still, that punishment stung more than any other. They might as well string the island with barbed wire.

Without his flight simulator, Robert was restless. The school district had ten days to set up his alternative placement. The residential school. He was starting to wish they'd hurry up.

He flicked through the twenty channels they got without satellite TV and only found soap operas and daytime talk shows. A grainy show where a man followed people around in a van to see if they were cheating on their wives or husbands. Arguments about paternity featured heavily in all three. Cooking shows.

One day Robert was inspired to make an omelet. He cracked four eggs against the counter. He smacked one too hard and wiped up the drippy mess with a paper towel. He mixed the eggs together with some milk and poured it into a scratched frying pan. The batter hissed and bubbled. Robert couldn't find a spatula so he hovered at the ready with a fork, waiting to flip the eggs over so they folded into a tasty envelope. He tapped the fork against the counter, against the steel sink. Yellow liquid still pooled at the pan's center. He turned the heat up as high as it would go to speed things up.

Then he heard Hulk barking, and realized that he'd forgotten his dog outside. He left the stove to let him back in, and even the fork still in his hand didn't help him re-member the eggs cooking on the stove when he saw a flash of brown at the edge of the evergreens. Twigs snapped and the brush shook. Too big to be a squirrel or a rabbit. A bobcat?

Robert strode closer, but whatever it was had disappeared.

Had they ever caught that bear? A whole family could live back there by now. How big would a bear cub be? Big-ger than Hulk, surely.

He waited, watching the woods, trying to detect

movement. He held Hulk back by the collar. The dog's ears stuck straight up. Birds tweeted, unseen.

Then Robert smelled smoke. The front door slammed behind him just as the smoke detector blared to life.

The eggs had burned into a charred blob. He ran water in the pan and left it steaming in the sink, blackened bits of egg swirling down the drain.

When Deb got home, he begged her for the computer power cord. "I'm so bored. Can I have it just for a day?"

"I threw it out," she replied. She sniffed. "Why does it smell like something burning in here?"

"You threw it *out?*" Robert moaned. He tugged at his hair and kicked the kitchen table.

The next day she left a list of chores on the counter, written on the back of a grocery store receipt. *Vacuum whole house. Do dishes. Give Hulk a bath. Dust whole house.*

"We don't have a house," Robert pointed out to Hulk. "We have a trailer."

Go to Laundromat had been printed and then crossed off. Robert guessed Deb didn't want him wandering too far.

Holt made a couple of calls and got the Kelley kid into Sea Brook Youth Home as part of his diversion agreement. Tucked into a sleepy beach town just over the bridge on the mainland, the "wilderness therapy" program focused on nonviolent kids and barred all media: no phones, no TV, no Internet. Holt liked the program's emphasis on nature and physical activity. The juvie in Seattle was a rough place, and soon enough the kid would be done with his punishment, and land back on Yannatok. Holt didn't want him learning any new tricks from the thugs in juvie. Besides, the kid could use a break, with the father he'd gotten saddled with.

"I was there when we caught the father," Holt had told Sea Brook's director. "I'm sure you remember that mess. The kid's like a lit firecracker. Can't sit still for five minutes. But there's something there. He's looking for somebody to please, in a way. And a change of scenery would do him good. I bet he's never been off this island."

That would change, Holt knew. The kid would get off Yannatok, eventually. Holt just hoped it wasn't with a one-way ticket to Washington State Pen. They'd eat him alive in there.

As soon as Robert heard his mother's truck pulling up, the trailer seemed to suck in its breath. Its walls constricted. Deb broke two days of silence by informing Robert that she'd spoken to a Sea Brook counselor who'd called her at work, and that he shouldn't bother packing much. Deb ticked off items on her fingers, her voice cold. "Socks.

Underwear. White T-shirts—no logos, no colors. Khakis. One pair of sneakers. No extras. The woman said not so much as a pack of gum. Start packing. They'll be here tomorrow morning."

"What am I supposed to put it all in?"

"A plastic bag, like from the grocery store," Deb instructed. "They don't want backpacks in that place."

Robert trudged to his room, started rifling through his drawers, but soon found himself planning for a different trip than the one he was about to take. One for which he'd certainly need more supplies than socks and undershirts.

What would he need to pack if he were to take off into the woods?

He abandoned packing, escaped from the trailer's thick, stale air, and stood near the flagpole, bouncing a mottled tennis ball for Hulk. The dog raced and retrieved it, boomeranging back every time. Hulk was a smart dog; Robert bet he could have been trained to sniff out drugs or tackle murderers.

If Robert was going to run away into the wilderness, he'd need some clothes he could layer on. Matches. Water. A knife, probably, for protection and hunting. He wouldn't need that much, really. He'd take Hulk. He could hike his way to Canada and leave them waiting for him at the "wilderness therapy" school, which was only called that to make parents feel better about their kids getting locked up.

Robert was going to jail, same as Joey in juvie, no matter what they called it.

He watched the trees and remembered, suddenly, one of the best and only books he'd read from start to finish the entire time he'd been in school. *Hatchet*. He remembered the cover, with the ax printed right over the kid's head, like the hatchet was part of his brain, and the tilted plane in the background, over the kid's shoulder. The slow classes read it in eighth grade, the year he'd almost failed. He'd raced through it in one sitting. A kid named Brian is on his way to visit his dad in Alaska, but the Cessna he's riding in crashes, and he has to survive in the wilderness with just this hatchet, catching rabbits and foraging for berries. Robert thought the book ended with Brian still out there, hunkering down for a long winter.

He was supposed to turn in a report at the end, which he never finished. He could have either completed a standard five-paragraph book report about the setting and the characters and how the book made him feel, or a fake newspaper article in which he pretended to interview the main character. Robert opted for the article, which was obviously easier; he could just make it all up.

He'd written a headline: *Brian Is a Hero!* And he'd scribbled out a few questions: *What did you think when the plane crashed? What did you think when you realized you were alone in Alaska? What did you think when you realized you only had your hatchet?* And he didn't remember if he ever got any further with the assignment, but he doubted it.

For his last dinner at home, Deb microwaved two frozen pizzas. She dropped two plates onto the table with a clatter, and let the steam waft off her dinner while she slugged a beer. Robert didn't wait. The gooey cheese seared the roof of his mouth.

"An army recruiter called. Asked for you." Deb glowered through rings of fatigue and smudged eyeliner. "You know anything about that?"

"I'm going to enlist. Like Dad." His mouth burned. He pushed back from the table to get a glass of tap water.

"Like Dad?" Deb's cigarette hung in the air.

"Yeah. He told me all about it once. Desert Storm." The cabinets were emptied of cups; food-encrusted dishes teetered in the sink. He considered slurping out of a bowl, Hulk-style.

Deb snorted. "Your father wasn't anywhere near Desert Storm."

Robert sighed. He should have known she'd react like this. "*Yeah*, he was. He told me about rescuing Daniel McQuaid, and getting a medal—"

"The military wouldn't even *take* him. He had a rap sheet miles long." Deb stubbed out her cigarette. "In and out of jail is where he's been for your whole life. You know that."

"Why would he make that up?" He slammed the cabinet shut. He knew his mom was mad at him, but who was she to call his dad a liar? He'd asked her, to her face, why she'd been stockpiling his Adderall and he knew she hadn't told him everything.

Maybe she knew where his dad really was. Maybe she's known all along, and she'd thrown Robert off the trail all these years, inventing a prison Robert Senior could never escape from.

"Why do you think?" his mother yelled back. "Because he's a loser! He was nothing and he wanted you to think he was something. He *killed* an old man! Thought he was playing some stupid prank, stealing a cop car, and then he hit a seventy-five-year-old man! And left him bleeding in the middle of the road. And forgive *me*, I never wanted you to know!"

"*You're* a loser! And you're a liar! He hit a *deer*." Robert stormed out of the kitchen and stomped into his sneakers. He called over his shoulder, "*You* were the one taking the Adderall! You should be going to prison, too!"

"If you walk out of here, plan on staying outside!" Deb crashed after him. The next trailer's porch light flickered on. "You don't think I'm tired at the end of the day? Have you ever thought for one second about how hard it is to work all day and then go to school? And you want to judge me over a couple of pills!"

"I knew it! I knew you were lying, just like you're lying about Dad," Robert yelled over his shoulder as he slammed the door. The porch was much colder than the cramped trailer, but Deb kept following him, pawing at his shoulder.

"I could have had my own horse by now! The only thing I ever wanted!" she screamed. "I spend all my money on you! All of it! And all you care about is your father. Name one thing he ever did for you!"

Robert shrugged out of her grip. "Get off me! Don't do anything for me ever again! I never asked you to!"

Deb stepped backward. "Where do you think you're going?"

"None of your business!" He whirled toward the road.

The door crashed shut. Robert stood by the road with his thumb cocked. He'd take any ride, to anywhere. But not a single car passed and soon he gave up and trudged back to the trailer.

Robert knew his mom had left the door unlocked, but he spent the night on the porch anyway, sleeping fitfully and listening to the wind in the spruces' branches. He wrapped his arms around himself to try and fend off the cold, but he shivered anyway.

In the morning, a van painted with a yellow sun rising over rolling waves came for him. He waited on the porch with his plastic bag at his feet, rubbing his aching neck. Every gull's squawk needled his forehead. His eyes hurt. Robert had packed his toothbrush, boxers, deodorant. He'd scrounged up the white shirts, though technically two of them were undershirts. He only had two pairs of khakis, though, one with cuffs so worn they trailed dirty threads like gray tentacles. He guessed the school would give him whatever else he needed. Deb hadn't been in the mood for a shopping trip.

His mom came out, bundled in her sweatshirt, its frayed cuffs pulled down past her chapped knuckles. She huddled beside him. She was hoarse. "I want you to think of this as a fresh start. It's not going to be fun. It's not supposed to be. But you need to listen to these people and try to learn something. You might be able to get on a different path."

Robert nodded, but he couldn't make himself talk to her. The van pulled up. Deb hugged him and Robert patted her stiffly.

Hulk barked and tugged at his flagpole-bound leash until the van had driven out of sight, Robert the only passenger on its long bench seat.

The van puffed along, the miles between him and the trailer widening.

Dunes Road widened into two lanes just before Yannatok Bridge. Robert had only been across it a few times: a class trip to the aquarium, a visit to his now-deceased great-grandmother's farm, a dentist appointment. On each excursion the allure of the mainland had had him bouncing in his seat. Even a fluoride treatment seemed exotic, compared to his sludge-paced school days.

Traffic crawled onto the bridge, paused atop it like Ferris wheel cars dangling at the ride's pinnacle. For twenty-five minutes the van inched across the bridge, Robert suspended between Yannatok and the mainland. Despite the van's wide bench seat, he started to feel trapped. He whipped his head from one window to the other. The ferry passed them and blasted its horn, a single, bloated note.

Then he was off the island.

Like a deep-sea diver, finally coming up for air.

He looked straight ahead, and told himself he'd never go back.

Every dude wore identical white tees and khakis, like they'd been drafted into the Hanes army. Sea Brook also gave each student two green sweatshirts printed with the same rising sun logo that had been painted on the van. Lights-out at nine thirty and a wake-up call at six. A basketball court without nets. A cafeteria without knives or forks. They ate sandwiches and apples.

The school was strict; the guys weren't allowed to talk as they marched between buildings in single-file lines, rotating through their regimented schedules. But Robert quickly discovered that everyone here was getting away with something. Kids offered to sell him Ritalin, Percocet, Vicodin, weed, E. Some sold clean piss. The counselors and teachers gave out carved wooden discs, bottle cap–sized, that could be traded for snacks, breaks from chores, and trips off campus. The tokens were engraved with eagles' wings, bear claws, shark fins. Guys sold those, too, though not for nearly as much as the other contraband.

Each of the school's housing units was named for a tree. Redwood was reserved for guys who'd been in fights or caught with drugs and put on twenty-four-hour lockdown; Robert was sent to Maple, the house with the most privileges. He'd been evaluated by an on-staff psychologist and determined not to have any substance abuse problems, major mental illness, or potential for violence, and so he was put in the house with the lounge and foosball table.

Robert slumped through his first math and English classes, and the only nature he saw was the bushes outside his windows and the weed his roommate smoked after lights-out. But, he had been told in orientation, he could start earning Greens, the tokens, right away.

His first day he got one for complying with lights-out at the first request. Robert flipped the Green over to see it was stamped with some kind of paw print; he couldn't even tell what animal the carving was supposed to represent. He slipped it in his pants pocket and couldn't find it by morning.

"Hey." Robert approached a counselor after breakfast, toast crusts piled on his tray. The food wasn't bad: fresh fruit and eggs, a buffet of cereal boxes. "Can I have another one of those things? The Green? I lost it."

The counselor shook his head. A silver whistle hung from

his neck. Every counselor had something dangling on a chain: whistles, stopwatches, compasses. *Just my luck. A school full of gym teachers.* "Sorry. We don't give out duplicates. Gotta be responsible for your things."

Robert walked away knowing he'd never hold on to enough of those things to earn a bag of Doritos, never mind a trip off campus.

He had to sit through a class three days a week about drugs and drinking, and he'd alternate between studying the floor and the ceiling.

"Do you have anything you'd like to share, Robert?" one of the sad-sack counselors always asked him. These guys drank so much coffee their mugs might as well have been welded to their hands, along with their clipboards, free gifts from pharmaceutical reps. Their pens, handy for note-taking, were also emblazoned with logos: Concerta, Wellbutrin, Lexapro.

Barry Lancaster had never asked him a dumb question like that. Robert shook his head and didn't say a word.

Time seemed to slow and stretch during the ninety-minute class. Robert found his mind wandering to what Deb had told him about his father. He heard her accusations over and over again. But Robert didn't believe his father had really killed anyone. Drank too much, no doubt. Gotten into fights, sure. Stolen a cop car, laughing as he did it, definitely. But when Robert thought back to that last time he saw his dad, he couldn't imagine that Robert Senior had, just minutes before rapping on his son's window, left another man to die in the street. And when Robert tried to imagine his dad locked in a cell like the one Holt had put him in, well, that just seemed impossible.

More likely, Robert Senior was still on the run, and his mother couldn't stand the fact that she wasn't going anywhere at all.

One day a van left for the woods, taking five guys and two counselors on an "overnight wilderness encounter." Robert watched from his window as they loaded rolled-up sleeping bags and tents. He thought of how Hulk used to wait for him to trudge off the school bus, his nose pressed to the trailer's screen door. Robert abandoned the window for his bunk bed and stared at a water stain spreading across the ceiling like a dirty cloud.

Four white cinder-block walls, two metal-framed twin beds, desks, and shelves built into the walls. A window over each bed, a beige shade, fluorescent lights. They were allowed to have books and crayons and paper. No markers, no pens, no pencils. All potential weapons.

Through his window, Robert could see a swath of trees,

and beyond that, vacation houses' peaked roofs. He'd finally crossed the bridge off Yannatok and the view still looked like he'd never left the trailer.

There wasn't a fence.

His roommate, Dalton, was quiet and gnawed at his nails until they bled. His T-shirt swallowed his lanky frame like a white whale. He'd stolen a car and snorted crystal meth. Once a week, Dalton forfeited his climbs up the rock wall for an NA meeting.

"Crystal makes you crazy," Dalton told Robert. "I was pulling out my hair, my eyelashes. Thought I had bedbugs."

They talked after lights-out while Dalton rolled joint after joint. Smoke curled up to Robert on the top bunk. Dalton said more in the dark than he ever did during class. He'd actually been living on Yannatok before his stint in Sea Brook began. His mother had hoped a move to the island from Seattle would keep Dalton away from his tweaker friends. He'd been enrolled in Yannatok High, but had only attended two days before hitchhiking back to the city to be reunited with his meth-smoking buddies. According to him, stealing a car, the transgression that finally landed him here, was the simplest thing Dalton had ever done.

"I did it with a screwdriver. Just popped it in the ignition," Dalton bragged. "People are so dumb. So many people leave their cars unlocked. And it's like 'I wonder where I should park?' Maybe all the way over here, where it's pitch black? And I know what I'll do! I'll put one of those magnetic boxes under my bumper with the key right in it! Or maybe I'll leave a spare in the glove box. And a lot of people out here never lock their houses." He flopped over, ruffling the beige blankets. "It's like they want their shit to get stolen."

"I really miss my dog," Robert said.

Dear Robert,
I feel bad about the last time we talked, but you
needed to know some things. I don't want you going
down your father's path, and I've tried to keep you off
of it. When you get home, we can talk more and try to
make things better around the house. I hope you think
about what you want to do in school.

Mom

Robert rushed through his work and was just as lackluster a student as he'd been at his old school, but "wilderness therapy" was a different story. Sea Brook's staff trained their charges with the goal of eventually sending them out to the cliffs and the dense woods. The school was equipped with a ropes course and a rock wall dangling with belays. They shot blunt-tipped arrows at rows of foam targets and practiced assembling and tearing down tents, a counselor with a stopwatch cheering them on to beat their previous times.

Robert ruled at all of it. Some guys rolled their eyes and zombie-walked their way through the tires, hung from the rock wall limp as damp shirts on a clothesline. But Robert high-stepped across fields of tires, shimmied up the rock wall, balanced atop a revolving log like he'd been practicing his whole life. His arrows soared and pierced. His tents were sturdy.

Mr. Drew, a counselor with tattoos snaking around his biceps and down his legs, asked him, "You play sports at your school?"

"Nah."

Robert stooped to help Mr. Drew gather errant arrows from the bases of the targets. Each counselor went by Mister followed by their first name—chumminess countered by deference. "Why not? You're a natural athlete."

Because I was always failing everything and never got a physical and couldn't listen to the announcements long enough to hear when tryouts were. "Sports are stupid."

Next Mr. Drew showed them how to construct basic water filters out of spare T-shirts and sand, and they all trudged through the firs to a murky creek to test them out. Robert drank greedily from his and wiped cold drops from his chin, amazed it worked.

"Never, ever drink your own urine," Mr. Drew told them as they gulped their sand-filtered water, and the guys busted up, Robert doubling over. Mr. Drew held up a hand and waited for them to collect themselves. "Seriously. Enough time alone in the wilderness and you get desperate. Dehydration and fatigue can even make you hallucinate. But urine will dehydrate you. Don't try to filter anything but water. You should always keep an energy bar or trail mix on your person while hiking or camping, too."

Robert raised his hand. He screwed his face up into an approximation of studiousness. "Excuse me, Mr. Drew. You said your own urine. But what about someone else's piss?"

They all whooped again.

Mr. Drew glared and continued. "Even candy will keep you alive and give your body some calories to burn. But something with a little protein is a better choice, and no piss."

DECEMBER 2009

———————

Robert had never had a friend like Dalton. They talked, after lights-out, Dalton game to discuss any random topic flitting through Robert's head. The merits of the X-Men versus the Avengers. What ink they would tattoo on their calves and forearms. Whose ass they could kick if they ever felt like it (everyone's). They'd play the band name game until Dalton's snores floated through the dark.

"Metallica."

"AC/DC."

"Coldplay."

"I'm going to have to tell Mr. Drew how you're secretly a girl."

When Robert was stumped on a letter, he'd try to slide a made-up name in, but Dalton called bullshit every time:

"What the hell band is Roadkill?"

"The Apaches are Indians, dumbass, not a band."

"If Killer Bees are a real band, sing one of their songs."

One night after Dalton had regaled him with a point-by-point summary of the plot of *The Texas Chainsaw Massacre*, Robert told Dalton all about the last time he'd seen his dad. The rapping on his window. The way his dad had said the cops were coming for him. How his mom had claimed Robert's father was a murderer.

"Don't you think he could have outrun them, though? The cops?" Robert asked. He picked at the wall, splintering his thumbnail. No answer. Robert added, "I don't know. I mean, he's probably not running around the woods, not after all this time. He probably had to settle down somewhere."

And then he realized his roommate was asleep.

Christmas Eve was marked by visits from a pastor and a priest, who conducted sparsely attended voluntary services. On Christmas Day, the guys in Maple were corralled in the cafeteria for a screening of *District 9*, a gift from Sea Brook to its inmates. Robert sat in a folding chair and watched aliens go berserk on Earth. He and Dalton cheered on the Prawns as they spat and hissed. By the next day, Robert couldn't have said what the movie's plot was, just that the aliens looked like shrimp. Afterward, the counselors passed out snowflake-patterned gift bags that held a fun-size

Snickers bar, a pair of white socks, and a Green. Robert's was carved with antlers, and this time he didn't lose it.

> *Robert,*
> *I wish you'd write me back, since I take the time to write to you. Hulk is doing good, but he misses you. I'm almost finished with my real estate law class. I think I'll get an A, do you believe that? Soon I will be able to visit, and I have a few Christmas presents for you.*
>
> > *Love,*
> > *Mom*

A counselor from Sea Brook contacted Deb and recommended that she also attend counseling, or perhaps a parenting class, to prepare her for Robert's eventual return home. They could establish new patterns, the counselor said, and she could learn new strategies to manage Robert's behavior and motivate him in school. When Robert was released, they might benefit from a few joint counseling sessions. Deb wrote down a local psychologist's phone number and even made a call to her insurance company. But with her minimal benefits, she'd need to kick in a fifty-dollar co-pay per session, and only three total visits would be covered. She was referred to some other program for low-income families seeking mental health care in Seattle. She'd have to apply, and between her late shifts and classes and wherever Robert would end up going to school, she couldn't imagine schlepping to Seattle three times a week to be told, she was sure, everything she'd ever done wrong as a mother by some psychologist who thought the degrees on his wall meant he knew all about her. She'd apply anyway, she swore, and she'd squeeze it all in, and no one would be able to say she hadn't tried. But days passed and she still hadn't found time to log on to the organization's website and find the forms. Eventually she lost the psychologist's phone number.

"He straight *bounced*. They couldn't keep him locked up! We were on the second floor, and Robert just jumped out the damn window like he was friggin' Spider-Man. I didn't hear a thing. I woke up and he'd just vanished, ninja-style.

"They didn't know he was gone until morning, and by that time he was *long* gone. Cops came around with his picture, asking if anybody had any information. Said all kinds of bad things can happen to teenage runaways, and if we knew anything, we better speak up. But nobody knew anything then. Anybody who said anything else was lying. He was *gone*. No trace. Until he stole that first plane."

JANUARY 2010

———————

*He squirreled away a stack of Greens. On days Robert re-*membered to make his bed, one would be waiting on his pillow like a hotel chocolate bar. The first time he raised his hand in algebra, the teacher slipped him one on his way out the door. He thanked a lunch lady for a steaming scoop of mac 'n' cheese, and she plonked one on his tray. Sea Brook's staff ignored his screw-ups and quickly recognized anything he did right. At first Robert thought the whole thing was corny and embarrassing, and he wanted to give this system the finger the way some of the other guys did, clogging the bathrooms' sinks with the discs and whipping them at each other between classes. But racking up points made each day like a video game, and he couldn't help but want to score as many as he could.

The counselors knew how much each guy had earned, but it was up to the students to hold on to them. Robert collected tokens imprinted with rhino horns, sharp antlers, elephant tusks, claws and paws of all kinds. He emptied his pockets at lights-out and dumped them into his sock drawer every night.

He cashed in tokens here and there for little rewards: a math homework pass, an extra twenty minutes of archery practice, a cold can of Mountain Dew, the best Snickers bar he'd ever tasted. But mostly he was saving them for a trip into the woods, though he'd never have admitted it to Dalton or any of the others.

In the woods, he wouldn't be able to see a single wall. He might not even sleep in the tent, if Mr. Drew would let him.

Robert had been at Sea Brook for eight weeks when a sign-up sheet appeared in the dormitory hallway, Scotch-taped to the wall. *Overnight Wilderness Encounter. 50 Greens. Counselor: Mr. Drew.* Five lines stretched across the page. One name had already been scrawled in red crayon, bumpy like the cinder block beneath it.

Robert rushed to his room to count up his loot. He thought he had enough.

He flung open his bureau's top drawer.

His Greens were gone.

He rifled through the drawer, tossing the dingy socks and thin T-shirts to the floor. He sifted through the piles of paper on his desk. He pulled out the bureau drawer, dumped it onto the tile, and peered into the cavity behind it. Dust, a computer-printed porno picture, an empty baggie. The used-up contraband of residents past.

He eyed Dalton's bureau, wondering. If Dalton caught him snooping through his stuff, Robert would confront an unpleasant living situation at best, an ass-kicking at worst. He whirled around the room, as out of hiding places as in an open field.

Finally Robert marched to the common area, where Mr. Drew was playing cards with Dalton and a few others. They bet M&M's, sliding them across the pockmarked table. Dalton gloated over a growing rainbow-hued pile.

"Yo, Mr. Drew, somebody jacked my tokens." Robert's voice seemed too loud.

Mr. Drew put down his cards and held up his palms like a traffic cop. "Robert, we don't make accusations."

"I've been putting all my tokens—"

"Greens."

"Greens. Whatever. I was stashing them with my socks and now they're gone. Somebody stole them."

"Did someone steal them, Robert, or did you lose them?" Mr. Drew asked. He rose from the sagging couch, suddenly towering over Robert. "One of the biggest lessons to learn here is to take responsibility for yourself."

"I didn't lose them!" Robert threw up his hands. But was he positive? He thought of his old locker, the mountain of crumpled papers inside it. *Had* he lost them? Could he *prove* someone took them?

"Who stole them, then? Are you accusing Dalton?" Dalton had put his cards facedown on the table. He stared at his roommate.

Robert's yelling had attracted an audience. Guys paused on their way to their rooms, their mouths twitching with stifled smiles. For the first time Robert wondered if he'd acted too proud of scaling the rock wall, of every bull's-eye his arrows had hit. Could someone have decided to teach him a lesson? Were his fellow inmates tired of him showing them up?

Or had he just lost them?

Even if Dalton had taken them, Robert wasn't going to be a snitch like Joey Kovach. "I'm not saying it was Dalton. I don't think Dalton even cares enough to take them."

"So who else had access to your room, then?" Mr. Drew's face softened and Robert felt the squirmy embarrassment of his pity. "Could you have moved them and forgotten?"

"Somebody took them!" Robert insisted. "You guys know how many I had. Why can't you just give me back what I had?"

"Dude, I swear I didn't take your Greens," Dalton said. He lowered his voice. "You stay here long enough, they *make* you go on the camping trips. You ain't really gotta buy them."

"I don't care about a camping trip," Robert lied. "What I care about is somebody coming into my room and stealing my shit!"

Mr. Drew just looked at him. Dalton picked up his cards again. The small crowd began to disperse. Robert hated to think about what they'd say about him later. *Kelley's a baby, whining about his stupid Greens.*

"Forget it," Robert said loudly. "I probably lost them. Who gives a shit."

Mr. Drew patted his shoulder. Robert stiffened. "You'll have plenty of chances to earn more. I bet you get some this afternoon."

"Whatever," Robert replied.

By the time he made it back to his room, four names filled the sign-up sheet.

That afternoon, while Mr. Drew demonstrated how to use a compass to find north, Robert looked out toward the rumbling highway, the roar like waves.

Dalton was to be released and shipped back to Seattle in ten days, and just as he'd predicted, Mr. Drew was making him go on the excursion. His name appeared on the sign-up sheet, at the very bottom, in someone else's handwriting.

The trailer was awfully quiet without Robert. She'd thought she'd at least be able to concentrate on her homework, but instead Deb found herself talking to Hulk.

"Should we clean his room?" she asked the dog. "He'll be mad if we do. But it smells like a locker room in there."

Hulk barked.

"Is that a yes or a no?"

The dog tilted his head at her.

She sighed and turned up the television to keep her company. She was supposed to be reading about tenant rights, but her mind kept wandering to Robert's eventual homecoming.

He'd be eighteen by the time he returned.

He'd be a man.

She had already sent one man into the woods. And she never saw him again.

Why had she let Rob Kelley talk her into dubbing her son a junior? At the time, she'd hoped that Rob's insistence on passing on his name meant he'd intended on turning himself around. On being a real father. Now the name seemed like a curse.

Of course she hadn't really thrown away her computer's power cord, like she'd told Robert. They weren't giving those damn things away like perfume samples. Deb left the kitchen table and booted up the desktop. Its hum filled the trailer. She googled local vocational training programs, flipped to a back page in her real estate notebook, and started writing down phone numbers and email addresses. She searched used car listings. She jotted down the next three GED testing dates.

She toggled between an ad for a 2000 Honda Civic and the course listings at Shoreline Community College. Her son was always on the computer. Maybe graphic design would spark his interest.

She darted from window to window until a misaimed click opened the shortcut for the flight simulator. For a second the monitor darkened, and the ghostly shadows of her nose and eyes emerged.

Then Deb blinked at the screen's sudden brightness. She tapped on the keyboard, but the view from the cockpit stayed spread before her. She clicked and clicked, and then suddenly the gray runway and the grass that framed it were whooshing by. A buzzer blared as she piloted straight into the field, never getting aloft. Her plane ground to a halt and then sat for a few minutes, the grass emitting a radioactive glow.

Try again? the program asked her.

"No," she said, but then a menu popped up. *Favorite destinations.*

Deb scanned the list. Barely a continent left out.

Robert's virtual alter ego had crisscrossed the globe, his path carving the world into jagged pieces. Such sweeping arcs compared to the well-worn trails he'd actually been traveling. School to the trailer. Trailer to school. Back and forth, back and forth.

Like if he could have, he'd have vanished into thin air himself. Jetted away to New York. Egypt. Paris. Alaska. Afghanistan.

"I'm sure he's on lockdown," she told Hulk. "He can't go anywhere. Where would he go, anyway?"

She'd call, though, on Monday. Ask to talk to him. Just to make sure.

FEBRUARY 3, 2010

He went to his classes and his therapy sessions and shuffled down the corridors and stared out the window and stood around outside and plodded through each afternoon's survival training, and finally one night when Dalton offered him a joint, Robert took a long drag and choked and coughed and hit it again. And they passed the joint back and forth, not talking, the paper getting sticky, his throat dry and clotted.

He got angrier and angrier about losing the Greens. How could he have lost anything in a room this tiny? He was banned from the excursion, just like he'd been banned from the library and then banned from his whole school. And what had been his crime, exactly?

How big was this room? Bigger than six by eight? Did it matter? A cell was a cell.

Dalton laughed and coughed. "You need to slow up, dude. Your eyes look like you're trippin'."

"When are they gonna have another camping trip?" Robert croaked.

Dalton shrugged. "I don't know. Probably not for a while. It's gonna get too cold."

"I'm not waiting," he said, and the second he heard his words, he knew he meant them.

While Dalton snored, he stuffed his khakis and white shirts back into the crumpled grocery bag he'd brought from home and slid into his sneakers. He wouldn't go back to Yannatok and that cramped trailer, splitting at the seams with his and his mother's frustrations, like their pent-up anger and secrets were gouging the leaking, rotting roof, searching for skyward escape. He'd disappear into California, where he'd trade Yannatok's waves for some real surf. Or maybe he'd camp out in the woods for a while. His dad had pulled it off, a Houdini in camo. Why couldn't Robert?

His mom would worry. Served her right.

About eight feet stretched from the windowsill to the ground. The thorny bushes tangled around the building were meant to discourage the jump, but Sea Brook wasn't alarmed, wasn't guarded. The reason only now occurred to him: there wasn't anywhere to go. Beach on one side and timber on the other. Prisons didn't always need bars.

He slung his bag over his shoulder and took a deep breath. Then Robert swung out the window, feet first, landing in the prickly brush below. The branches broke and brambles tore at his calves and arms, but the night air cleared his lungs, refreshing as a cool drink of water. He looked back up at his window, where he'd launched himself from, half expecting to see Dalton gaping in amazement. But just like every time he'd surfed a giant wave, every time he'd landed a simulated plane, Robert celebrated this victory alone.

He kicked his shoes off, crammed them into the bag, and let the wet grass stick to his feet. Quieter that way, as he sprinted for the trees. When he reached them he didn't hesitate before crashing into the woods. Beneath a woven cover of branches, Robert paused to catch his breath, resting his hands on his knees and waiting for a siren, a police car's revolving lights, a barking K-9 unit, but only the full moon and a scattering of stars beamed down on him. Waves crashed beyond the boughs. He wriggled his shoes back on and headed that way, pushing aside branches like curtains.

He had expected the woods to wrap miles along the coast, a pointy maze to Canada, but the beach unspooled through the thinning trees only a few minutes later. The shore was deserted. Rows of beach houses hibernated, dark and quiet. Robert ran for the ocean, kicking up the spray, punching the air, miming a watery victory dance.

A raindrop spattered his shoulder. Thunder rumbled, and then rain pelted the sand. The pink scratches winding down his arms and legs stung. Suddenly he was cold in his dripping pants, hugging his chest and ducking his head. The beach left him without any cover, and he hadn't actually brought what he'd need to camp in the forest. He hadn't planned at all. He was only armed with his five white tees and two pairs of khakis. So much for survival training.

For a moment, he considered tiptoeing back to the dormitory, slipping in the front door and under his sheets. Reporting to archery tomorrow smuggling a secret.

But then what would he do? Bust his ass for Greens until they decided he was cured and shipped him back to Yannatok? Another island prison, just like Rikers, Alcatraz.

He wouldn't do it.

Robert crept closer to the house at the row's end, his feet sinking heavily in the sand. Only one neighbor. No cars in this driveway or the next three. He circled around to the street-side front door and waited beneath the deck, crouching against a plastic trash can. Rain beat against the planks over his head. A painted piece of driftwood hung from the front door. *The Petersons'*. Seashells and beach rocks bordered the house's walkway. He left his shelter, an arm shielding his face.

The key was under the first rock he turned over. Like they were inviting him in.

He ducked again and broke for the door. He looked over his shoulder before sliding the key into the lock. Nothing following him but rain. A wave of stale air hit him as he opened the door. No one had been home for a while, maybe since the summer. Pine needles, sand, and dirt were caked onto his shoes, like a wild animal's paws. His left heel bled. He wiped his feet on the welcome mat.

Robert closed the door gently behind him, but his footsteps still rattled framed pictures on a table in the foyer. A tan boy and girl showed off boogie boards and squinted into the sun. In the next, the same pair posed, a little older, the boy's sapling arms thickening, and the girl with a more complicated haircut. They toyed with the controls of a two-seater plane. Maybe these people were rich enough to have their own plane and flew from Seattle whenever they craved some sun and surf.

The living room and the open kitchen could have swallowed his whole trailer. The kitchen had room for an island and a table. Another glass-topped table in the dining room. He couldn't picture Deb sitting there, sipping her coffee, savoring her cigarette, but he could imagine Hulk curled up under the table. If Robert lived here, he'd take Hulk to the beach every day.

His reflection shone in the microwave, ghostly in the dark. A twig was tangled in his hair. His forehead and nose were smudged with dirt.

He didn't belong here, either. The only way he could get into a house like this one was to break in.

In the pantry, behind some Cap'n Crunch and a chip-clipped bag of Tostitos, Robert found a bulging plastic bag full of dime-store candy: Atomic FireBalls, jawbreakers, Now and Laters, Dum Dums. Easily three pounds' worth. Robert tore open a fireball and let it burn the roof of his mouth and stain his tongue red. He tucked a few misshapen Now and Laters in his pocket and replaced the bag.

The candy had probably been abandoned since last summer. Who'd ever miss it? Robert reopened the cabinet and swiped it all. Then he crept through each room. Couches and tables hulked in the moonlight. Three bedrooms, beds tightly made. Shelves of loose-spined, sun-faded paperbacks, Monopoly and Scrabble, decks of cards. Bikes and plastic beach toys in the garage.

He was too keyed up to even think about sleep.

He unwrapped a sour apple Dum Dum and popped it in his mouth.

Robert ambled back to the kitchen and opened a cabinet. Rows of clean glasses winked back. He poured himself a tall glass of flat Coke, drank it in three gulps, and refilled his cup.

No *Law & Order*. No Hulk padding around. No Dalton snoring. Robert had never heard such quiet.

He knew what some of the guys from Sea Brook would do. Ransack the place for hidden cash, credit cards, jewelry, electronics. Soap up the mirrors. Shred the couch cushions, smash every window. Piss on the walls, take a shit on the bed. Run away laughing, the front door gaping like a broken jaw.

Robert rinsed his glass in the sink and dried it with a seashell-embroidered dish towel. He might be staying awhile.

In the garage he found three surfboards crusted with last summer's salt.

Robert stood on the deck until the rising sun stained the ocean orangey pink, a sour apple Now and Later melting on his tongue. Then he crunched down on another fireball and snuck a board from the garage. The sand cooled his bare feet as he crept down the deserted beach. Waves hushed the shore with their frilly spray. The insides of his cheeks burned. He left his khakis and tee on and waded into the water. Icy spray soaked his pants. His skin stung.

He stepped back onto the sand, cold as wet cement, and propped the board beside him. He so wanted to paddle out, watch the house shrink behind him. But the foam alone numbed his blotchy, purple feet. He withstood the pins and needles as long as he could, until the sun hovered over the water, before he turned back to the house.

Robert hung his wet pants from the shower curtain rod and borrowed gray shorts and a hooded navy sweatshirt from his hosts. He wiped sand from the board, returned it carefully to its spot in the garage. He napped restlessly on the deck, a gritty lawn chair cushion for a bed.

Interview with Mira Wohl, Willamette University cafeteria, October 2, 2010

From *Flight Risk: The Robert Jackson Kelley Story*

"School was just chugging along like normal. I was getting ready for play auditions, trying to pick a monologue, and rereading *Twelve Angry Men*. The play's kind of a big thing here, since sports are such a hassle. We don't have a football or baseball field, and even for basketball or volleyball you have to go across the bridge to play another school, and it takes all night. So like a lot of us, I was trying to decide which juror I wanted to be.

"At first no one cared whether or not Robert had disappeared, because there was other breaking news: *Mira Wohl and Alex Winters broke up! And then she cut all her hair off because she was so depressed! She's tweeting all these, like, Taylor Swift lyrics and he's already hooking up with Olivia Donovan! Girl's ready to jump off Yannatok Bridge!* Which, like, yeah, right. Everyone just couldn't stop talking about it, everywhere I went, and there were, like, a couple people saying Robert had run away from juvie, but it was mostly coming from Joey Kovach, who had gotten expelled but was still hanging around, showing up at basketball games, being pathetic. No one listens to him anyway."

FEBRUARY 4, 2010

A honey-voiced woman named Gloria Whalen, apparently Sea Brook's assistant director, phoned Deb, waking her in the early afternoon, after a long night shift. Deb's first question was the obvious one: "What did he do?"

But as she listened to Ms. Whalen's euphemisms, her heart quickened and her hands shook. Gloria told her that Robert was very likely still on Sea Brook's grounds, that he certainly had not crossed back over the Yannatok Bridge, that between the Seattle police and Sea Brook's staff, he would certainly be located swiftly, dirty and hungry but otherwise with only his pride injured. Perhaps then, Gloria had allowed, they should discuss another facility more appropriate for Robert's rehabilitation.

But Deb knew better. Her son wasn't going to be found anywhere near Sea Brook. He'd end up retreating home, to the island he'd lived on since he was a small boy, if for nothing else than his dog. Deb cut Gloria off in midsentence. "I knew it. I goddamn knew it."

Then Deb hung up the phone, grabbed her cigarettes, and drove circles around the island. The Sea Brook staff and the police could keep wasting time looking for her son on their side of the bridge. Deb would find him herself.

But where would Robert go? Who were his friends? And why didn't she know?

Joey Kovach. The only name she had, but Lord knew she wouldn't be welcomed at that house.

As she drove, she rewound a memory of her son, before the terrible grades and the discipline problems and the prescriptions and the expulsion. A boy running circles around the flagpole, chasing his dog, throwing a tennis ball. A little boy in race car pajamas.

After a day cooped up in the house, Robert's nerves were cranked as tightly as a jack-in-the-box. He'd peeked into every bureau drawer, every kitchen cabinet, every closet. He'd messed around with some sort of weather station, which displayed the temperature and the humidity and the times for high and low tides, but its batteries quickly drained, and Robert couldn't find a power cord. He paged through a few creased magazines from last summer, with their expired coupons for free slices of pizza and discount board rentals.

No computer.

He started itching to get outside. Why did his life seem like a giant game of hopscotch, with him leaping pointlessly from box to box?

He peeked through the blinds' slats at the frothing waves, at the slash where the water darkened the sand.

A trash truck clattered down the street, not making a single stop. Did that mean nobody was home?

He decided to sleep inside, on the living room carpet, and tossed and turned through a too-quiet night, the ceiling above him smooth and white as the lid of a closed coffin. He woke at four, as suddenly as if he'd set an alarm. Outside the house was a curtain of black, pierced only by the low moon.

This time Robert scurried low around the other side, away from the shore and toward the road. He crouched and ducked behind trash cans and cars, like a raccoon foraging for scraps, like a bear lurking at the trees' edge.

The summer homes were hollow skulls, their windows darkened eye sockets. The street was so empty a blowing tumbleweed wouldn't have been out of place. Robert stuck to the evergreens' shadows for a while, then pulled his hood over his head and walked along the road's shoulder. A car approached. Headlights loomed. Robert kept walking, hunched, not too slow and not too fast, until it whizzed by him.

He kept walking, straight, so he could find his way back easily. Sunlight trickled into the sky, and Robert was about to turn back and hunker down when he saw the sign.

A yellow triangle. Black letters. *LOW-FLYING PLANES*.

He was that close to an airstrip. Maybe he could find a spot nearby and watch the early morning commuters take off. All the years he lived on Yannatok with its airstrips lacing the island, he'd never actually seen a plane rise from the ground. He walked a bit farther.

The boxy building was topped with a gently sloping roof. The hangar so resembled a warehouse that Robert wouldn't have been surprised to find stacked cardboard boxes inside instead of planes, if it weren't for the sign in the front office window. *Come fly with us! Ask about our lessons! Take the controls on your first flight!*

The building was fenced in by loosely knit wire diamonds, maybe eight feet high. No barbs.

How hard could it be to climb over?

He shimmied up easily, rattling the metal, and landed feetfirst on the other side. His hood had fallen away, and Robert ducked back beneath it. Spider-Man couldn't have done it better.

He lapped the building. Five doors, wide like a garage, the runway stretching and looping in front. Traffic cone—

orange windsocks flapped and snapped with each wind gust. On the far side from the road was a Dumpster and a back door. A few parked planes in various states of disrepair, a tethered and tarped flock. He threaded between their metal shells, beneath their contoured wings. He peered into an open hatch, ran a thumb over some greasy, coiled parts. Thick oil coated his fingertip, nothing virtual about the way it seeped into his fingerprints' every crack and spiral.

Robert wouldn't have been able to say how, but before he even tried the cold metal handle, before he even gave it a tentative tug, he knew the back door would open for him. And it wasn't that it wasn't locked, because it was, in fact, locked, but it hadn't been shut properly. Someone in a hurry hadn't checked, had let the door slam shut behind him, and Robert Jackson Kelley slipped right inside.

Dalton had said it. Sometimes it seemed like people *wanted* to get their shit stolen.

Robert turned on the buzzing, flickering overhead lights and discovered a storage area with boxes stacked six feet high. Scratched metal lockers lined one wall, their doors hanging open like stunned mouths.

One more door, and then he found what he had come for.

Five Cessnas hunkered down, each before an exit to the airstrip. Robert circled the dormant machines as though they were sleeping beasts. The planes were snub-nosed, sleek, each about thirty feet long from nose to tail. A ton or more of metal that could defy gravity. He tentatively stretched to touch one, his fingertips brushing the wing above his head. He lapped the hangar again, and then a third time, peering in the oval windows, standing on tiptoe to spy a pilot's seat, a hibernating control panel.

A darkened computer sat atop the front desk. A wall calendar full of bright skies and shining wings hung behind it. Robert opened each desk drawer quickly. Rubber bands, pens, thumbtacks. A battered beige tackle box sat beside a stack of tattered flight manuals. Robert flipped through the diagrams and instructions. He picked up the tackle box and its contents jingled. Keys, labeled. *Cessna* imprinted on the silver, a slim plane wing gliding above the letters.

He slunk around the hangar, matching each key to the proper plane. N71387S. N97681H. N2008SC.

More than a dozen keys hung from another heavy ring. Some were labeled with pieces of tape; others were unadorned. A brass key was labeled *Master*. Robert slid it from the ring, used his fingernails to scrape off the tape, and then wrapped it around another brass key. He slid the master key into his pocket.

He took two manuals, too, and locked the hangar behind him.

_____

As morning dulled into afternoon, Robert sat at the kitchen table and read the manuals, even the penciled-in notes some novice pilot had scrawled in the margin, studying like his classmates must have for their school tests. For the SATs. He dog-eared the first pages of two chapters. *Taking Off. Landing.*

He ate his way through the box of stale Cap'n Crunch, three DiGiorno pizzas, two gooey paper cups of watermelon Italian ice with splintering wooden spoons. He poked a straw through the pouch of a Capri Sun and sucked down the juice in one gulp. He left his dirty dishes and ringed glasses on the table, and he spent his third night sleeping again on the deck. He actually felt more comfortable on the patio chair than inside. He shook sand from his hair when he woke up, the sky still dark, the leftovers of someone else's summer embedded in the cushion.

FEBRUARY 6, 2010

The four a.m. sky was bleached by clouds. Most com-
muters were still cocooned in their beds. Robert went
back to the airstrip and, emboldened by his study session, filched N2008SC's corresponding key. The door
opened with a whispered mechanical click. He slid behind
the controls, leaning forward in the tan leather seat,
running his hands over the levers and switches. His slick
forehead and dirty hair and nose were ghostly in the
dark Garmin screen. He caught himself exhaling, pushing air between his teeth and imitating the whir of the
engine.

He had to forcefully stop himself from acting like an elementary schooler dropped off at the arcade. Planes weren't
toys, at least not to him. For the rich people who owned
them, maybe it was different.

Still, he stayed behind the controls, and through the windshield he saw not the gray hangar walls, but the blue, pixelated, simulated sky.

Interview with Joey Kovach, Gold's Gym, Seattle, October 10, 2010

From *Flight Risk: The Robert Jackson Kelley Story*

"The sheriff only goes after local people. Everyone knows it. Summer people spend their money and are allowed to do whatever they want. Drink on the beach, set off fireworks, park wherever they want. Speedin' down Dunes Road to get to the highway, jammin' up the bridge every Sunday night with their giant minivans, leanin' on their horns, beepin' at nothing, like they expect traffic to part just for them, so they can get back to their important shit on the mainland. So sunburned they can barely move! Meanwhile, I get caught with twenty Addies and it's 'Lock 'im up!'

"Yeah, you pass the sheriff's cruiser out there, lights spinnin', and he's got somebody pulled over, fumbling for their registration or trying to touch their finger to their nose or slammed up against the hood of the car, well, you know that's not a summer person."

FEBRUARY 6, 2010

———————————

Deb called in sick and then drove down each and every winding island road. She didn't sleep, nicotine and coffee fueling her next workday. She brought Hulk on her drives, both for company and the hope the mutt could pick up Robert's scent, chase him down and tree him if that's what it took. She thought about using the copy machine at work to make flyers, but then was mortified to realize she'd only captured a few blurry snapshots of her son since he'd shed boyhood like a too-tight skin.

Every search ended at the beach, where she took off her shoes and surrendered to the shadowy scenarios she otherwise fought off. Her son's broken body washing up on the shore. Mangled by the side of the road. Hanging from a beam in some abandoned Seattle building.

She never should have told him about his father. Who

knew what crazy ideas that had put in his head? When he came back, she decided, brushing sand off her toes, she was going to sell the trailer and anything else she had to and move them off the island. To somewhere with open fields instead of thick forest, grass instead of sand.

Robert tried to study by the television's blue light, afraid to draw attention to himself by turning on a lamp. Quick pencil strokes next to a diagram of an altitude meter. Chapter after chapter after chapter about flying at night, flying in bad weather, in high winds, with glare in the pilot's eyes and thick, churning clouds. So much to know, but his thoughts scattered as easily as those geese back at the airfields, his own brain firing shot after shot. One word sent his attention flapping away. *Altitude needle* reminded him of getting a shot at the doctor's and the doctor's office reminded him of Barry Lancaster's office, which reminded him of the Adderall he was supposed to be on and his mother and getting kicked out of school and what was he reading about again? Robert tried to will himself to stop tapping his pencil, stop bouncing his trampoline knee, and read. Were the kids whose names were printed in the paper when they made honor roll, report card after report card, the kids with their homework finished and their permission slips signed and their binders tabbed and divided, were they really that much smarter than him? Could he truly not read a manual?

He flipped back to the first page. He didn't realize he was grinding his teeth until his jaw began to ache. He read the manual straight through, underlining, tattooing the pages with his scrappy printing, and he didn't remember a word of it.

He threw down the manual. He watched a sitcom for a few minutes but couldn't tell why the audience was laughing. Then he checked out a basketball game where he didn't recognize any of the players. Then local news. A bank robbery. A car accident. A local forecast coming right up!

No reports of a boot camp escapee.

Was anybody looking for him? Sure didn't seem like it. In the movies, squads of searchers would be deployed, scouring the beach with flashlights, distributing flyers, driving red-tipped pushpins into a map of the coast. His mom would have been on TV, pleading for his safe return. Robert pictured Holt in a war room, a walkie-talkie pressed to his ear, pointing platoons of officers into the woods. But during the off season, summer towns grew desolate, and Robert could easily pretend he was the last person on Earth.

He was just the tiniest bit disappointed.

He'd face a heavy punishment at Sea Brook, he was sure. Goodbye, lounge. Catch ya later, foosball. They'd lock him up in Redwood, without a roommate. Those guys only left their floors for classes and therapy and had to slowly earn the privileges Robert had already enjoyed, like the ropes course and archery practice. Knowing that Dalton and the others were outside while he was trapped in his room would make his sentence that much worse.

Or maybe they'd kick him out, ship him back over the bridge to Yannatok. And then where would he go? If he didn't complete the terms of his diversion agreement, would they send him somewhere else? He imagined diminishing rooms, one fitting inside the next, his room at Sea Brook nestled inside the trailer, tucked into the high school, each place he got booted from smaller and smaller.

He couldn't go back to Sea Brook and he didn't want to go back to Yannatok, so he stayed put all day, TV and manuals, manuals and TV, until the allure of the airstrip pulled him back for a third visit. This time he didn't skulk along the edges of the building, didn't feel a jolt of adrenaline at the fence's rattle, didn't ease the door closed. His footsteps thudded and echoed around the hangar as he strode toward the desk and its tackle box, luring him in with its key-stuffed compartments.

Robert grabbed the keys and tested out the pilot's seat of N97681. He put himself through the paces of an entire imaginary flight, takeoff through landing, maneuvering through some thick cloud cover. The blue-gray sky, the cottony cloud swaths could have been painted on the hangar's wall, Robert saw them so clearly.

An hour raced by, and his concentration never wavered. Something about those controls, those gauges, washed out the tide of distractions.

He was returning the keys, jangling them against his thigh, strutting through the hangar, congratulating himself on a successful flight, when the hangar door swung up and open.

Heavy footsteps.

Flashlights swept over the room.

Robert ducked behind the desk. He closed his eyes, afraid their animal shine would give him away. He should have waited until three or four a.m., like he had for his other visits. Being here at eleven o'clock was obviously a mistake.

"Who's there?"

The loudest silence Robert had ever heard. His blood roared, his veins throbbed, his heart hammered.

Footsteps again. More than one guy, he could tell now.

He would burst from behind the desk, rush them, knock them over, push them down, and run for the woods.

"I know I heard something."

"Gotta be an animal."

"Tomorrow let's check for nests upstairs," the second man said. "Which locker did you need to get into?"

Robert sat frozen, tense, ready to spring, until their footsteps faded and the door slammed shut behind them. He waited an hour, his legs cramping, his neck stiff, before he slipped from the hangar and ran back to the house. Later, as he was trying to get to sleep, he couldn't remember if he'd returned the keys to the right spot, or simply left them flung under the desk. The kind of mistake that could cost him his freedom.

NORTH COUNTY—A 17-year-old Yannatok teen has
been reported missing from the Sea Brook Youth Home.
Robert Jackson Kelley was last seen wearing a white T-shirt,
khaki pants, and sneakers. Kelley is 5 feet 10 inches tall and
weighs 165 pounds. His mother reports he loves dogs.

North County police are asking for help in finding Kelley. Anyone with information about the case should call the
North County Sheriff's Department.

FEBRUARY 7, 2010

After three days, Robert's food supply was dwindling. He ate the last DiGiorno with a side of cereal and washed it down with tap water. Tonight he'd have to go forage.

Beneath a densely cloudy sky he walked past empty house after empty house, but was hesitant to go so far as to break a window or bust down a door. He was hungry, but he wasn't a burglar. At two a.m., on the next street over, Ocean Avenue, he found a garage door cracked open, hovering just a few inches off the cold cement. Robert peeked beneath it, into a dark cavern, silent except for a freezer's hum. He eased the door up just enough that he could slink under it. A chest freezer hunched against the wall, but first he knelt and checked out the motorcycle parked a few feet away. Red chrome. Robert paced around it. He thought of the posters in Barry Lancaster's office, back at his old school.

He opened the freezer. Chicken patties. Sheets of those

cheap popsicles, the red and blue and purple flavors in plastic tubes. Steak-umms. Robert took a package of chicken patties. Six sandwiches would hold him for a couple days at least.

Back to the motorcycle. Robert ran his hand over the smooth seat. Was it gassed up? Where were the keys? Could he take it for a spin? Just zip down the street and bring it back?

He should go in the house. Who knew what else these people had?

Robert turned the knob, waiting for the lock's catch, but it spun easily.

Did beach house decorations come in a kit or something? Same big, pearly conch shells, same sunset paintings, same wicker furniture. Robert's eyes adjusted to the dark and he took in the open floor plan. Kitchen morphing into living room, tile meeting carpet.

Robert headed toward the kitchen cabinets, then stopped short. In the living room, a guy and a girl were snuggled on the couch, nestled under an afghan, her head cozied against his arm. The guy snored, mouth open. The girl's hair was a blond tangle, hanging like soft, beckoning seaweed. Her big toe stuck out from the blanket's edge, revealing chipped red polish.

Robert froze and wondered at his own stupidity. The door was unlocked because the owners were *here*. Of course.

He crept backward, hands up like he had already been caught.

If these people were to open their eyes right now, who would they think he was? A prowler? A murderer? Robert wasn't going to wait around to find out.

He tiptoed backward out of the room. The man shifted his legs and the girl sighed, nuzzling closer. Robert held his breath, mannequin-still. When the couple seemed settled again, he hustled for the garage door.

The only traces he left were wet footprints stomped across the garage and the missing chicken patties. That night, he would make sure he locked his doors.

FEBRUARY 8, 2010

Robert woke up on the summer house's floor. He counted forward from the last time he had been sure of the date and realized that today was his eighteenth birthday and no one on earth knew where he was.

He told himself that he'd forgotten about his own birthday, that birthdays were for kids, and that it was a sign of his maturity how little his mattered to him. But really the milestone had been nagging at him, a splinter at the back of his brain.

He was too old now for juvie. Too old for his mother to be held responsible for him.

His loot from the previous night was stacked on the kitchen table and in the fridge. After the first near-disaster, he'd gotten lucky at two more houses, one with a key under a rock and another with an unlocked garage. Cans of soda, chicken nuggets, cheese curls. If only he'd been able to carry more. Stuffing his haul in his hoodie's pockets had slowed him down, and he had been afraid someone would hear him clinking down the street.

He rummaged around in the kitchen drawers and found some stubby birthday candles, streaked with ash and hardened icing flecks. A book of matches from the Pine Tavern. He bet his dad, wherever he was, had a book just like it getting flattened in his pocket, or in his truck's glove compartment.

Robert microwaved a plate of chicken patties and mashed all twelve candles into the biggest one. The patty split, its breaded coating crumbling. Robert quickly lit the candles, burning his fingertips and throwing the spent matches in the sink. He hummed one verse of "Happy Birthday to Me," waving his hands like a conductor over the flames. Wax puddled on the counter. He puffed and blew, but the candles wouldn't go out. He tossed the whole mess into the sink and ran the tap over it, then wolfed down three more patties. Dinner finished, he inventoried his food again, proud of his spoils.

Whatever he didn't eat, he'd leave as a gift for his hosts.

He knew it couldn't last forever, but what the hell? Robert would visit the hangar one last time, creeping in around midnight, when it would be deserted. He'd have his fun, and then he'd get out of town while he still could. That couple in the house had been a warning shot; he needed to make like a goose and take off. Maybe he'd borrow a surfboard and go down into California, try out some real waves. He'd hitch, or he'd sneak onto a bus.

He shoved the remains of his candy stash into his pocket and headed for the airstrip. He crunched on a sour apple Dum Dum while he walked. He'd also brought the manual, glad he'd remembered to return it.

At the hanger, Robert slid behind the yoke of his favorite, N2008SC. Yellow stripes streaked across the plane's nose, lit up the wings. The tail dipped in citrus paint. Just like his surfboard. He drummed on the steering wheel. He tried to imagine another takeoff scenario, but tonight he was bored with just imagining.

Wouldn't it be awesome to put this beast in motion?

All he would do was drive the plane down the runway, just to see what it was like.

He would never have another chance.

If his final destination ended up being a lockdown somewhere, at least he would have this.

Robert jumped from the plane, sprinted around to the front of the hangar, rolled up the door, and then hopped back in.

He turned the key and taxied onto the airstrip. Slowly, tentatively, nudging into the darkness. The engine hummed.

His seat back vibrated. He cruised down once, then back, slowly at first, then a little faster on the return. Taking the turns wide, pumping the rudder pedals. Faced with the hangar's open door for the second time, he spun into a U-turn, and this time he floored it. The plane leaped forward, like a cheetah springing toward its prey. Dashboard needles shot skyward. The white runway lights blurred. Robert's hands quivered. His jaw clenched painfully.

Then, without exactly deciding to, Robert yanked on the throttle.

Happy birthday to me.

Accelerating. Ripping down the short runway. The tarmac was covered in hieroglyphic lines, circles, Xs. Sweat ran down his forehead, his neck, puddled beneath him on the seat. His legs thrummed like just-strummed guitar strings. A hoarse growl rose over the engine's roar, and only his raw throat hours later let him know that the noise had come from him, yelling. He bit his lip and tasted blood. Flat fields blurred by him, whizzing past on each side. The runway shortened, disintegrated beneath the plane's wheels.

Three warning-shot-accustomed geese flapped and scattered. Their shadows stretched in the runway lights.

He pulled up, sharp, the yoke so much weightier than a joystick. He didn't think to look at the manual, at the pages he'd marked. At the takeoff basics. At all the checklists, the

186

inspections, the navigational charts with the earth split into halves like an orange. He didn't think. Air pressure glued him to the seat. The hangar's single open door winked behind him.

And then Robert Jackson Kelley was flying.

Interview with Mira Wohl, Willamette University cafeteria, October 2, 2010

From *Flight Risk: The Robert Jackson Kelley Story*

"So here's the truth. My older brother actually worked at the hangar sometimes, on their computers, and he heard it all from his boss, the very next morning.

"First time Robert took off, the owner was hot on his heels. Guy gets a call in the middle of the night. Somebody's poking around the hangar. He gets up out of bed, throws on some clothes, and grabs a flashlight, goes to check it out. Takes a lap around outside, doesn't see or hear anything, until suddenly there's a plane barreling down on him. He ducks, he rolls, the wind's blowing his hair back. The heat from the engine leaves blisters on the guy's stumpy neck. He's, like, an inch away from getting decapitated!

"The owner runs inside, grabs a shotgun, and starts shooting it off at the sky, shaking his fist, cursing the moon. But Robert's already gone, winging it, looking down and laughing from twenty thousand feet."

FEBRUARY 9, 2010

At first Robert simply moved through the simulated operations he'd completed a thousand times. He lowered the plane's nose and flaps, checked his alignment. He oriented himself via the GPS. He didn't select a destination; he was too busy concentrating on merely keeping the plane aloft. Fifteen minutes ticked by before he seemed to take a breath.

As long as he stayed in motion, in the air, checking gauges, adjusting the yoke, watching the GPS, he didn't have to think about what'd he really done.

A hundred and thirty miles an hour. Alone.

His world had shrunk to the black sky, the engine's buzz, the lights flickering below him, the GPS screen's blue-and-green collage.

Calm washed over him. He had never felt so focused.

Like surfing, only better. The cockpit a cocoon, the sky a thick blanket settling over him.

Robert followed the coast, attempting to keep the waves lapping down the middle of the windshield. Flat beach house roofs dotted his right; the blue-black ocean stretched out to his left. Eventually the houses grew farther and farther apart and the forest thickened. The boundary between sea and forest blurred as the beach sharpened into the crags.

His knee, still.

Winds bumped the plane along. He pulled on the elevator control to the keep the plane's nose up. Inside the aircraft it was surprisingly quiet, the engine reduced to a hum like the ocean's lull. His eyes flicked between his hypnotic digitized progress on the Garmin and the black night outside.

Ten more minutes rushed by, but Robert wouldn't have known if he'd been piloting for minutes or hours. He'd become so engrossed in the silvery clouds, the blinking stars, that the next time he checked the GPS he was disoriented. A blob of land was coming up on his left, and he didn't know what it could be. Could he already be approaching Vancouver?

The yellow balloon moon hovered, so close Robert felt like he could point the plane's nose at it and touch down. He tried to arrange the twinkling stars into the constellations he knew were there: a bear, a hunter. He chewed a grape Now and Later to relieve the pressure in his ears.

And then Robert began to consider how he'd get out of the sky.

He wondered at first if he could simply turn around and land back at the airstrip. Cruise back into the hangar and return the keys. Walk away with a story, though who he'd tell it to he didn't know. He'd certainly one-upped Dalton.

The aircraft's gauges spread before him, numbers and lines and measurements he didn't fully grasp. The Garmin was easy enough, similar to the piloting he'd done in front of his computer. But he hadn't thought to check how much fuel he'd had when he'd taken off. He didn't know how much he'd need to get back. He was afraid to take his hands off the controls to flip through the manual.

Plan B would be to ditch the plane on the beach. The shore was just as open as the runway, bumpier, but coasting to a stop there might be less risky than trying to execute a turn he'd only ever completed on a simulator.

And what if the two guys who'd dropped by the hangar a few nights ago were waiting for him if he tried to return? He had a head start miles long; backtracking would be stupid.

He congratulated himself on his planning.

He wished that he could glide by his old school before he had to land. The trailer park. He wished he were trailing a banner, like those planes that skimmed the beach all summer long, advertising the Pine Tavern and Nino's Pizza. *Robert Kelley Is Flying This Plane!*

He extended the flaps and began powering down. He had flown far enough that he was coming to the end of the sandy stretch. Needles, bark, and crags on the horizon.

He'd fly up and down the whole coast, the whole continent, if his dad could see him. *I did it, Dad! I did get away. They couldn't catch me.*

Suddenly the spindly tops of the spruces and the firs loomed larger, and he was still approaching too quickly.

He'd closed the throttle too soon.

He was going to overshoot the shore. The last yards of beach unspooled beneath him, fraying as sand trickled into rocks and trees.

He tried to jerk the nose back up, regain altitude, but he was too late. Branches snapped against the windshield. The moon was swallowed by the woods' dense darkness. Metal groaned, and a wave of dirt and grass and pine needles rose and coated the windshield as Robert threw down the wheels, though the move was futile, he knew. The plane rocked left, then right, then left again. Robert braced himself, afraid it would tip.

He had not buckled his seat belt. One more forgotten detail, the last directions he'd ever forget. Finally, his wandering mind would kill him.

N2008SC shuddered to a shaky stop. The sudden silence echoed with the cacophony he'd created.

Robert smelled gasoline.

He leaned over and retched, throwing up on the passenger seat. Purple and sour, tinted by the Now and Later.

Robert pushed open the door, immediately tripped in the brush, then rolled away from the wrecked plane. Broken tree limbs dangled from the twisted propeller. The cowling hung open, bent, revealing the engine's coiling intestines. Cracks webbed the windshield, and scratches exposed the silver aluminum beneath the plane's paint.

Robert lay on the ground. He couldn't feel his legs or hands, and he wondered if he'd broken his spine. Then invisible pins and needles pricked his limbs, and he slowly rose to his feet. Sweat drenched his clothes, and he shivered in the misty woods. He looked left and right for a trail, a break in the trees. The sky was the color of a fresh bruise, the pine branches sutures across the moon's flesh.

He staggered in a circle around the N2008SC, mouth agape at the damage. The crumpled nose dipped to the forest floor. A chunk of the left wing had been thrown a few feet into the brush. The plane's back end tottered into the branches, like the tip of a seesaw. Ribbons of sheared paint waved from the rudder like forgotten party streamers, curling up the plane's underbelly.

Robert limped back around to the pilot's hatch. He reached in and grabbed the manuals, shaking bits of glass from the pages. He wasn't about to lose them like his stupid Greens.

Then he heard a rustling from a patch of shadow in the forest that somehow seemed darker than the rest.

A rustling that exhaled steaming clouds.

A bear stood up on two legs, his mouth open and nostrils flaring with great pungent puffs of breath. His inky black ears pricked the air. A white fur crescent moon bloomed over the bear's chest. He was taller than Robert, at least six and a half feet, with broad paws.

They stared at each other, neither making a sound.

A triangular chunk was missing from the bear's right ear.

He knew what he was supposed to do if he encountered a bear. Mr. Drew had told them: avoid eye contact, clap his hands above his head, back away slowly. As a last resort, play dead.

But Robert and the bear had locked eyes, and instead of aggression, Robert saw a single word in those dark, still pools. *Run.* Even though Mr. Drew had said not to, even though Mr. Drew had said that to try to outrun a bear was certain suicide.

In that instant, Robert saw his father turning from the bedroom window and running, running, running into the forest, shedding the cops and the trailer and Deb.

Robert's every nerve crackled.

Blood crashed through his veins, his heart a bass drum.

He turned and ran, and in between heaving breaths he laughed, panic burbling from his throat. Crashing through the brush, briars scraping his skin, not looking back for fear of seeing a raised paw and bared teeth, until he reached the sand. He collapsed on his knees, his chest heaving.

Robert was already half a mile down the beach when he realized he'd left his stash from the house in the glass-dusted passenger seat.

Just a bunch of candy. He wouldn't go back.

He wasted who-knew-how-long trying to figure out where he was. Robert searched the sky for the stars and signs Mr. Drew had told them about, the navigational touchstones he'd been taught to find. But clouds shrouded the stars and the pine-edged streets all looked the same, and soon he found himself back on the beach.

Suddenly, like a key clicking into a lock, he realized his location exactly. A pin pushed into his mental map.

The same sandy stretch he'd spent his boyhood surfing. The dim house he stood in front of was the one that those teenagers had commandeered for so many long, hot days, ambling between it and the waves. The place he swore he'd never return to.

The dark combined with his inexperience had led to a serious navigational error.

Robert cursed and kicked sand at the sea. He pulled at his dirty hair.

He was back on Yannatok.

ACT II

A ZONE OF TURBULENCE

From *The Beginning Pilot's Flight Guide* (p. 28):

Students complete their lessons in aircrafts equipped with two sets of controls: one to be used by the instructor and one to be used by the student. In an emergency, the instructor can and should take control of the plane. There should never be any question as to who is flying the airplane at any time. Numerous accidents have been caused due to a miscommunication about who actually has control of the aircraft.

Robert shimmied up the house's piling and swung onto the back deck. Eagles swooped and squawked over rolling, gray waves. The distant spruces gave no hint as to the secret they now contained.

He tugged on the screen door until its rickety frame bent enough for him to slip his hand through. He tugged on the sliding glass door's knob, rattling the lock. Another Dalton trick: shaking those things hard enough jimmies the lock.

Robert let himself in and closed the door behind him.

He half expected to discover the remnants of a keg party, but the house's former teenage inhabitants hadn't left a trace. He rinsed off in the shower. Dirt and blood swirled down the drain. He borrowed a fluffy towel and a pair of khaki shorts a size too big; they hung loosely off his hips. He assessed his injuries and found nothing too severe. Scrapes, bumps, bruises, and aches, more of which seemed to be from his rampage through the brush than the actual crash. Then he stretched out on the sectional, carefully moving a half dozen or so taupe throw pillows onto the floor. He was sore enough from his escapade that sleeping on the floor was out.

The remote was nestled in the cushions. Buttons rioted over the black rectangle: oval ones, yellow ones, two different sets of numbers. Of course these people had digital cable. The trailer had twenty channels.

He could fly a plane, but he couldn't work the television.

He rummaged around in the fridge and cracked open a Pepsi, then toyed with the remote until the TV flickered to life.

He wondered if he would see his adventure on the news. Robert flipped through the channels, but within fifteen minutes he was restless and found himself back out on the deck. He watched eagles dip and dive, finished his soda, and relived his flight. In the pilot's seat, his rushing brain had finally been in sync. He'd always been told to slow down, calm down, focus. When he was flying, the world had finally caught up to him, accelerated to match his pace. He was itching to do it again. If he had another chance, Robert knew he could land a plane.

From the *Yannatok Tide*: "Stolen Plane Crashed in Woods," February 10, 2010

YANNATOK—A Cessna 182 was stolen from North County Airport early last night and crash-landed in the woods near Highway 41 on Yannatok Island sometime before dawn Tuesday morning.

The plane is owned by Gary Stanton of Overlook Township.

"I heard a loud crash around two, two fifteen," Conrad Porter of Portland reported to local authorities. "I'm just glad no one got hurt."

Porter owns a vacation home near the crash site.

No other witnesses have come forward, but physical evidence left at the scene, including vomit found in the cockpit, is being investigated.

"Drug cartels are often behind the theft of smaller planes," Sheriff Holt of the Yannatok Sheriff's Department commented. "We are looking into every possibility, and that includes heroin running into Seattle. But the way the plane was left doesn't fit that pattern. This would be the work of a very inexperienced drug runner."

He added, "The trees are so dense out here, it's lucky no one was killed."

Sheriff Holt encouraged the community to report any suspicious activity witnessed in the area near the scene.

Interview with Gary Stanton, North County Airport, October 19, 2010

From Flight Risk: The Robert Jackson Kelley Story

"I had always dreamed of flying. When I was growing up, airports were shopping centers. You could finesse a business deal over a round of drinks, meet your lady with flowers, put your nose to the glass and watch those giants take off. I collected miniature bombers and jets. I even slept on sheets patterned with planes. But I'm blind as a bat without my glasses, so the air force was out for me. I became a history professor instead. The military buffs, the boys who watched the History Channel, would linger after class and we'd talk about the real story of the Red Baron, look at Raptors and F-16s on the computer. And I played around with simulators, too, the same ones I read the Kelley kid learned from.

"My dad was a carpenter. Built his own house. All the furniture, too. Then he got arthritis. His hands started to look like old trees, all gnarled and swollen. Had to retire. And I feel it in my joints, too. Scary, when the stiffness, the pain starts to set in. Then my wife surprised me with flight lessons for my sixtieth birthday. Behind the controls, my fingers felt loose again. And I admit it, I whooped like a boy when I first took the controls. Nothing like it. For the kid to want to experience that, well, I understand. I don't condone what he did, but I understand it. I pulled money out of my retirement savings to buy that plane, thinking my wife and I would fly on the weekend. Seattle, Portland, Los Angeles, even.

"And then Robert Jackson Kelley crashed my plane."

FEBRUARY 10, 2010

Deb drove and waited, drove and waited. For the call that Robert had been found, to come get him at the hospital, the trailer, the county lockup.

But she didn't see so much as a cruiser. She was the only one looking.

She spent an afternoon watching the line for the ferry to Seattle twist down the docks. Behind her sunglasses she checked every face. A group of kids boarded, the girls in high leather boots over their tight jeans. Like riding boots. Deb bet at least one of these glossy-haired girls kept a horse at the stables where Deb traded three hours of scooping dirty hay for an hour of riding. Sweating and wrecking her back on her day off. The boys slouched in their hoodies, and every one of them tapped on their phones and didn't even look up as the ferry pushed away from the shore.

And she knew, as the ferry shrank, the kids blurring, that her phone would only ring when her son had been arrested.

It'd be for something petty, like trespassing, she reassured herself. And if Robert was in one piece, even in handcuffs, she'd be relieved. A present for them both.

She'd even wish him a happy birthday.

Back at the house, Robert rounded up his belongings, which weren't much: the flight manuals, the stolen navy hoodie and gray shorts, his waterlogged sneakers. He rummaged around the garage for anything that would come in handy and scored a tent. He borrowed that and whatever food he could carry.

He might get lucky, and the home's owners might not show up for months. Years, even. But Robert couldn't count on it. He had to skip town before he was caught by the owners of the plane or the house. Yannatok was one small island.

He had to disappear.

Robert pushed into the forest along the road and walked until he could only see furrowed bark and spiky green needles in every direction. He started clearing out an area to pitch the tent, snapping off branches and hurling them into the woods. He wished he had a hatchet. Thunder rumbled, and soon rain streamed down his face. The tent was harder to set up than Robert had bargained. He tried to remember the steps he'd practiced back at Sea Brook, when he'd been assembling these things in record time, but ended up crouching beneath a sagging nylon roof. Holes in the tent had been patched with peeling duct tape. He stared at the blue tarp as raindrops spattered the tent, and pondered his own stupidity. Why hadn't he grabbed matches? A knife? A blanket? A flashlight?

Sometimes Robert had to wonder if he really did have a mental disorder.

Water dripped onto his flight manuals. He should have sealed them in baggies. Once the sun set, the already dim woods were plunged into pitch-black darkness. Thick branches blocked any moonlight.

Robert remembered the bear.

He tried to stay dry while he thought about his next maneuver. He had to figure out a way off the island. Tomorrow he could abandon his campsite and try to hitchhike to the ferry. In Seattle, he'd be able to blend in, and he could stake his claim on a more hospitable patch of wilderness somewhere near the shore. He'd lie low for a while, then return home to pick up Hulk.

He slept fitfully, tossing and turning. He might have been asleep five hours or five minutes when the crunch of branches snapping beneath an invading army of boots ripped open the night. Hunters? A gang of stoners searching for a place to get high? Robert bolted up. His neck ached, a reminder of his airborne misadventure.

A walkie-talkie's crackle. Cops? More lumbering footsteps. Definitely cops. The only question was how many.

Robert's tent would give him away. He was trapped there unless he made a run for it. Once he was in the thickets, disappearing would be easy.

He rose to his knees, crouched, and unzipped the tent. He rolled the flight manuals into a loose, thick tube and stuffed them into his pants.

If the police mistook him for a bear, would they shoot him?

Robert took a deep breath and crashed into the woods. The tent collapsed, and he shook the nylon from his foot. He could hear the police trampling the brush behind him.

He leaped over a rotting log, caught his toe in the splintered pulp, stumbled, and kept running. The slick pine needle carpet stuck to his sneakers.

He glanced back just long enough to see an arm, a leg, a boot clad in brown and black. The cops were tangled in green spruce needles, slowing as the boughs snagged their clothes, tore at their skin. Robert let the branches lash against his face, scratch his arms, claw his clothes. Each scratch, each slash widened the distance between him and his pursuers. He plowed ahead, blood smearing his forehead, dripping into his eyebrows.

The cops were running for their reputations; Robert was running for his freedom.

You're a natural athlete, Mr. Drew had said. This race through the woods was the track meet he'd never run in. His feet slid over the needles, barely seeming to touch the ground. Would there be a finish line? Would he know when he reached it?

After a few minutes, Robert's own thundering, ragged breath deafened him to the noise of the cops. He had to pause at a clearing, clutching his knees, to see if they were still behind him, and if so, how far.

Stillness, not even a bird's rustle. Scattered raindrops still fell, mingling with the blood on his forehead. He wiped his eyes.

He had lost them. For now.

The plane must have been found, or at least reported missing. What he didn't know was if the police were looking for him, or just looking.

The ferry could be crawling with cops. Set like a trap. He'd have to dodge the eyes of the other passengers, the crew. He'd have to wait in line, standing still. The ferry would crawl over the water like a bug trapped in thickening sap.

Might as well paint a target on his back.

He had to get off the island. And how could he do that on the ground?

Robert started for the house. He had studying to do.

"So Robert was out there roughin' it, serious survivor stuff. Like catching fish with his bare hands and building fires with sticks. Wearing camo and infrared goggles like special ops do. Blending into the trees so that bears would just walk by him. Cops would stomp around where he was hiding, and half the time he was right there, a couple of feet away. One time the cops all stop. They can smell the candy on his breath. Sour apple. So they're sniffin' away like drug dogs, trying to figure out where it's comin' from. They're craning their necks, looking in the trees.

"Then a cop steps in a wad of gum from a Blow Pop. Bright green, shiny little bits of lollipop still stuck to it. Cop's cursing, dirt's sticking to his shoe. And Robert's ghosted *again*."

FEBRUARY 11, 2010

Holt was beginning to wonder if the trailer park and the woods creeping behind it were cursed. He swore that since he'd been here looking for Rob Kelley the trees had snaked closer to the trailers, reaching for the yards, the porches, the front doors. One day, these folks would wake up to tree branches rapping on their windows, nudging their way inside.

The trailer hadn't changed a bit. These lots were landscaped with beer cans and cigarette butts. Gravel driveways dissolved into stumpy porches. If Holt lived here, he'd be looking for a flight out, too.

Sure, the park looked down on its luck, but Robert Jackson Kelley had gotten very lucky. Who walked away from a crash like that? And then to outrun three men! Ragged scabs still dotted Holt's own face from their race through the woods. After that, Holt had ordered his department not to speak to anyone about the case.

But the kid was no master criminal. His fingerprints were on the plane's controls. He'd puked in the cockpit. And he'd left a bag of candy, of all things, in the passenger seat, from which they'd been able to lift even more prints.

But still, when Holt had opened the email from the technician at the crime lab and started scrolling down the list of possible print matches, and there, right there, had been Robert Jackson Kelley's name, his birthday, a link to his record, Holt had been sure there'd been a mistake.

He'd called the lab, in fact, spoken to the technician. "This match, here. This is for a juvenile runaway. Are we sure on that one?"

He could practically hear the technician's shrug. "The computer doesn't lie."

"Does it make mistakes?"

"Not often, sir. Not often."

The other possible matches linked the prints to a thirty-four-year-old already doing twenty years for armed robbery, a twenty-two-year-old convicted of a DUI three years ago and living in Detroit, and a forty-two-year-old fugitive wanted for assault, whereabouts unknown, but arrested for a prior assault in Dallas. All of whom had probably never even heard of Yannatok.

Which left Kelley. Which meant Holt was issuing a warrant for the arrest of a high school student, accusing him of stealing a plane. Which was undoubtedly the most unbelievable event of Holt's entire term as sheriff, which had otherwise consisted of visits to the schools, arresting drunks, and issuing tickets.

Holt wanted to bring the kid in quietly and avoid embarrassing Sea Brook, whoever was in charge of North County Airport's security, and of course, his own department. Sheriff O'Shay had lost his job over another Robert Kelley who'd known how to run and hide.

But Holt knew that was the extent of the similarities between father and son. Robert Jackson Kelley was a kid. A kid who, despite a thin tough-guy act, couldn't disguise how hurt he'd been when his mom had decided to let him spend the night in jail. A kid who'd gawked at the cruiser's console and practically had to sit on his hands to refrain from fiddling with the tantalizing array of buttons and levers. A kid who, every single time Holt saw him, asked him about a bear, a bear who had in fact never been caught by the sheriff but had surely by now migrated away or been hunted down, a bear that hadn't been spotted in over a decade. *Did you catch that bear yet? Did you? Did you?*

Robert Kelley had lit up like a puppy greeting his master every time he'd bumped into Holt, including when the

214

sheriff was booking him. Holt wanted to find him before his luck ran out.

A lean little dog meandered over. The old guy was slow, but his tail wagged like a much younger pup's. Holt reached down to scratch his head.

He pocketed his sunglasses and rapped on the door.

Deb answered so quickly that Holt had to assume she'd been watching from a window, and she stayed behind the wobbly screen. He recognized her, of course. He was the lucky one who always got to haul in her men. The dog scratched at the door.

"Can I help you?" she asked flatly.

"Ma'am, I'm Sheriff James Holt." She knew who he was; he wasn't sure why he was being so hesitant. Maybe it was the bags beneath her eyes or her knotty, unwashed ponytail. She looked like a walking headache. "I need to talk to you about your son. I suspect he's in a bit of trouble. May I come in?"

"Trouble like what? Did you find him? Is he okay?"

"I'd really like to come inside to discuss the specifics."

Deb snorted. She lit a cigarette. "You know, I have a feeling that if he was one of those kids driving around here in a Beemer, he'd have been home before breakfast."

"Ms. Kelley—" Holt bristled. No matter what he did for the community—all that work he put into the aquatics program—he couldn't shake the islanders' scorn.

215

"Ms. MacPherson. Never was Ms. Kelley."

He knew that. Something about this case had him off his game. "Ms. MacPherson. Could we continue this conversation inside?"

She glared, exhaled, and opened the door. The dog scampered in after him.

The trailer was small and cluttered. Shoes scattered near the door, dishes and ashtrays littering the table. Eat-in kitchen, living area. The curtains were drawn over every window. Holt peered down a short hall. "Where's your son's room?"

"I don't want you back there."

"Ms. MacPherson, your son is accused of some very serious crimes—"

"I don't give a damn what you say he did."

Holt raised his voice. "Ma'am, we have physical evidence that links your son to a plane theft. A *plane*. The one stolen from North County? About five miles down the road from Sea Brook? He's lucky he didn't get himself killed."

Deb laughed shortly. "A plane? My son doesn't know how to fly a plane. What's next? He's Al Qaeda?"

Holt looked around. He didn't tell her that the possibility that Robert Jackson Kelley was a budding jihadist had already been brought up, namely by loudly concerned citizen Conrad Porter. "Is there a computer in the house?"

Deb narrowed her eyes. "Why?"

"We'd like to see what's been searched. What's on the hard drive. See if there's any clues to where Robert might be."

"You want my computer—because it's mine, not my son's—you're going to need to come back with a warrant."

Holt held up his hands. "We both want the same thing: your son to be found before he hurts himself. Isn't that what you want?" Her face didn't change. He tried another angle. "Look, you work dispatch. I consider the operators part of the department. The last thing I want to do is come back here with a warrant against one of our own."

She paused, just enough for Holt to note her hesitation. He added, "We have his prints. A match on a bag of candy he left in the plane. We have him. The question is whether or not we'll catch him before he gets hurt."

Deb spread her hands and smiled. "Look. He's off the island. I put him on the ferry myself. Drove him and watched him get on. He was heading for San Francisco." She exhaled a thin stream of smoke. The dog padded over and curled up at her feet. "So start looking there."

FEBRUARY 11, 2010

Tomkins Airstrip was just down the pine-lined road. He'd spied it from the school bus for years. Now the building seemed to greet him like an old friend, its window winking, an American flag waving hello from atop the hangar roof.

The flight to Seattle was only twenty minutes. Robert had stayed airborne that long on his first attempt. He could be landing on the coast by four thirty, before sunup. He wished he could simulate the trip on his computer—impossible now, of course—but he had a little experience under his belt. He'd be fine. The only question was where to land. Ditching in the evergreen forests was certainly dangerous, and loud. The beach would probably be safest, but so out in the open.

Might have to decide on the fly. Wherever looked good.

Robert waited in the woods until long after nightfall, for

as long as he could stand it, hoping it was at least one or two a.m. Then he emerged from the trees, pushing back branches, and sprinted for the hangar.

Security was tighter at Tomkins than North County Airport. No unlocked doors welcoming him here. Robert hopped the fence without any trouble, but pacing the squat building's perimeter didn't reveal any openings. He pulled on door handles and ran his hands along window ledges without any luck. Even the dilapidated shed at the back of the property was padlocked. Robert tugged at the tarnished lock, frustrated. The splintering door looked flimsy; he wondered if he could kick it in.

Three tries and the door swung open, the hinges breaking and falling to the dirt floor. Rusty flakes sprinkled the grass. Inside was a mower and an assortment of dusty tools: hammers, pliers, saws, screwdrivers. Tin cans filled with nails. He grabbed a hammer and swung it like a baseball bat, like he was Thor. Robert wouldn't have known what to do with half the tools, but a crowbar was easy enough to operate. He traded the hammer for it, tossing it from hand to hand, enjoying its heft.

Prying open the back door wasn't so painless. Sweat dampened his shirt and his arms ached by the time it swung open. The crowbar clattered to the floor, and Robert waited, his heart thumping in his ears, for an alarm to sound. But soon his blood slowed and the silence calmed him, and he went inside, hefting the crowbar, like he was ready to brain someone. He wasn't.

Tomkins was laid out much like North County Airport: the warehouse look, the planes in the hangar, the roll-up doors. A lounge with plush couches, a bathroom with a shower, a foosball table and three computer stations, though, seemed to cater to a different breed of pilot. Robert could upload a flight simulator, try his planned run, scope out a landing site, and practice the whole flight a few times before he took off.

He searched for keys, opening desk drawers and checking shelves. He found manuals, binders filled with various logs and time sheets, atlases. Boxes of Reese's Peanut Butter Cups, Snickers bars, gum, and lollipops were stacked on another shelf, along with a can labeled *Honor System*. That he could snag a meal here along with a ride hadn't occurred to him, but now his stomach gurgled. He didn't want any distractions in the air. He found a back office with another bathroom, a small TV, and a mini-fridge. He slid his sleeve over his hand and opened it. Bread, lunch meat, cheese, a few apples, some cans of Pepsi. Robert slapped together two sandwiches, passing on the mustard, not wanting to dirty a knife. He awarded himself an imaginary Green for attention to detail. He devoured the meal right there and brushed the crumbs into the trash. He took a Pepsi for the road.

Then he remembered the crowbar and the prints he'd

left there. He was on his way to wipe it down as well when the candy beckoned. He shoved a Snickers bar, two peanut butter cups, and a fistful of Dum Dums into his pocket. Dessert.

That's when he saw the camera's roving eye in the corner above the desk. A beady red light blinked steadily. Robert cursed under his breath. He should have thought of this, should have checked the whole hangar.

Just one more reason to get out of town. Since he was already caught on film, Robert winked. Then he retrieved the crowbar from the floor, stalked back to the camera, and took a swing. Glass and metal sprinkled the floor. A busted piñata of wires and parts remained.

But he still didn't have keys, and now he knew he might have been seen. What if they kept the keys in a safe? He spotted a toolbox and took a screwdriver instead. He thought about Dalton's stories of stealing cars.

He decided on a TTx, N1980TT, a sleek plane, lime-green paint sweeping across the top half and down the wings. Robert walked the wingspan before opening the cockpit hatch. Unlocked. Butterscotch leather interior. The plane seated four. Fewer buttons and knobs peppered the control panel. Robert wasn't sure if that was a good or bad thing, but the Garmin was close enough to what he'd used on his last flight. The console's cup holder cradled a paper cup printed with golden arches, full of melted ice and watery

Coke. Robert threw it in the trash on his way to the hangar doors.

He buckled up. Safety first.

This time Robert's stomach lurched, knowing what he was about to do. His hands shook as he jammed the screwdriver into the ignition. The resulting metallic crunch made him sure he'd broken something. He rattled the screwdriver and tried to turn it, but it wouldn't budge.

He looked wildly around the hangar. What else could he use to start this plane?

He desperately jimmied the screwdriver a final time, and suddenly the handle turned. The engine revved. He was half-thrilled and half-terrified. Now he had to go through with it. Robert unwrapped a Dum Dum and shoved it in his mouth, biting down on the hard candy. The cherry lollipop cracked into candy splinters, sharp as glass shards, which he worked furiously with his teeth as he taxied out of the hangar.

Stars twinkled over the airstrip and sharp pine branches pierced the horizon. On one side was the ocean; on the other were the trees. He'd swoop over them, skip across the bay, and land back on Washington's shore. The cover of night would last long enough for him to distance himself from the plane.

He told himself he had a plan. He told himself he was ready.

The plane's speed increased and Robert wrenched the throttle. N1980TT jerked into the air, punching up through gravity. He waited for the adrenaline rush to boil down. For that feeling of control to steady his hands. His first flight had been pure impulse, but now all he could do was think. *Am I doing it right? Am I following the directions? Am I doing everything in the right order? Am I paying attention to the gauges, the meters, the signs?*

The altitude meter lurched and dove, as though the air itself had become bumpy. Wind tossed the plane left and right. Robert tugged at the throttle again. He yanked on the elevator control, and the nose came up too sharply. The runway danced across the windshield as he pushed the rudders and overcorrected. Too late he thought to lower the flaps, a worthless move now. He did it anyway. *I thought I was good at this, and now I'm screwing the whole thing up.*

At around 100 feet, the altitude meter stopped climbing, and the needle hung suspended. If he couldn't gain any more altitude, the plane could tangle in the trees' ancient tops like a stuck kite. He could end up impaled on a branch.

Something wasn't right. Something was engaged that should be disengaged, something was down that should be up, on that should be off. Maybe he'd broken something during the rough takeoff. Maybe he'd broken something with the screwdriver. Robert's eyes skimmed the windshield and the control panel. He tried to pull up on the throttle but it might as well have been sunk in concrete. All his computerized flights that had ended in flames flared before his eyes. One more time he jerked the elevator.

The beach narrowed.

Seattle might as well be the moon for as close as he was going to get to it. He had to land, and the place least likely to kill him was the sand. He threw down the wheels, extended the flaps, and trimmed the elevator quickly, quickly. He closed the throttle, kept the nose up, and shut his eyes, bracing himself for impact.

A blooming cloud of grit coated the windshield as the plane gouged the shoreline, cratering the sand. Waves broke against the wheels, and salt water sprayed the windows. The carriage thudded, bounding along the beach. The plane finally skidded to a stop, leaning on the right wing. The left was bent, a broken bone in the plane's metal skeleton. The engine sputtered and died. The nose wheel was crushed beneath the plane; the landing gear had snapped off and lay a few feet down the beach, among the shell shards and smooth stones. The propeller spun frantically, whirling up a small sandstorm, until it, too, lost momentum and was still.

He'd crashed only a few miles from Tomkins. A few lousy miles.

Robert pushed against the pilot-side door, smashing his shoulder against the frame until he realized the bottom was blocked by a six-inch-deep trench gashed in the sand. He climbed over the controls and beat on the passenger-side door until it finally lurched open. Robert scrambled from the plane, lost his balance, and fell into the sand. Grit filled his mouth and coated his nose and chin. He rolled over and blinked at the stars and the full, round moon before blacking out.

ACT III

BRACE FOR A CRASH LANDING

From *The Beginning Pilot's Flight Guide* (p. 36):

A flight is not considered finished until the engine is shut down and the airplane is secured. A pilot should consider this a critical part of any flight. After engine shutdown, the pilot should complete a postflight inspection. Any parts that need to be checked or repaired should be noted.

FEBRUARY 12, 2010

He wasn't dead, but pain shot through his neck when Robert tried to get up. The seat belt had carved an angry burn across his chest to his shoulder. His top lip was torn. He rose to his knees and spat blood-speckled sand.

How long had he been lying there? Robert scrambled to a stand. He had to go.

When the cops eventually stumbled across this scene, they'd question how he made it out alive. Maybe they'd spend days searching for his body, assuming he'd been mortally wounded and had crawled into the trees to die.

Maybe that was a good thing.

He wrenched the screwdriver free of the ignition and slipped it into his pocket. He kept the candy, smashed and flattened as it was, for later. His halting, limping footprints disappeared into the dunes.

Steve: So for our listeners who haven't tuned in to the news yet, let me be the first to share this gem, making headlines in both Yannatok and in Seattle this morning.

Mac: Beep, bah-beep-beep-beep. Beep, bah-beep-beep-beep. Breaking news. Dateline, Yannatok.

Steve: Enough. So everyone already knows about the plane stolen from North County Airport and then brought down ever so gently in the middle of the damn forest over on this side of the bridge. Well, the intrepid reporters at the *Tide* have confirmed the rumors running wild all over this island that indeed the same culprit—

Mac: The Red Baron.

Steve: Hold that thought, because you've already been outdone in the nickname department.

Mac: The Jesse James of the sky.

Steve: This Jesse James of the not-so-friendly skies filched another aircraft from Tomkins and managed to smash it to bits on some oceanfront property and—

Mac: Wait for it.

Steve: Walked away again! Survived the crash and skedaddled fast enough that he's still at large. So who is this master pilot, you're asking? Who is this renegade flier, this Houdini hijacker with nine lives? This master of escape, who can crash two thousand pounds of metal without being seen by a single person? Who has the sheriff running through the woods in the dark, begging for somebody, anybody to come forward with a tip that will save his ass come the November election?

Mac: Wait for it!

Steve: Eighteen-year-old Robert Jackson Kelley.

Mac: Who?

Steve: Exactly. A kid. A kid without any type of flight training. And apparently he's been leaving a sugary parting gift at the scene of his crimes, and so, the oh-so-clever *Seattle Times* has dubbed him the—

Mac: Here it is!

Steve: The Lollipop Kid.

Mac and Steve (singing): We represent the Lollipop Kid!

Steve: You know, you look just like one of those

Munchkins. On the *Tide*'s website, the story's blowing up with comments. It's got more hits than anything I've ever seen posted up there. And we've found a Facebook page that is apparently Robert Jackson Kelley's—

Mac: You gotta say all three names. You just have to.

Steve: You can just see it on a wanted poster, can't you?

Mac: Well, we're gonna pay the bills with a quick commercial break and then we'd love to hear from you. Do you know where the Lollipop Kid lurks this morning?

"You tell me: how does Robert keep walking away from plane crashes? He just walks away! They don't even find his footprints! What? Are his bones made of adamantium or some shit, like freakin' Wolverine? Does he parachute out? Can he friggin' fly?

"He was driving everyone crazy, and he knew it. That second time he arranged the Dum Dums in this big smiley face, right next to the plane. Like, have a nice day, suckers."

FEBRUARY 12, 2010

Holt ran his hand over his stubbled chin and wished fervently to be back in his warm bed. Instead, rain spat on him and sand worked its way into his boots.

He couldn't believe he was standing in front of a second wrecked plane, as big an eyesore as a beached whale. And again, no sign of Robert Jackson Kelley. He got away— alive—again.

The Sheriff's Department was a small one: the deputy, four detectives, and the sheriff himself. Dispatch, which also directed calls from across the bridge in North, Doby, and Womset counties, employed at least double. Without the summer's influx of tourists, Holt doubted his position would exist at all. But Holt's entire outfit had been called out to the beach, and they were combing over the wreckage, wearing gloves. He'd sent two guys into the woods. Holt stood in the middle, watching, his stomach roiling. He wished he had Tums.

"There's blood in the sand over here." Holt pointed with his toe. "You guys getting this? Don't let the rain wash it away."

"We're taking samples, Sheriff."

Holt knew he'd have to spend the next several hours on the horn, playing up a terrorist threat he didn't believe existed, in order to rush these specks of Robert Jackson Kelley's blood through one of Seattle's crime labs. If these two crashes were chalked up to just a local punk, the samples would languish in the state's backlog of nonviolent investigations. He'd have to make the case for an island-based sleeper cell, a delicate dance of convincing the lab and not making himself look like too much of a fool when he arrested a local punk after all.

Deputy Hauser stuck his head through the plane's bent window frame, like an annoying sitcom neighbor popping his head over the fence. "Check this out, Sheriff."

There were his men, stumbling out of the trees, one with his arm slung around the other's shoulders, leg awkwardly bent. Sweat stains bloomed under their arms. Did they have pine needles in their hair? "We thought we heard him, went tearing through the trees. McMullen blew his knee out."

McMullen shook his head, panted. "And it wasn't even him. Damn raccoon."

Just what Holt needed. Down a man, looking out of shape, bumbling, small-time. What if a lack of manpower forced him to deputize citizens?

If Robert Jackson Kelley tried this stunt one more time, the results would be disastrous for both the kid and the sheriff. How many times could an untrained pilot cheat death?

Holt hadn't found a body since Rob Kelley Senior had left one in the middle of the road.

He had no choice now but to release Robert's name and photo to the public. Someone, somewhere on this island, knew where the kid was. Someone was feeding him. He wished he had a photo other than Robert's mug shot, snapped by Holt himself, grinning for the cameras, full-out cheesing, wide and proud. But the mother had lied to him already; he knew Robert had never been anywhere near the ferry. Holt doubted she'd offer up a snapshot.

Interview with Joey Kovach, Gold's Gym, Seattle, October 10, 2010

From Flight Risk: The Robert Jackson Kelley Story

"There was this time the sheriff thought he saw him. He'd been pushing his cart full of groceries across the parking lot at Shipley's Market. Toilet paper and Hungry-Man dinners, I bet. He was off duty, out of uniform. Jeans and a Mariners T-shirt. Maybe he's even whistlin', grinnin', thinking back on all the speeding tickets he gave kids that day. Then suddenly he thinks he spots Robert Jackson Kelley, on the other side of the lot, and he takes off running, faster than you'd think for an old guy like that. The cart rolls away, clattering into a minivan. A bottle of Coke rolls out, stops against the van's tire. The sheriff's full-out sprinting, haulin' ass, going for this kid in a pair of cargo shorts and a black hoodie up over his head. He's yelling, he's waving his arms, other shoppers are stopping whatever they're doing, thinkin' they're really gonna see some action. Getting out their phones so they can film it all and put it all over

YouTube. The kid stops walking and the sheriff grabs his shoulder and spins him around.

"Of course it's not Robert. Sheriff's standin' there looking like Paul Blart. You almost start to feel sorry for him. All he has now is a shook-up bottle of Coke.

"Kelley's long gone, a ghost, vapor."

From the *Seattle Times*'s website: "The Lollipop Kid: Yannatok Teen Steals 2nd Plane, Taunts Police," February 12, 2010

YANNATOK—A Yannatok teenager, identified by police as Robert Jackson Kelley, Junior, 18, is suspected of stealing a second Cessna TTx, owned by Ted Jenkins of Tacoma, from Tomkins Airstrip early this morning. Kelley is also wanted in the theft of a Cessna 182 belonging to Yannatok resident Gary Stanton from North County Airport only three days prior. Yannatok police have released a photograph of Kelley. Residents are warned to consider Kelley armed and dangerous and to contact police immediately with any information regarding his whereabouts. Kelley was reported missing from the Sea Brook Youth Home on February 4, where he was being held on misdemeanor drug charges. His whereabouts since that time are unknown.

Nicknamed "the Lollipop Kid" by locals, Kelley has become notorious for leaving Dum Dum lollipops at the scene of each plane crash.

"Everyone's calling him the Lollipop Kid," confirmed Mira Wohl, a seventeen-year-old former classmate of Kelley's. "I'm not sure who started it, but now everyone's saying it. Someone spray-painted it on the side of Shipley's, and then it started showing up in bathrooms at school, on the lockers, in that Sharpie that never comes off."

"Mr. Kelley seems to think he can thumb his nose at the law," Sheriff James Holt of the Yannatok Sheriff's Department said in a statement released yesterday. "He needs to be brought to justice, for the safety of everyone on the island as well as his own. I want to urge the citizens of Yannatok to keep their eyes open and take common sense precautions such as locking their doors."

"I would like restitution," Stanton commented. "But I'm glad no one was hurt."

Regarding the Sheriff's Department's ongoing efforts to apprehend Kelley, Stanton added, "In a place this small, all the deputies ever deal with is drunks and domestic calls. There's no helicopter, no SWAT. The K-9 unit is the sheriff's own dog. You can't see fifty feet in front of you in those woods. It wouldn't be hard for somebody to disappear."

"I come here with my family every year," Jenkins, owner of a vacation home, stated to reporters. "We eat at the restaurants, go the shops. It's quiet. Now I feel like I might as well stay in the city. This guy needs to be caught.

"Catch him and let me deal with him," Jenkins added. "I'll show him what he can do with his lollipops."

Not everyone on Yannatok Island shares Jenkins's sentiments. Bill Greer, a retired contractor and lifetime Yannatok resident, says, "These deputies go after us for all sorts of piddling stuff. You don't have a permit to burn this, you can't just go and build that. I'm glad to see someone sticking it to 'em."

FEBRUARY 12, 2010

Robert hobbled along the road, sweat-glazed, dizzy. His throat was so parched it hurt to swallow.

He knew he could land one of those planes. He'd done it a thousand times on his computer, in his head. He could picture it now, like a movie. Smoothly gliding onto the beach. What happened after that, the next frame, was what he couldn't see.

He staggered in the vacation house's direction, but he wasn't sure if that was the best plan. Would the cops start to nose around the empty houses? Call up the owners and tell them to check on their places? He pictured Holt cruising down the shore roads, his classic rock on low. Maybe if Robert talked to him, in secret, he could explain that all he wanted now was to get off Yannatok. Maybe Holt could help him. How could Robert get in touch with him without walking into the sheriff's station and winding up in cuffs? And Robert wouldn't try it with any other cop; it had to be the sheriff. Holt had been cool to him when he'd been busted, or rather, when Joey Kovach had been busted and thrown Robert under the bus. And he was the one who always came to Robert's school, telling the kids that the police were there to help them. At this point, Robert would happily pack his bags for Sea Brook, shoot arrows, and swallow little blue Adderalls and sing "Kumbaya."

The sun had come up, fat as a juicy orange, and Robert was still lingering by the road. Maybe he could hitchhike. Maybe he'd get picked up by someone on their way to work in Seattle, and there he'd be, over the bridge. For a while, not a single car passed. He hobbled in the house's direction, thought better of it, turned around, shuffled back the other way. He couldn't think. A handful of those little blue pills he'd been so cavalier about unloading might help now. His stomach ached, empty but for candy.

He was so roughed up, so dirty, with sand in his hair and the skin between his mouth and his nose scraped and his clothes stinking and wet, that whoever offered to give him a ride was probably someone he should stay away from. Or someone who would recognize him and drive him straight to the police.

Something was coming down the road. His old school bus was huffing along. And there was Mira Wohl's BMW, nipping right behind. The road was too narrow to pass. The bus screeched to a halt to pick up a few elementary school-ers. Mira braked and banged on Stella's steering wheel in frustration. Her strawberry hair was shorter, angled into twin chin-skimming points. A kid in the back of the bus stretched his mouth wide and stuck out his tongue. Mira's girlfriends laughed and waved their middle fingers. Alex Winters was missing from his passenger seat perch.

Robert pulled up his hood and kept walking. When he snuck another quick peek at the car, it was crawling behind him and the girls in the back were whispering. One of them leaned forward to talk to Mira and pointed in his direction. A flush spread from his neck to his ears, and he walked faster. The car slowed to match his pace. The girls in the back, Justine Pierce and Riley Brennan, were also his former classmates.

"Hey!" one of the girls called, and they all laughed. Robert burrowed farther into his sweatshirt. Justine leaned out the window. "Got a lollipop?"

Now the girls were in hysterics, clutching one another. The bus was long gone. Robert didn't get it. Were they making fun of him?

Justine yelled again. "Hey! Why are you walking? Don't you have a plane?"

They knew. He wasn't sure how, but they knew. He put his head down and broke into a run, thinking of the girls gathered around that pink phone in the cafeteria, the slim rectangles Justine or Riley or Mira were surely going to whip out to call 911 and report the fugitive hobbling down the road. Why wouldn't they? He was just a free lunch kid with a telltale apple sticker on his ID.

The car matched his pace, rolled along beside him no matter how fast he tried to outrun it.

"We won't tell," Mira called.

Robert looked up just in time to catch her wink, and then they sped off.

For the first time in his life, Mira Wohl had talked to him. All he'd had to do to get her attention was steal a plane. For just a second, he really, really wished he had had a lollipop. Three, even.

Interview with Mira Wohl, Willamette University cafeteria, October 2, 2010

From *Flight Risk: The Robert Jackson Kelley Story*

"I could have whipped out my phone right then and taken a picture. Had it on Twitter in like five seconds, right there under my name, @mira_mira_on_the_wohl. And probably would have gotten like a hundred thousand new followers, too. Or sold it to the newspapers. There wasn't any reward money yet, but a few days later, I could have gone to the sheriff and my tip still would have been worth something. Could have told them what he was wearing, where he'd been prowling around. I bet Vera Hunt would have interviewed me.

"But of course I didn't do any of that. Justine wanted to, but I told her no way. I'm not a snitch, for starters. Plus, he looked so beat up, like a homeless person or like he'd been in a fight. And he was wandering around like he was lost, like he totally didn't have a plan. He looked like he didn't know who we were for a second, and I thought, 'How long has he been out here, all wet and dirty?' Turning him in would have been just mean, like kicking a puppy or something.

"And this might sound crazy, but I totally got what he was doing. I scored the part of Juror Number Eight. The best part in the play, the most lines. I sat down with my English teacher and went over all of it, so I could really act, like Kristen Stewart or Emma Stone. My teacher thought I was a natural! But I could barely even be happy. Because you know what people were saying? That I cut my hair because really, the jurors are all guys, and I thought it would help me get a part. People in this school just make up whatever they want. I cut it because I've had the same long hair since I was, like, five, and Alex and I broke up, and I just felt like a friggin' change. So many of my so-called friends turned on me after the breakup, and I was tired of being my same old self, basically, and doing what everyone expects me to do. If I could have stolen a plane and flown off this friggin' island, I would have done it, too."

From the *Seattle Times*'s website, in the comments section for the *Times*'s article "The Lollipop Kid: Yannatok Teen Steals 2nd Plane, Taunts Police," February 12, 2010

Posted by TruPatriot911 at 3:40 p.m., February 12, 2010
This kid could be planning anything. They need to catch him and quick. You know who else liked to screw around with planes? Hang around airports? Mohamed Atta.

Posted by Airman45 at 5:58 p.m., February 12, 2010
Fly, Robert, fly! Who do you think will play him in the movie?

Posted by PacSunn, at 9:52 p.m., February 12, 2010
Where is this kid's mother?!?!?

Deb planted a sign in front of the trailer. No trespassers. *Beware of dog.* A reporter spotted Hulk on the porch, though, wagging his stubby tail, and after that they didn't hesitate to snap pictures on the lawn.

Yellow police tape wound through the Tomkins fence and across the front door like a finish line Holt thought he'd never cross. He and his deputies had been combing the place for hours, while Walt Meehan, the airport's general manager, hovered nearby, making his scorn for the Sheriff's Department known. He trailed them around the hangars, questioning every photo they took, every surface they swiped. Holt had brought along Bandit, though he didn't think the dog would unearth any evidence. He still missed Copper, his first

K-9 partner, but loyal, smart, energetic Bandit made a fine replacement. Something about the animal put a swagger in Holt's step. But Walt kept glaring at Bandit like he had shit on the floor.

Holt and the dog joined Walt in his office, a neat little cubicle lined with shelves displaying various logbooks and a dozen or so intricate model fighter jets. Walt's certifications hung over his desk. Not a stray paper, not a single wrapper or Coke can. The thought of Kelley's grimy hands on his keys was probably driving Walt nuts. Probably wasn't thrilled about Bandit's paws on the carpet, either. Holt took a notebook from his pocket. "In any B and E, the first question is, what's missing?"

"Besides a plane?"

Holt wished he carried a Taser. "Money? Electronics?"

Walt sighed. "No. Computers don't look touched. Didn't use the shower. There's food missing, though. Candy. I only realized it because I counted up the change in the can just yesterday. It was short, which usually doesn't happen. Guys around here are honest."

Holt clicked his pen and kept his expression neutral. "Candy?"

He nodded. "Reese's. A Snickers bar, I think. Some lollipops, just like everyone's saying." Walt stood. "Look, I gotta tell ya, I'm not happy with how this is being handled. Is the FBI going to come out here? Homeland Security?

Because your deputies seem out of their element. And I want this guy caught so I can get some kind of restitution."

"Mr. Meehan, we are conducting an extremely thorough investigation. In fact, you're going to need to cease operations while this facility is considered a crime scene. And I also ask that you not speak to the media about *any* aspect of this investigation. We are being very careful about what information is released to the public."

"And why is that?" Walt barked. "And how I am supposed to cease operations? I need to pay *rent*." Walt shook his head. "I'm going to stay here, sleep here if I have to, until this guy's in handcuffs. How do you know he won't be back? And when will I get restitution? What about the camera he smashed?"

"Where is the footage kept?" Holt asked, attempting to steer the interview away from the missing lollipops. Walt sat back down, answering the rest of Holt's questions petulantly but thoroughly, providing logs and phone numbers, computer passwords and keys. He continued to eye Bandit, but didn't complain.

An hour later, Holt stood in the open hangar door, gazing down the runway, absently scratching behind Bandit's ears. He surveyed the view Robert would have stared down right before he took to the sky. Black tarmac reaching toward the horizon, spruces pointing skyward. Holt tried to imagine Robert's mindset. Would the kid have been scared?

Excited? Holt had come of age in Culpepper, a rural Washington town. As a teenager he'd made a general nuisance of himself. Smoking dope, firing his father's guns, hot-rodding past the apple orchards. He and his buddies would smash mailboxes and get into drunken fights, until one night young Jimmy Holt got picked up by the cops and charged with drunk and disorderly, along with, to his mother's horror, public urination. His parents had the good sense and savings to ship him to an East Coast military school, where he'd had the punk saluted and marched and drilled right out of him.

He knew that a change of scene, pure and simple, could do a kid good. Why on earth would Robert have come back to Yannatok? Why hadn't the kid flown east from North County, to Las Vegas or even St. Louis, as far away as that plane could carry him? He would have had such a huge head start, he might have actually stood a chance of getting away with the whole thing.

Holt led Bandit down the runway, taking deliberate steps, closing in on where Robert had left the ground. What if the kid just wasn't thinking? If Holt threw out any notion of Robert planning, then the first flight must have been a lark, a dare Robert Jackson Kelley had challenged himself to.

Then maybe he got into trouble in the air; maybe he got scared. Maybe he just put the thing down wherever he could.

But why try such a potentially dangerous stunt again? Why not get on the ferry and go, before he'd been identified? He could have been caught at Tomkins. He could have been killed trying to take off in, or land, another plane. Why take the risk?

There was only one answer: because the kid loved it. Pure and simple.

And if his theory was correct, Holt knew he would try it again.

Oreo Cake 5.99

Chocolate cake topped with Oreo cookie crumbles, vanilla ice cream, hot fudge, and whipped cream

The Triple 5.59

Three scoops of ice cream (vanilla, strawberry, and chocolate) topped with hot fudge, whipped cream, and a cherry. Gluten free!

The Lollipop Kid 6.59

NEW! Two scoops of vanilla ice cream floating in a frosty mug of root beer, topped with two Dum Dums. Flavors vary.

Add cherry vodka 2.00

The walk back to the house had been long and painful. His crash-induced aches, along with his blistered toes inside his tattered, sodden shoes, slowed his pace, and he kept having to stop and rest. His thirst was painful. He'd decided to go back to the house. He'd take the chance that it was crawling with cops, and that he'd have to retreat to the woods. The prospect of a bed was worth the risk. The sun was melting through the pine branches by the time his destination came into view.

When he'd thought about hiding out in the wilderness or imagined his dad on the run, Robert had never considered the long hours with nothing to fill them and no one to talk to. All the kids he went to school with were sitting at their desks, gathering around cafeteria tables, shooting hoops in the gym. As he trudged down the road, he wished he'd talked to Mira. Maybe she'd have given him a lift. He believed her when she said she wouldn't turn him in. She was popular, sure, but she had never seemed like a goody-goody. He could have told her he liked her haircut.

The screwdriver knocked against his leg, deep in his pocket. The tool was evidence now.

If a patrol car had come upon him, he probably would have surrendered.

Back at his home base, he showered until the water ran cold, leaving wet footprints on the tile as he searched for a towel. Robert once again pawed through a stranger's bureau for a change of clothes. This time he could only dig up a polo rugby shirt, gray with maroon stripes, and black track pants. He swished downstairs.

The adrenaline had drained from him like a dying battery, and now he was too exhausted to do anything other than watch television. He lifted the TV from its spot in the entertainment console, bear-hugging it and setting it gently on the floor. Now the light wouldn't give him away. He flipped through the channels, landing on the Olympics' opening ceremony. Robert hadn't even realized the games were this year. The Parade of Nations was long, but Robert liked to see the waving flags, hear the made-up-sounding names of countries he hadn't known existed. Of course he rooted for the United States, but he liked the small teams the best. From the leather sectional belonging to a family he'd never met, Robert clapped as the lone skier from Ghana took his lap.

"Tonight brings both the pageantry of these opening ceremonies and tragic news from the Whistler Sliding Centre, where this morning Georgian luger Nodar Kumaritashvili was killed during a training run. The twenty-one-year-old athlete was—"

And here was footage of men encapsulated in their sleek suits, ricocheting feetfirst around frosted corners. A hundred and forty miles per hour! One fifty! One fifty-three!

Then Kumaritashvili flew off the track, his sled bouncing to the finish line without him. Robert suddenly had to abandon the TV to get a glass of water. He tried not to think about Kumaritashvili's last moments. Whizzing, winging through the icy turns, the air rushing, the banks on either side a blur, and then panic rising like bile as the last twist came up too fast. The speed suddenly terrifying. The risk of launching down that icy track suddenly foolhardy.

The opening ceremony continued, but the anchors interjected the news of Kumaritashvili's death seemingly between every delegation, interspersing the parade with footage of the lugers shooting down the icy track. Robert flipped through his manuals each time, skimming a paragraph about engine maintenance here, about defrosting there.

He thought about sleeping on the bed in the largest

bedroom, on top of the covers. He paused over the green-and-white-checked comforter and finally decided to sleep on the couch. He kept the TV on, a second airing of the Parade of Nations flickering over his face.

In his dreams, Kumaritashvili took off from the gate and careened down the icy track. The short sled hopped and then crashed down, but Kumaritashvili steered and braced, his body a streamlined shot of navy blue. He crossed the finish line, and Robert gave him a high five.

The town hall meeting was not Holt's idea. The state attorney general's office sent down word that Holt needed to quell the "public's growing anxiety about fugitive Robert Jackson Kelley." The meeting was staged in the same room where Robert Jackson Kelley had been expelled. His former principal was there. His mother wasn't.

The sheriff, over the phone with the AG's second-in-command, had tried to explain. The chatty boy he'd arrested only a few months ago, who'd grinned for that mug shot, who'd asked him if he had kids—that kid might love being the subject of this much attention. The press might be egging the Lollipop Kid on.

Holt stood behind the unfurled American flag. Someone from his office had also hung a large banner behind him, emblazoned with a replica of the star-shaped sheriff's badge. Holt couldn't remember the last time he'd seen that thing out of the storage closet. A microphone perched atop a polished wooden podium. All of the room's fluorescent lights blazed. Holt was already sweating. Reporters representing all three network affiliates were there, as well as the *Seattle Times* and the *Yannatok Tide*. Holt recognized Sara Ortiz from Channel Eleven, and he'd been interviewed several times over the years by Channel Four's Lisa Kennedy. But the younger guy with the coffee, the lady in the purple blazer—Holt would have to ask around later to find out who they were. He'd be shocked to learn the man was working on a story for *Outside* magazine and the woman was a low-ranking Fox News correspondent.

"Are we calling this a town hall or a press conference?" Deputy Hauser asked. He hiked a thumb back at the reporters. "Lady wants to know."

"Town hall," Holt said quickly. Locals were filtering into the back. Gary Stanton. Kirk Oden, who taught flight school at Tomkins Airstrip. Holt nodded at Lorraine Simena, flanked by her sister, Renee Flores, who lived in a neat little house near the shore, not far from where the first plane had crashed. Gerri Kovach, arms folded stiffly across her chest, trying to catch him with her glare. And about a dozen others he knew by sight, though not necessarily by name: the butcher at Shipley's, the guy who ran the ferry ticket window, the lady he saw power-walking down Dunes Road at sunrise most mornings. Frankly, people for whom he wasn't sure what could be at stake in this mess.

Hauser nodded. He leaned in closer. "Do you have notes?"

"Notes?"

"Do you know what you're going to say, I guess," Hauser said.

"Of course." Holt had never needed notes before. Why would he need notes now?

Hauser slung a thumb over his shoulder. "There's a guy out there I swear is from Vera Hunt. You've seen her show, right?"

"I guess." Holt shrugged, very much doubting a national cable news network had sent a correspondent from one of their top-rated shows to his town hall meeting. Tongues were definitely flapping all over the island, but surely there were bigger news stories nationally. Hadn't the president just passed a budget? Weren't the Olympics under way?

"She sure nailed that bastard Jack Benson." The deputy lowered his voice. "I'd watch that guy."

Holt nodded, straightened his badge, and approached the podium. He'd shined his shoes and ironed his uniform that morning. "Let's get this over with."

Holt cleared his throat and began. "Good morning." Immediately flashbulbs exploded. He paused until the lights died down. "At approximately two fifteen a.m. the Sheriff's

Department, including myself and Deputy Hauser, responded to a 911 call regarding a small aircraft crash on the beach near Dunes Road. Upon reporting to the scene, it was discovered that there were no injured persons." He paused. "We believe the plane was stolen by Robert Jackson Kelley, the missing youth wanted in connection with the theft of another plane in North County. We are using all available manpower and resources to locate Mr. Kelley and bring him to justice. Island residents should report any suspicious activity and are encouraged to take simple steps to secure their property and homes, such as locking their doors. I would also like to emphasize, however, that Yannatok Island remains a safe place to live and work and residents should continue to go about their normal routines." Holt eyed the clock on the room's back wall. He'd said all he had to say in less than three minutes. He reluctantly added, "I have a few minutes to take questions."

Hands shot into the air. Holt didn't recognize the first speaker Hauser handed the mic to. Odd-looking guy. Wiry, with a shaved head and a twitchy smile. Thin-framed glasses. Dressed in all black. He smiled when he said, "I'll bring you your boy. Within forty-eight hours. Alive and well."

Holt leaned into the microphone. "We, too, intend to bring Mr. Kelley in alive. There is no call for the public to hunt for Robert Jackson Kelley." He paused, then asked, "Would you care to introduce yourself, sir?"

"Travis Tennant. Fugitive recovery specialist."

"You're a bounty hunter?" Holt blinked. A few in the crowd chuckled. A flush warmed Holt's neck. He hoped it wasn't noticeable. "Are you a resident of the island, Mr. Tennant?"

"No, I am not."

"Well, at this time, we have no need for your services."

The man smiled again. He was smaller than his profession might imply. "Certainly seems like you do."

Holt raised his voice. "Let me be clear that there is no call for vigilantism and citizens are not advised to approach Mr. Kelley—"

"What are we supposed to do? Wait for him to crash into our living rooms?" a woman cried out. Holt cringed, recognizing her. He'd picked her son up for underage drinking out on the beach, though he'd let the kid off with a warning. Didn't stop the woman from marching into his office the next day, claiming a detective had pushed around her boy.

"Citizens are always advised to call law enforcement officials rather than take the law into their own hands like Mr. Tennant suggests."

"He's on Facebook saying 'Eff you!'" the woman continued. She shook her head, disgusted. "Did you know that? He's turning you into a joke."

"We're looking into Mr. Kelley's Internet presence," Holt

said shortly, knowing full well that Robert Kelley had not had a Facebook page prior to his escape from Sea Brook, and that he almost certainly had not created one himself while he had been on the run. So who was posting under Robert's name? That was something he'd have to investigate later. Holt turned back to Travis Tennant. "I'd also like to point out that Mr. Kelley has not violated the terms of any bail. Citizens, including yourself, don't have the authority to arrest him or pursue him on private property. Next question, please." He pointed to a glossy-haired reporter in a starched white shirt and a pressed gray suit punctuated with a bright blue tie.

"Jonathan Richards, *Hunt for Justice with Vera Hunt*." Whispers rippled through the crowd. Holt kept his face frozen, as if the TV program meant nothing to him. Deputy Hauser had been correct, for once. "How are you this morning, Sheriff?"

Scattered laughter. Holt allowed a tight smile and replied, "I have certainly been better."

Richards nodded. "Fair enough. Is the Sheriff's Department investigating Robert Kelley's ties to terrorist organizations?"

Holt paused. He was certain that if he said no, simply because Robert Kelley wasn't a terrorist, someone would turn up a molehill to make a mountain out of. One unfortunate google on the kid's hard drive would be enough.

And there were the insinuations he'd made to the lab, a means to justify an end. The sheriff made sure to look Jonathan Richards in the eye. "At this time there isn't any evidence that would tie Robert Kelley to a terrorist cell, but we are continuing to investigate all aspects of this case."

"Have you been able to access his computer?"

"I'm not able to answer that at this time."

Richards grinned again. "Wouldn't Robert Kelley's computer be an essential piece of evidence in this case?"

"That is not an aspect of the case I can discuss at this time." Holt searched for someone else to call on. The reporter in the purple blazer raised her hand, waving her pen. Holt nodded to her.

"Are you concerned about copycat behavior?"

Holt couldn't help but smile. "Most people would be pretty hard-pressed to copy what Mr. Kelley has done." He had one more ace up his sleeve, a nugget sure to win the public to his side. "The Sheriff's Department has also established a reward for any tip that leads to Mr. Kelley's capture. Fifty thousand dollars."

Once a price had been stamped on Robert Jackson Kelley's head, calls to the tip line and the police department increased by 300 percent. Kelley had been spotted among a group of homeless kids crashing under a Seattle bridge, lounging on the beach in Los Angeles, exiting Las Vegas's MGM Grand Casino. At airports in Portland, San Francisco, Salt Lake City. Fleeing a car break-in right there in Yannatok, making off with an iPod and a GPS. That time the real culprit left a Dum Dum at the scene, rolling around under the driver's seat among some spare change and dry pine needles. But that guy got caught a few miles down the road, and Robert Jackson Kelley remained at large.

He's on Facebook saying "Eff you!"

After the town hall, Holt shut the door to his office and opened his computer.

Though he knew it was unlikely, Holt was just the tiniest bit hurt to think that maybe Robert Kelley, who'd been so impressed by his cruiser and his bear traps, could be mocking him online.

He checked the *Tide*'s site. The paper was now reporting that their story on the Lollipop Kid had received more views than any other in their history. And embedded in the article was a link to Robert Jackson Kelley's supposed Facebook page. His mug shot was being used as a profile picture, which was only the first indicator that Holt wasn't going to take seriously anything he found here.

And there was what that concerned citizen had been so

loudly referencing. Robert Kelley's status was a lyric from that controversial N.W.A. song, "Fuck Tha Police."

The status had received 2,598 likes.

The kid hadn't written this, but whoever had wasn't doing Robert Jackson Kelley any favors.

Holt sighed and pulled open his top desk drawer. Some joker in the department had been putting lollipop bouquets on his chair. One had been waiting for him when he returned from his trip to Tomkins. Five Dum Dums, all wrapped up with a curling, frayed ribbon. Something about this candy-chomping kid had made the deputies ornery. Like since Kelley was sticking it to the sheriff, they could get their kicks in, too. Someone more sympathetic to Holt's plight had posted Kelley's picture, the one with the smart-ass grin, in the urinal, but Holt ordered it removed. Couldn't let it get around that his men were pissing on a kid's face.

Holt had always had a sweet tooth. A pudgy kid, he'd been the type to scarf all his Halloween candy in one sitting. And he'd never had the patience to suck a lollipop down to the end. He always bit them, let the hard candy pieces fly.

He liked the green ones, but he'd lie under oath before he'd admit it.

Interview with Dalton White, Seattle Community College, October 15, 2010

From *Flight Risk: The Robert Jackson Kelley Story*

"This part's true. The whole thing's on film. You can find it on YouTube, if you don't believe me. Tennant was tryin' to do a reality show.

"The first place Travis Tennant comes is here, because he can't believe that Robert's acting alone. He's gotta have help. He figures it's gotta be me, the old roommate. Criminal mastermind. And I was out of Sea Brook by this time, crashin' at this other dude's house out on Barrens Road. So Tennant comes around, trying to shake me up and get me to snitch on Robert. Now, I don't know *anything*, but I flip him off and say I know *exactly* where Robert is, but I'm not going to tell him. And then the dude went completely nuts. Bam! He slams me on the floor, gets in my face, spits on me. Waves around a Taser. But I just laugh. I'm no snitch, I'm not talking no matter what, and finally Tennant gets tired of looking like an idiot, and shoves me one last time for good measure and storms off.

"So of course now I start thinking, just what the hell has Robert been up to? I'm not the type of dude who watches the news, and we don't have the Internet. Half the time, we barely have the lights on. So I actually took a bus to the public library, which turned out to be kind of cool. Did you know they have movies? Anyway, I got on a computer, and bam! There's Robert all over the place. He's got like a million Facebook friends. There he is on the cover of the *Seattle Times*. There he is on CNN.

"I'm reading this and I actually start talking out loud like I'm completely tweaked. 'Robert stole a *plane*? Are you serious? He stole *two*?' And the best part was that he was getting away with it.

"Some band wrote a song about him. I started playing it, turning it up and up because I couldn't believe what I was hearing. 'Ballad of the Lollipop Kid,' it was called.

"*We represent the Lollipop Kid!*

"That was when they kicked me out of the library. And that was when I started thinking about T-shirts."

As he rummaged through the beach house this time, Robert pretended he wasn't an idiot and tried to find supplies he could actually use. The teenagers who'd last vacationed here had actually left behind plenty. He hit the jackpot in the kitchen, where he pocketed a book of matches and a small but sharp kitchen knife. Robert found a dusty pair of binoculars in a hall closet, ensconced in a slick black case. He slung those over his shoulder, wincing as the strap dug into his raw skin, and kept looking. A flashlight and a folded nylon poncho were hidden in the coat closet. And finally, behind the light jackets and sweaters, a navy JanSport backpack was waiting for him. The zipper stuck, but he packed his findings and set out again.

An hour and a half later, his feet ached so badly he was limping, but he crouched in a ring of cedars around the

Yannatok County Airport, the second airstrip he'd watched pass by him from the school bus window. He'd walked close to the road's edge, ducking in and out of shadowy tree cover. Bruises and scratches swelled his arms and neck, pink and puffy as balloons.

He watched planes come and go. The binoculars left sweaty rings around his eyes and a divot across the bridge of his nose. The airport was busy; he counted eleven planes taking off and eight coming in. The flights must be chartered, probably into Portland and Seattle. Guys in suits, hauling briefcases and suitcases, boarded and disembarked until about six o'clock. Cars remained in the parking lot for another few hours and were still there when Robert turned back. Could he get inside the place? Something told him that this wasn't a keys-in-the-drawer operation. He worried about cameras and alarms. An octagonal blue-and-white ADT sticker was prominently affixed to the front office door. Of course, if he moved fast enough, he could be in the air before the police even waddled out to their cars. And this time, he knew exactly where he was going.

Canada. Vancouver.

The city was packed with people for the Olympics. He'd land the plane and be able to hide among the tourists, the influx of fans and athletes. So many eyes glued to TVs, to the floors of rinks, to the tops of mountains, to finish lines and medal podiums. Who'd notice just another dude in a hoodie?

He pushed Kumaritashvili's last sled ride from his mind. His gamble would pay off. His final flight was going to be a victory lap.

He'd learned all he could from the outside. He'd go back to the house and lie low until nightfall. He wound his way through the thinner trees near the road, and he had almost made it back when a cop car sped by, lights flashing, siren blaring. Robert dove into the trees. He rolled to the ground and his knee collided with a crushed beer can, the grimy mouth slicing through his pants and biting into his skin. He buried his face in the needles, afraid to show even his eyes.

The siren faded. Robert counted to one hundred, then stood and brushed himself off. Sap gummed his fingers and scabs rusted over his knuckles. Blood stained his sweatshirt and his cuffs were caked in gray muck. Robert trudged to a spot where the trees weren't so dense, and trained the binoculars over the road, scanning the horizon until he found the ocean, then located the house.

Cops were everywhere, like ants scurrying over an anthill. Black-and-white cars lined the street. Flashlights swept over the porch. Orbs of light bobbed across the windows. And there he was, walkie-talkie up to his mouth, wide-brimmed hat pulled low despite the evening dim. Sheriff Holt. His hair had grayed around the edges, but he was still clean-shaven. His badge still shone among the medals and patches that adorned his tan uniform. The fittest guy among them, possibly the only one with a chance against Robert in a race.

Robert crouched despite his aching calves, not daring to move. Shadows flitted inside the house.

He'd have to wait here until dark, until after midnight but before the morning commuters started heading for Yannatok County Airport. He shrouded himself in the poncho, trying to barricade against the damp chill. The cops came and went, stringing yellow police tape across the front walk. Holt paced around. Every time Robert thought the sheriff had called it a night, he popped up again, talking to the other cops and on his walkie. A news van from Channel 11 pulled up, and a red-suited reporter spoke into a mic outside. Robert wished he could hear what she was saying. Were they investigating *him*, or investigating a break-in? Was he on TV?

After a few hours, waiting out the police didn't seem like such great idea. He was freezing, his fingers numb and clumsy. The air seemed filled with needles, pricking his neck, his eyes, his cheeks. His nose was running and he thought he'd have thrown up if there'd been anything substantial in his stomach.

He didn't know if he'd survive another night in the woods. He wasn't going to be a body somebody's dog sniffed out of the woods, asleep forever on a bed of Douglas fir needles.

He could go back to the trailer. The place he'd sworn he'd left behind for good.

But sleeping in his own bed, his dog warming his feet, sounded like heaven. Even one of those crappy microwave pizzas, the Deb dinner special, would hit the spot. One night. Not even an entire one. He'd set his old alarm for two a.m., get back into the woods, wait for his chance to fly away.

His mom would be glad to see him.

Robert stuck to the trees as he made his way down the road to the trailer park.

Everything from the rusty mailbox to the bare flagpole was the same, but Deb had put up a sign: *No trespassers. Beware of dog.* She didn't mean him.

"Hulk!" The dog launched himself at Robert's legs, and Robert knelt down to hug him. Hulk licked his face, his tail drumming the ground. Robert scratched behind the dog's ears, ruffled his bristled haunches.

He rapped on the door. Deb answered on the first knock and yanked him into the trailer. "Get in here! Get in here right now!"

She peered out before locking them in. Hulk scurried under their feet. "Did anyone see you?"

"I don't think so." His mother must have just gotten

home. She looked tired, like after a busy shift. "You're filthy. Are you hurt?"

Robert shook his head and Deb wrapped him in a hug so long that Robert started to squirm. She sniffled, her shoulders trembling. Finally Robert stepped back and awkwardly said, "Everything's fine, Mom."

Deb shook her head and unearthed a cigarette from her pocket. She sniffled again, wiping her eyes. "They came for your computer. Did you know that?"

"No," Robert replied. "Did you give it to them?"

"Of course not," Deb snorted. "It's my property, and I haven't done a damn thing. I'm thinking about taking it outside and smashing it to bits. The sheriff and I have gone around and around. But he'll be back. With a warrant, I'm told."

Robert shrugged. "Let him have it. What do they think he'll find?"

Deb stared and shook her head. "You don't get it. Just the fact that you have that stupid simulator on there is incriminating. There's a fifty-thousand-dollar reward on your head. Fifty thousand dollars! There are people around here who would *kill* you for fifty thousand dollars."

The same clothesline divided the living room. The dirty dishes stacked in the sink. A bucket half-full of scummy water beneath a leak. The dingy linoleum floor.

"I gotta go," Robert said.

"I'm feeding you."

Deb cracked four eggs on the side of the stove, dumped their contents into a bowl, and stirred them with a fork. Then she poured the yellow liquid into a sizzling skillet. Robert stood awkwardly by the table. He started to speak, to launch into his epic tale, but Deb shut him up with the palm of her hand. "Don't tell me. Less I know the better. You were never here. You're gonna eat this, and then you're gonna catch a ferry, and then you're probably gonna go to Seattle or up to Canada. I won't know and I won't tell. You're not gonna draw any attention to yourself. You're gonna keep your mouth shut and your head down. Aren't you?"

"I am." Robert swallowed. He didn't tell her how he'd been trying to do just that on his last two flights, but something about this island, the forest, Yannatok's very air conspired to weigh him down and keep him imprisoned here. Landlocked. "Canada was already my plan."

"Canada would be the smartest thing." She turned back to the skillet. "And when you get there, you won't call for a while. And maybe if you do all that, after a *long* while, I'll bring Hulk up for you."

"That'd be great," Robert said. He had thought he could take his dog with him now, but obviously that wouldn't work. He was running from the law, and Hulk would be hard to hide.

Deb scooped scrambled eggs and toast onto two plates and poured orange juice while coffee brewed. Hulk sat at Robert's feet, nudging his shins while Robert polished off his breakfast. His mother talked about her real estate classes, the housing market, the neighbors. She stopped her chatter and looked at him. "What are you doing with these lollipops?"

"Lollipops?"

"Everyone's saying you're leaving candy behind, in those planes." Deb shook her head. "They're calling you the Lollipop Kid, like you're a smart-ass. Like you think you can't get caught."

Robert couldn't help himself. "I haven't been caught."

"Yet."

Robert stood up from the table. Deb said, "One more thing," and then hustled to the back of the trailer. She came back with his old school backpack, the cracked faux-leather bottom covered in peeling Wite-Out and inky doodles. She stuffed one of his sweatshirts inside. "There's two pairs of socks in there, too. Underwear. A clean towel. T-shirts. Toothbrush." She rifled through the cabinets. "And take some granola bars." She glanced at the kitchen window. "You gotta get out of here. I wouldn't be surprised if a cop is watching this house." Deb searched through her purse and pressed a crumpled twenty-dollar bill into his palm.

"You get on that ferry, Robert. Or if you don't want to do that, get on the bus. Buy a ticket and get off this island."

Robert pocketed the money and stooped down to muss Hulk's brown head. He was on his way out when he saw a newspaper clipping, torn from the paper and stuck to the refrigerator. "Lollipop Kid on the Loose: Yannatok Manhunt Continues."

Deb nodded toward the article. "See for yourself."

He couldn't concentrate enough to read the whole thing. He scanned it, taking in phrases: *theft of two airplanes, evidence recovered from the scene, mocking the police, combed through the woods.* He couldn't comprehend anything, until his eyes rested on *Dalton White, of Barrens Road, knows Kelley personally from his time at Sea Brook Youth Home.* "He was a good roommate," White said. "I hope he gets away with it."

"They interviewed Dalton," he said. Like that was the most important thing.

Deb's eyes shone with tears. She blinked. "I didn't even know who that was."

Robert swallowed and nodded. Then he tapped the article's third paragraph. "I didn't even leave any candy the second time. I took it all with me."

"Don't you see?" Deb's voice thickened. She raised her palms. "No one cares what the truth is. They just want a good story."

A good story. Like a father who laughed, who howled at the moon as he got the best of those cops, and then outran them through the woods and didn't stop until he reached Canada.

A story with a better ending.

Who was the real liar? Robert or his mom?

He never should have come back. Every time he talked to Deb, her words piled on him, buried him alive.

"*I* care what the truth is," Robert said. "I care that people—that *you*—make up stories. About me. About Dad."

She met his eyes, and where he expected anger, he just found sadness. "That's right. Blame me. You and everyone else." She pointed at the door. "Go. And for God's sake, don't come back. To this island or this house. You're not welcome here."

"Cool. Awesome. I'll be on the next ferry."

He was half a mile down the road when he realized he'd in fact told his mother the story with the ending she wanted to hear. He'd lied when he said he was going to take the ferry off this island.

He was going to stick to his original plan and fly to Canada.

His mom could read all about it in the paper.

But first he was going to drop in on Dalton White.

He was going to cross the finish line, break the tape in Vancouver's sky, he knew it, but if—*if*—the odds weren't in his favor, he couldn't bear to have his story die with him. He finally had a tale to tell, a true one, and finally, he had a friend to tell it to. He would choose the ending.

YANNATOK—Robert Jackson Kelley, also known as the "Lollipop Kid," continues to elude authorities despite a two-day search of Yannatok Island that Sherriff James Holt called "exhaustive."

A warrant has been issued for Kelley's arrest in connection with the theft of two airplanes: a Cessna 182 from North County Airport on February 7, and a Cessna TTx from Tomkins Airstrip on February 9. The first plane was found in a wooded area adjacent to Sandy Spruce Lane; the second, on the beach near Dunes Road. Kelley appears to have been unharmed in the accidents and is still at large.

Kelley was reported missing from Sea Brook Youth Home, where he was enrolled in a residential program for juvenile criminal offenders, on February 4. Evidence recovered from the scene of both crashes implicates Kelley in the thefts. Kelley has gained notoriety both on Yannatok and in the national press for leaving Dum Dum lollipops at the scene of his crimes, leading some to believe the suspect is mocking the police.

The Sheriff's Department is making use of a K-9 unit and is being aided by the Seattle Police Department.

Sheriff Holt stated, "Our men have combed through the woods surrounding both crash sites as well as several vacation properties in the area. We are utilizing all available personnel and following up on every lead. We're again advising residents to take simple precautions to secure their homes and property, and report any suspicious activity to the sheriff's office."

When asked why Kelley was proving so difficult to capture, the sheriff added that he was "confident that Robert Kelley will be caught, and soon."

Not all island residents, however, share the sheriff's confidence.

"We are talking about a teenage kid," commented Gerri Kovach, whose son is a former classmate of Kelley's. "He should have been brought in by now. Someone has to be helping him out, and that person should also be thrown in jail."

Dalton White, of Barrens Road, knows Kelley personally from his time at Sea Brook Youth Home. "He was a good roommate," White said. "I hope he gets away with it."

When asked if Kelley should be considered dangerous,

White replied, "I don't think so. Dangerous to a plane, maybe."

"I think he's just getting lucky," stated Kirk Oden, a flight instructor at Tomkins Airstrip. "And that luck's going to run out sometime."

The suspect's mother, Debra MacPherson of Dunes Road, did not return requests for comment.

FEBRUARY 13, 2010

He was sweaty, sticky, itching to keep moving, but he waited until night fell to make his way toward Barrens Road. The house wasn't hard to find. Dalton's squat home swarmed with teenagers. Cars were parked haphazardly under the trees. A lit joint's earthy smell hit Robert before he could see the kids smoking on the porch. He wound through the crowd, making his way inside, the backpack his mom had given him heavy, bulky.

As soon as he was in, he wanted out. The kitchen was packed with people, brushing by him, balancing full plastic cups. Partygoers stood dense as a forest between him and the living room. Girls shrieked and hugged. Cigarette smoke fogged the room, quilted the ceiling so that it seemed a foot lower. A guy emerged from the refrigerator, clinking bottles, passing them to his buddies.

Did he imagine it, or had the guy just elbowed his friend and nodded toward Robert?

He ducked his head and shouldered his way into the living room, where the stereo was thumping and a bunch of guys were crowded around a muted television. Was that the back of Dalton's head? If Robert didn't find him in the next five minutes, he was going to leave.

A girl yelled. "It's him!"

The party quieted. Then the news rippled through the crowd. A few kids raised their phones, snapping pictures. Robert smiled stiffly. This visit had been his stupidest idea yet. A crowd surrounded him.

Dalton leaped up from the couch to bump Robert's fist. Skinny as ever, though he'd buzzed his shaggy hair and was wearing a hoodie instead of Sea Brook's uniform tee and khakis. "Dude!" He patted Robert's back. "The Lollipop Kid himself!"

Dalton whipped out his phone and began frantically thumbing and tapping. Robert leaned away from the flashes. He wished Dalton hadn't used that nickname, that alias. "Dude, don't take a picture."

"No, look. Check it out. What do you think of the merchandise?"

Dalton held up his phone. Onscreen was a picture of a T-shirt, baby blue with red words circling a red drawing of a Cessna—*Where Would Robert Fly?*—flanked by two little illustrated lollipops. Across the back, in that bright red: *The Lollipop Kid.*

"They're fifteen a piece. I'll cut you in," Dalton explained.

I'll cut you in. A promise that, in Robert's experience, was meant to be broken. Robert shook his head.

Dalton slapped him on the back again. "Anyway, the shirts are selling, man. I've got *preorders.* Can you believe that shit?"

A dreadlocked kid pushed Dalton back on the couch. "Yo, can you just let him chill? Everybody. Stop taking pictures and shit. Christ, he wasn't in *Twilight.*" He held out a cup of beer. Foam sloshed over the side. Robert waved him off. "I'm good."

"Good call, man. Don't drink and fly," Dreadlocks grinned. Suddenly, Robert recognized him. Adam Neff, another member of the slow kids' club. They'd had science together back in the fall, but never really talked. He wondered how many other partygoers he knew.

"Christ, you *look* like you just climbed out of a wreck. You're so dirty," Dalton laughed, pointing at Robert's shirt. Then he asked, "So what are you gonna do, man? Leap the border?"

"That's the idea," Robert replied as Dalton showed Robert his phone again.

"Here. Check this one out." Same concept, except this one had Robert's mug shot in the center instead of the Cessna. Beaming his lottery-winner grin. The photo was recent enough, and yet somehow Robert didn't think it looked all that much like him anymore. He ran his hand over his prickly, grown-out hair.

Still he said, "That's awesome, man."

"So how'd you learn to fly a friggin' plane, man?" Dalton asked, shaking his head. "I mean, Mr. Drew didn't go over that shit."

"I just—" Robert turned toward a flash of light, like an exploding firecracker. Some girl had taken another picture. He'd wanted to tell Dalton the whole thing, beginning to end, but there was no way he could do it here, with all these people. "I don't think I should say. Actually, I gotta get going."

Adam pointed. "Ain't that you, man?"

Robert looked at the television just in time to see that same mug shot. Then his trailer flashed onto the screen. On TV the dumpy mobile home looked smaller, squatter. The blue tarp on the roof flapped like a flag. He hadn't given the patched ceiling much thought in a long time, but now he wished his mother would get it fixed.

"Turn it up!" Adam scrambled for the remote. "The police were up at your place, man."

"It's not really my place," Robert mumbled. Certainly his

mother had just made that very clear. Now he wished he had a cup of beer to stare down into.

"Sheriff What's-His-Nuts, man, this guy's a dick." Dalton waved his beer at the screen. "He thinks he's, I don't know, fuckin' Robocop."

"*Kindergarten* Cop," Adam said, and everybody busted up. Robert laughed, too, but he studied Holt. That gray he'd spotted from his copse of trees was more evident on TV. He must have polished his sharp-cornered badge every night.

"How is it, Sheriff, that Robert Jackson Kelley has been able to evade the law so flagrantly, on such a small island?"

"Cuz he's the man!" Dalton held up his palm and Robert smacked it.

Holt answered quickly. "I can assure the residents of Yannatok that my office, partnered with resources from the state, are working around the clock to bring Robert Kelley to justice. We've just announced a reward for any tip that brings about his capture, and we urge the public to remain vigilant."

"Is the sheriff's office working with Travis Tennant?"

"That's the guy!" Dalton yelled, pointing at the TV. He sloshed beer over the side of his cup. "That dude came here and tried to fight me!"

"At this time, Mr. Tennant is working privately," Holt replied. "Again, we urge anyone who sees anything suspicious to call the tip line. I wouldn't try to approach Mr. Kelley yourself, as he may be dangerous."

Dangerous? He'd been in maybe one fight in his whole life. Even in his mug shot, he was smiling. And now Holt thought Robert was dangerous?

The party busted up, cheering and laughing, so Robert laughed along. Dalton slapped Robert's back and flopped against the couch cushion. A phone number flashed across the screen while the reporter intoned, "With a fifty-thousand-dollar price on his head and Travis Tennant on his tail, Robert Jackson Kelley's flight from the law might soon come to an end."

"Fifty thousand dollars!" A big kid crumpled his red cup. He glanced back at Robert. Had they had algebra together? "Sorry, man, but fifty thousand dollars! I might turn you in!"

They laughed. Adam said, "Naw, man, we ain't gonna. Shit, though, I wanna be on a shirt. I'm going down to the docks. Steal me a boat and call myself the Tootsie Roll Kid or some shit."

Suddenly, the TV flickered and went dark. A guy in an oversized white tee and black jeans was wielding the remote. He was bulkier, like he'd made good on his plans to start lifting weights, and his hair had grown out, but Robert would have known him anywhere.

Joey Kovach.

"C'mon, dude," Dalton complained. "We were watching that."

Joey dropped the remote, like an MC hurling a mic. He took a long gulp from his plastic cup. He nodded in Robert's direction. "You think you're the shit now." Spit flew from his lips. "Face on T-shirts. You look like the same old asshole to me."

Robert raised his hands, retorting, "*I* didn't put my face on a shirt."

Joey continued. "Here's what I know. I steal a road sign, I spend a night in jail. I sell pills, I get kicked out of school. And I didn't get sent to no Girl Scout camp. I spent two months in juvie. Do the crime, do the time. You're stealin' planes and walking around like it's nothing." He turned to Dalton. "What's so cool about that? You were locked up, too, and had to stay there until they let you out, and this dude just up and goes."

"Joey, dude." Robert spread his hands wide. "I didn't get you caught. *You* wanted those pills."

Joey sneered and kept talking to Dalton. "If I were you, I'd turn his ass in. Make yourself a lot more money than these stupid shirts," he spat. Then he jerked his chin at Robert. "Snitch."

A few guys snickered. Eyes crawled over him, watching to see what he would do.

What *the Lollipop Kid* would do.

Robert raised his voice. "The truth is that you ripped me off. You're either the worst Addie salesman ever or you stole from me."

"I didn't steal nothing!"

"Did you pay me? Did you ever pay me anything?" Robert stepped toward Joey, and to his total surprise Joey took a step back. Was he actually scared?

I wouldn't try to approach Mr. Kelley yourself, as he may be dangerous.

Robert raised his shoulders. "What do *you* call it when you take something and you don't pay for it?"

"Don't ask Joey complicated questions like that," Dalton cracked. A smattering of laughter rose from the group clustered around them.

Joey flushed. He started to speak, but Robert cut him off. "And then *you* snitched on *me*. The first chance you had, you squealed. And *I* was locked up for your stupid idea."

"But they can't keep him locked up!"

Robert swiveled to see who'd yelled, but soon everyone was cheering again, raising their plastic cups. So he repeated it. The ending they all wanted. "But they can't keep *me* locked up."

Dalton slapped his back like he was a boxer ready for his next round.

Joey scowled. "Whatever. I'm leaving. And I'm no snitch,

so don't think I'm gonna turn you in. When you get caught, it'll be on your own dumb ass."

Robert said his goodbyes to Dalton at the end of the house's gravel driveway. They shook hands, slapped each other on the back. Robert slung his bag over his shoulder. He should ask Dalton for more food, some clothes, but somehow that seemed uncool now.

"So, uh, don't get killed or nothing," Dalton said.

"I'll try not to," Robert replied. "You could make a sweet T-shirt out of it, though."

Dalton grinned. "In memory of the Lollipop Kid. R.I.P."

"'He said they'd never take him alive, and he was right,'" Robert joked, but when a car peeled down the driveway, he jumped.

Would Joey turn him in? Could any one of his former classmates have already made the call?

Was there anyone he could trust?

They shuffled around in the porch light's shadows. The party was winding down, but shouts and laughter still drifted outside.

"Hey, why don't you come with me?" Robert asked. He hadn't planned on offering. He wasn't even sure what he'd do once he landed in Canada. Was he suggesting he'd take Dalton up in a plane?

"What?" Dalton laughed shortly. "Dude, I mean, I can't. I can't get in any more trouble. I'll go to, like, *jail* jail. Like don't-drop-the-soap jail."

"Yeah, I understand," Robert said quickly.

"I mean, I'm getting hooked up with a job. Just construction, but the pay ain't bad," Dalton continued. "And I'm thinkin', like, with this T-shirt thing, if I could be a real artist or something. Like, come up with some more and do that for a job eventually."

"No, I get it."

"It's cool, though, what you're doing," Dalton said. "Like, everyone thinks it's cool as shit."

"Yeah." Robert offered his hand for another handshake, another shoulder bump. "When I get settled somewhere, I'll look you up."

Then he headed for the woods.

Interview with Mira Wohl, Willamette University cafeteria, October 2, 2010

From *Flight Risk: The Robert Jackson Kelley Story*

"I saw him, and so did Riley and Justine.

"Dalton White saw him.

"And *everyone* has a story from that party, whether they were really there or not. But no one turned him in. They coulda made it a hundred thousand, half a million, wouldn't have mattered. Nobody wanted to snitch on him. Team Robert!"

Vera: Before we get to our lead story tonight, the bombshell dropped in today's testimony in the case of wife-killer Jack Benson, we are also following a disturbing breaking story involving a possible terrorist cell on the West Coast. Our own Jonathan Richards is live from tiny Yannatok Island, where a small town has been plunged into a nightmare! Jonathan, what's going on out there?

Jonathan: Vera, Yannatok is pretty much a ghost town during the winter, home to only about five thousand people once the tourists head home, but the country's eyes have been on this West Coast island since photos were released yesterday of a teenage suspect wanted for the theft of two small aircrafts, both of which were found crashed not far from where they were stolen, and, unbelievably, the thief appears to have simply walked off.

Vera: Unbelievable!

Jonathan: And the story just gets stranger. The suspect, Robert Jackson Kelley, is an eighteen-year-old runaway, a Yannatok native, who escaped from Seattle's Sea Brook Youth Home only last week. And at both crime scenes, the suspect has left behind Dum Dums, the lollipops I'm sure you're familiar with, and some are saying he is mocking the police by leaving this evidence.

Vera: And look at that crash site! It's a miracle no one was killed by this recklessness! The audacity to leave *candy*, of all things! So what I want to know, Jonathan, is how does this young man even know how to turn a plane on, let alone get one up into the air? I'm shocked that this is even possible!

Jonathan: Well, not a lot of information regarding the specifics of the crimes is being released, for fear of copycat criminals. But a spokesperson from the Yannatok Sheriff's Department has told us that they are working on gaining access to Robert Jackson Kelley's computer, as they believe flight simulators may have played a role in these incidents.

Vera: Flight simulators, like the kind the 9/11 hijackers used to prepare for the World Trade Center attacks. Is this young man a terrorist? Is this the work of a terror cell? Perhaps a trial run for something much more sinister?

Jonathan: At this point, Vera, no one really seems to be sure, though of course a serial plane thief is certainly a major concern, post-9/11. And people on this island are wondering how Robert Jackson Kelley could possibly be acting alone, given his lack of formal flight training.

Vera: And no one on this island can catch an eighteen-year-old? Where are the police?

Jonathan: Vera, the sheriff's spokesperson assured me that all manpower has been focused on this case and bringing Robert Jackson Kelley to justice before he can cause any more destruction. But I spoke to some citizens who felt that the manhunt had been botched and were outraged by the sheriff's response thus far. They were certainly locking their doors.

Vera: I'm sure no one will sleep well on that island tonight. Thank you, Jonathan, and we will certainly continue following this explosive situation. Up next: what did Jack Benson's mother, Dottie, know, and when exactly did she know it? Bloodshed in the heartland, coming up!

FEBRUARY 14, 2010

The party had drained him so much that Robert was actually glad to return to the woods. Robert had talked more to Dalton and his buddies than he had in days. Now the forest's darkness, thick as a blanket at one a.m., felt more like home.

He shrugged into the sweatshirt his mom had packed and unfurled the towel. The cheery yellow shade wouldn't make good camouflage, but he might be able to hang it from some branches and fashion a makeshift tent. After a few minutes of trying, Robert rolled it back up to use as a pillow.

And then there was the fight with his mom, returning like a muscle cramp, like a side stitch, slowing him, winding him. One minute she was making sure he had clean underwear, the next she was telling him to never come back.

Could she have actually meant that?

Whatever, he told himself. Didn't matter. He was leaving anyway. He just wished he'd made it clear it was *his* choice, his plan all along to be rid of Yannatok forever.

He knew he needed to think, to plan, but his head bobbed with exhaustion. Before he went to sleep he dug through the pine needles, darkening his fingertips, until he hit damp dirt. He smeared his forehead and arms with pungent earth, hoping to conceal any exposed flesh. Dirt mottled the rim of his hood and sweatshirt cuffs. Pine needles clung to his eyebrows.

He drifted in and out of a fevered sleep, the sting of insect bites interrupting his dreams. In one he had two hatchets instead of hands and kept accidentally scratching his face. An owl's screeching morphed into the shriek of torquing metal, a plane's squealing stop.

The trees were still wrapped in darkness when he gave up on sleep and woke for good. Robert stood, pressed his hands to the small of his back, unwrapped a granola bar, and chewed despite the gritty foulness of his unbrushed mouth.

Going to the party, getting his picture snapped, acting like a celebrity, had been a major risk. If anyone from the party had called the sheriff, then they'd know he was still on the island, hadn't somehow hitched a ride or slipped onto the ferry. They'd be waiting for him at the airstrips right now. Yannatok County Airport, which he'd taken care to scope out, the only place he'd yet to break into, was probably lit up like the Fourth of July. A cop convention.

But what about Tomkins?

Surely they'd bulked up their security. Surely they'd warned their pilots, their staff.

But would they really expect him to return to the scene of his most recent crime?

No. They'd be waiting for him at Yannatok County, because they wouldn't think he'd have the audacity to lift a second plane from the Tomkins airstrip.

But Robert Jackson Kelley, the Lollipop Kid, who they couldn't keep locked up, most certainly did.

He sat up. Better to go now, while the darkness still hid him.

Yellow police tape fluttered across the door he'd jangled, bullied, and finally kicked in, three nights before, when he'd stolen his second plane from this very airstrip. The door hadn't been replaced, the splintered wood still gaping like he'd left it.

Perhaps they were preserving evidence, but it certainly felt like they were inviting him in.

He stepped over the tape, but he knew he hadn't crossed the finish line just yet.

Then he scrambled for the hangar door and pulled it up,

rattling on its track. Cold air rushed by him into the cavernous room, chilling his clammy skin.

This time he had to move fast. No rummaging for food. No thumbing through the manuals. Pick a plane.

The Cirrus SR22, its nose tipped in sea-green paint, wasn't what he'd flown before, but it seemed close enough. The ignition looked just as simple to jimmy with his screwdriver.

Robert jumped into the pilot's seat and cranked the ignition, the grooves of the screwdriver's handle twisting between his fingers. The engine roared. He taxied out and stopped just short of the runway.

A goose lazily flexed its wings in the middle of the tarmac. It stretched its curved neck and cocked its head at him, blinked one black eye.

"Shoo," he said. "C'mon."

He rolled a few feet forward, and the goose didn't budge, turning to examine its own wing like it was performing a preflight inspection. It nibbled at a feather.

Robert leaned toward the windshield. Why wasn't it flying away? Was it hurt? Had its flock abandoned it?

"Dammit. Move."

He tapped the gas and inched closer. Would he have to get out and scare it off?

He wouldn't run it over, leaving it bloodied and bent on the runway.

"Freeze! Don't move!"

Three cops rushed from the trees, crouching low. Robert's vision seemed to expand to take in everything: the heavy black vests that weren't worn by any cop he'd ever seen on Yannatok, the weighty holsters, the shiny boots. Faces beneath plastic shields.

And there must be more, because a burst of static had punctuated the command to halt, and none of these guys had a megaphone.

Because they all held guns.

"Shit, shit, shit!" Robert stayed still, but his heart stampeded and his hands trembled. He touched the screwdriver, realized the plane's engine was still rumbling. Its shuddering jolted his every cell. His eyes vibrated.

One of the cops stepped closer. The black point of the gun's muzzle blotted out everything else, like a solar eclipse.

The goose flapped its wings and disappeared into the sky.

"*Slowly* raise your hands over your head!"

Six feet by eight feet. He'd walked around a jail cell before. Six steps. Eight steps. A window without a view, just a hole in the bricks. A ceiling, blank as a movie screen before showtime, where he could rewind every mistake he'd ever made. If Deb hadn't come to bail him out, Robert wouldn't have lasted the night.

His dad had outrun them.

The. End.

Robert stomped on the pedal.

Out of the corner of his eye, he saw the officers dive for cover, as though he might mow them down. But he was blazing past them in one direction only.

Up.

He bounced down the runway, like he was hitting the tarmac's every divot. He heaved the throttle. His knees rattled. The meters' needles veered.

Popping like fireworks on his left.

Were they shooting? Were they trying to *kill* him?

Had they *missed*?

Or were these warning shots, like those fired at geese to hurry them off the runway?

"Go! Go!" He shouted at the plane, at the runway that flashed past.

And then that subtle snapping, that lift, as he left the ground. He stole just a glance out the window and saw the cops shrink as he pulled back on the yoke.

He panted. Wheezed. His ears popped. He clutched the controls so tightly his palms ached.

No way Holt had been there. Because if the sheriff had been in charge, they wouldn't have shot at him.

And now he wasn't paying enough attention. He hadn't even entered a destination into the GPS.

Was there a way to make the plane fly faster?

He freed his hands just long enough to plug Vancouver into the GPS, clicking on the map and zooming in on a clear patch of Canadian land.

Forty-five minutes. In forty-five minutes he'd ditch this plane and run. The race would be over. He just had to stay in the air until then.

He would not think about what could be waiting for him on the ground.

He was going to land this one. He was going to leave it whole, on this, his last chance. He would only think about that. He willed his fidgety brain to cooperate and it submitted as he scanned the GPS, checked the view through the windshield, turned his attention to the meters. GPS, windshield, meters. GPS, windshield, meters, until his heart slowed. He told himself this was just a simulation, that if he looked to his right, he wouldn't see the black night sky, but the trailer's television and his mother watching *Law & Order*.

"Bring around the beverage cart. What's for dinner tonight? Lobster or steak?" He had no idea what pilots ate on planes that weren't stolen, but he tried to joke, turning to address an imaginary smiling stewardess with bright red hair and straight white teeth like Mira Wohl. His voice shook like a frightened puppy. He made himself smile despite the pain in his neck. Then he called to the invisible passengers, comfy in their gray leather seats. "And you buckle up. We could see some more turbulence ahead."

He forced himself to write his own headline. "Lollipop Kid Steals Third Plane, Is Never Seen Again, Leaves Cops and Islanders Baffled. Gets Away with It."

And then there was a flash, so quick he wasn't sure he'd seen it at all, but for the blue afterimage that danced before his eyes. Then a cloud to his left lit up again, flickering and then fading. A lightning bolt. The cloud cover thickened from stretched-out cotton balls to denser, bulkier thunderheads. The flashes came faster, thunder rumbling in their wake. The plane jerked to one side. Robert overcorrected and wrenched back the opposite way. The bumps jolted him in his seat. He'd jinxed himself by joking about turbulence.

The plane plunged. Robert felt the roller-coaster drop in his stomach.

He hadn't buckled up.

He jerked the throttle and the plane's nose held steady, then climbed, recovering. Another flash illuminated the ashen clouds. Could lightning strike the plane? If lightning struck the plane, would it strike *him*?

His focus was shot. Could he go under the storm? Above it? Around it? How?

He wasn't going to reach Vancouver. That plan had been destined to fail. He couldn't make it to *Seattle*. What made him think he could flee to a different country?

Because just for a little while, he'd believed he was the damn Lollipop Kid.

He pounded his fist against his knee. He was still so close to Tomkins he could see Yannatok's beach, but he couldn't turn around. The cops' shots still rang in his ears.

He banked to the right, away from the darkest clouds, tilting the ailerons. The storm shook the plane so hard he bounced in his seat. Robert slid his sweaty fingers over the screwdriver, making sure it was secure. What would happen if the damn thing fell out?

Another flare, so close it temporarily blinded him.

The beach, the same beach he'd crashed onto on his second flight.

Should he try to land here, where he knew he had a chance at fleeing into the woods?

All he'd needed was forty-five minutes. The trip was a sprint, an errand, a commute. But now he was a giant moving target, a bull's-eye with wings.

His dad had made it on foot, ditching that cruiser.

Robert would have to ditch the plane, but he would try to land it. His A+, his honor roll report card, his diploma. Even if he was the only one who knew he'd earned it.

But his indecision had cost him precious yards of sand. He threw down the landing gear and lifted the nose. Nudged it higher, higher, trying to break his speed. He raised the elevator. Still he was coming in too fast.

He clattered onto the shore, bouncing down the beach before heaving and wobbling to a complete stop.

For half a second, he thought he'd done it. The landing had been bumpy and clumsy, for sure, but the plane was in one piece.

Then Robert heard a whoosh and suddenly all was white. The plane's air bags had ballooned into his chest and chin.

Gasoline burned his lungs. The fuel tank must have ruptured. Another pop, this one so much louder than the cops' guns, and then only the air bag kept his face from igniting with the tank. He couldn't see the flames, but he felt them, the scorching reddening his cheeks, his arms.

Like the snowy plane crash in *Hatchet*, the smoke billowed into the cockpit, deadly and thick as an avalanche.

What did you think when you realized you were an idiot? What did you think when you realized you were going to die?

The Lollipop Kid was going to kill Robert.

He coughed, choking, as heat rose before him.

Had Mr. Drew ever talked about how not to burn yourself alive?

The smoke jammed its sooty fist down his throat, snatched his breath. His eyes teared, stung, burned.

He gagged and fumbled for the door handle. Flames crackled and hissed. His throat burned. He kicked at the air bag, white and solid as an unmarked tombstone. Something dripped down his forehead and he couldn't tell if it was sweat or blood or his own melting face.

He'd always heard that before you died, you saw some light. You were supposed to move toward it, up to heaven or whatever. But all Robert could see was thick gray. He felt for the door handle, the metal hot, searing his hand. He pushed, he jammed his shoulder against it, he strained against the window, the glass that wouldn't break and set him free, and suddenly he remembered pushing open the window the last time he had seen his father.

His whole life didn't flash before his eyes: just a few choice scenes. His dad drumming on Robert's windowsill, chuckling about how he was sticking it to the sheriff. The grin before he took off into the woods. That sour drunk smell.

Robert Senior had never been to Iraq, never flown a plane, never saved anyone. Never dodged gunfire.

Blisters rose on Robert's fingers, at the tip of his nose.

His father hadn't outrun anybody. He hadn't hit a deer.

The truth threw sparks. Robert burned with it, like the engine fire had blazed a path through his memory banks, his blood.

Robert Jackson Kelley Senior had killed someone that night. And then he'd decided to cruise by and brag to his boy. He'd decided to tell his son a different story.

And Robert knew now how it could happen. How a risk could go wrong and end in a body.

How eventually, everyone got caught in their own traps.

His lungs seized, his chest straitjacket tight.

Robert flashed back to the sleeping couple whose house he had broken into. Standing there in that house, about to be caught, he'd probably never looked more like his dad. Like he'd been in a fight—and in a way he had been: with the planes, with the island, with the sea and the sky. With the truth.

His mother hadn't been lying to him. He'd been lying to himself.

He had to tell her, to say he was sorry, that he finally got it, before he lost his chance to one more miscalculation, one more gamble.

Robert threw himself at the door, his whole body ramming against the metal as the smoke shrank the cockpit. Pain ricocheted up his arm and through his neck.

And then he tumbled onto the sand, cool as a bedsheet. His eyes teared and ran, and he wanted to close his heavy lids and just lie there. Let the ocean chill him on one side and the fire warm him on the other.

He decided then that he wouldn't take the chance of dying in a flaming bird, or drowning in a steel winged cage in the icy Pacific. But still, before he blacked out, he couldn't help but think:

I know I could do it.

I could land one of these planes.

If I tried one more time.

310

ACT IV

FLIGHT RISK

From *The Beginning Pilot's Flight Guide* (p. 114):

The obvious and best response to any electrical, weather, or fuel-related emergency is to land the plane as soon as possible. Any delay in getting the plane back on the ground can have grave consequences.

FEBRUARY 14, 2010

He jolted awake, pain a siren blaring through him.

His head swam when he tried to sit up, but the plane might explode, and the cops were probably on their way, and so Robert stood slowly, bone by bone.

He trudged in what he thought was the trailer's direction, relying on his internal GPS, trying to propel himself faster despite his seared lungs. He stopped and doubled over every few minutes. He might have been coughing broken glass. For long stretches of road he nearly crawled.

He wouldn't make it tonight; his pace was too slow. He'd have to spend the rest of the night in the woods, so he burrowed as deeply into the thicket as he could. He'd lost his bag, the one his mom had packed for him. Probably reduced to ash by now. Robert pulled on his gray-smeared hood. He tried to let the night air soothe his throat. The storm he'd flown through finally broke, though the canopy over him was so dense only stray drops splashed his face, carved grimy paths down his cheeks.

His mother would be mad that he had come back, no doubt, but once he apologized, he knew she'd forgive him.

At first light, then.

And when he'd settled things with his mom, he'd hit the road, conscience clear.

This time, he was heading south. Los Angeles. Mexico. Canada kept repelling him, tossing him back toward the island. And they'd be looking for him at the Canadian border, but not at the country's southern line. At the trailer maybe he'd take the time to shave his head. He could pick a new name for himself. He might go with Brian, like the kid from *Hatchet*. Not sharing a name with his dad would make him kind of sad, but the time was right. He was ready.

He would go with Brian. Brian Kelley.

Operator: 911. What is your emergency?

Caller: Yeah, I'm parked out by Dunes Road and I just saw a plane crash.

Operator: A plane crash?

Caller: Yeah, a plane just, like, crashed right out of the sky, and tipped over on the beach. Part of it's on fire.

Operator: Goddamn. Goddamn.

Caller: Hello?

Operator: I'm here. Where is the pilot? Is he hurt?

Caller: What's weird is that I don't think anyone is here.

Operator: Thank God. He's one lucky son of a bitch.

Caller: Huh?

Operator: Can you repeat your location? We'll be sending someone out there. Lucky son of a bitch.

Steve: So it's 6:15 in the a.m., bright and early here on beautiful Yannatok Island, and you're here with Steve and Mac on KRAW 91.3. It's a foggy one out there, getting up to around 48 this afternoon. And how's the traffic, Mac?

Mac: Backed up on the Yannatok Bridge toward Seattle, free and clear everywhere else.

Steve: Everybody headin' to the city. And I can tell you one more person probably looking for a way off this island this fine morning, and that's Robert Jackson Kelley.

Mac: Always three names with these guys.

Steve: Well, someone in Yannatok is waking up to find themselves short one airplane, after our very own Robert Jackson Kelley's latest misadventure, which ended in him crashing not his first, not his second, but his third stolen puddle-jumper sometime last night.

Mac: And of course, they haven't caught him yet. Did he at least leave the owner some candy?

Steve: You bet they haven't caught him yet. And word is he did leave another Dum Dum for the Sheriff's Department to suck on. I'll admit it, I'm sort of rooting for him.

Mac: Rooting for him? What are you, twelve? What middle school do you go to?

Steve: I mean, the kid's got some balls, you know. Lots of kids are just sitting around, playing video games.

Mac: This kid's out becoming a felon. What's not to love?

Steve: I know. Easy for me to say. It's not my plane that's getting crashed. But there's something kind of cool about it.

Mac: Well, Steve, the whole reason I allowed you to sully our program's fine name by mentioning Mr. Kelley is because unfortunately you're not alone in your foolish thinking. A little tune by local band Gull Trouble has dropped into my hands, called "Ballad of the Lollipop Kid." We're gonna take a listen to their homage to Robert Jackson Kelley, then we're gonna take some calls.

FEBRUARY 14, 2010

At first light he roused from a sleep deep as hibernation.
He coughed and spat gray phlegm. He lifted his sodden,
filthy sweatshirt and saw a patchwork of bruises, his skin
mottled and tender as bad fruit. Clear fluid seeped from
his nose. A scab crusted over his bottom lip. His fingertips had ballooned, raw and swollen. Dirt and pine needles
caked his knees. Sand and soot clogged his ears, and over
the birdsong and twigs snapped by eager squirrels, a dull
roar that grew and then faded, grew and faded. An engine,
revving. Surf lapping a Mexican beach. The part of him
that refused to die.

You weren't lying, he'd say.

I know what the truth is, he'd say.

I love you, he'd say.

Robert Jackson Kelley started for home.

"The Olympics were, like, what, fifty miles away? So some of these guys who'd been on border patrol were sent down here to try to catch Robert. They set up a checkpoint at the bridge and they're looking in every car, thinking someone's going to smuggle Robert across. I'm grocery shopping with my mom and there's a dude in fatigues, peering in the window of Shipley's. I took his picture, posted it on Facebook. Everybody smart stopped partying, especially on the beach, since Homeland Security was, like, hiding in the trees. They were supposedly listening to our phone calls, too, so we'd say stuff like, 'Hey, did you see Robert down at school? He's talking about stealing a school bus!' Just to see if, like, a Black Hawk would land on the roof.

"And then there was the neighborhood watch. My dad joined up, put on the orange vest they gave him, and walked around from when the sun went down until they all decided it was too cold and they'd rather be in someone's hot tub, having drinks and talking big talk about what they were going to do when they caught Robert Jackson Kelley. My dad even told me that people were talking about trying to lure him to their house, like leaving a window open or their car unlocked, so they could get the reward money. Or even leaving food out on their porches, like he was a stray. Some of these dads were packing, too, and, like, couldn't wait to shoot him. Like bagging a bear. They were going to all be as famous as he was. Part of the legend. The guy who caught the kid. A story they'd make their grandkids listen to forever.

"Each night when my dad was getting suited up, I'd start stalking around outside his room like it was the stage and yell some of Juror Number Eight's most famous lines: 'Are you his executioner? What it must feel like to want to pull the switch!' He would roll his eyes and call me Meryl Streep and tell me to go make myself useful elsewhere.

"So basically no one could get away with anything or go anywhere and everyone's dad was prowling the street in the dark with a gun. It was sort of the most exciting and most boring time we'd ever had. And I'm thinking, 'Really? All this over the dirty-lookin' kid I saw stumbling along the road?'

"And then the government shot him out of the sky, and

blamed it on the weather. Tried to cover it up. But it was antiaircraft fire, sneaky Homeland Security stuff. They must have been so pissed when they realized he was still alive.

"There's movies and books about Billy the Kid and Jesse James, right? But Robert didn't kill anybody, didn't hurt anybody. People say he was a terrorist, ready to join up with Al Qaeda and fly into the White House, but they have no clue. Robert was free, doing whatever he wanted, flipping off everyone, basically, and when somebody does that, they always got to try to bring him down. It's, like, the American way."

FEBRUARY 14, 2010

By Deb's count, Vera Hunt had shown her son's mug shot four times in a single report. Deb certainly hadn't done her son any favors by refusing to give the Sheriff's Department a photo of Robert. She'd thought anything she could do to drag her feet, slow the sheriff down, would give Robert a better chance to get away, but that strategy had backfired. She'd only given Travis Tennant time to show up on the scene. Time for the island's men to decide they needed to arm themselves and prowl the streets, like a serial killer was on the loose.

And Robert looked handsome in that mug shot, but too pleased with himself.

He hadn't listened to her. When had he ever? She'd told him another lie, that he wasn't welcome in her home. Those words had sliced into her heart, would rise and redden and thicken and scar. And for what?

So Robert had time to damn near blow himself up.

She had studied herself in the mirror, scrutinizing her crow's feet and roots, and then started making calls.

Vera Hunt could get her on that night. Jonathan Richards was still on Yannatok, interviewing locals. They could patch her in via satellite. They'd even bump some expert witness from the Jack Benson trial.

Now there was a guilty bastard.

She filled her next hours so she didn't have to think too much about being on national news, beamed into houses with living rooms where armchair psychologists would shake their heads at what an atrocious mother she was and kitchen-table judges would find her guilty. She borrowed a light blue shell and cardigan from Laura Roth that could have been worn by the widowed grandma who'd raised her. She kept her jeans on, though; they'd only shoot her from the waist up. And she paid for highlights and a layered haircut at La Vita Bellisima, the island's one classy alternative to Supercuts. She splurged on some new makeup, too, Revlon and Covergirl. Doe-brown eye shadow instead of her usual steel gray. Petal-pink lipstick.

When she next studied her reflection, she saw Debra MacPherson, someone you could trust to find your dream home.

She'd seen Vera Hunt's show before. She knew the story she needed to tell to save her son.

*   *   *

He staggered for hours in the wrong direction, only realizing his mistake when the Yannatok Bridge hovered in front of him. Robert hunched in the trees by the shoulder, his throat scraped by thirst, and stared at the road. He couldn't see the spot where the bridge finally crossed the finish line in Seattle, of course, but he knew it was there.

Somebody had tagged the island side of the bridge again. *WWRF.* Robert squinted, not sure if he was reading the letters correctly. Because what the hell did *that* mean?

What if he just kept walking? What if he gathered his last remaining bits of strength and ran over that bridge, dove for the opposite coast, went as far into Seattle as his feet could carry him? Wouldn't that be the best move?

No.

He would make it home.

He would make things right with his mother.

He turned around, and hobbled on.

Vera: Tonight, an explosive *Hunt for Justice with Vera Hunt* exclusive! Debra MacPherson, the mother of notorious airplane thief, fugitive, and suspected terrorist Robert Jackson Kelley, otherwise known as the Lollipop Kid, joins us live via satellite from Yannatok. Ms. MacPherson, welcome to the show.

Deb: Thank you, Vera.

Vera: Now, Ms. MacPherson, you know I have to ask you some tough questions tonight. The ones our viewers deserve answers to. So I'll just get right to it. Do you know where your son is?

Deb: I do not.

Vera: Have you been harboring him, Mom?

Deb: I have not. I haven't seen my son since before

Christmas. I find this all as hard to believe as everybody else.

Vera: So set the scene for us. How did you find out your son was a wanted criminal?

Deb: It was the middle of the day, and I was asleep. I work nights as a 911 dispatcher, so sometimes I'm asleep during the day. I had gone to bed with my phone right on my pillow in case the sheriff called, because they were supposed to be out looking for my son. He was already missing. So when the sheriff did call, I was hoping for good news, but very worried about a bad outcome. I obviously didn't expect something like this.

Vera: Your son was missing and you were still going to work? Business as usual?

Deb: Well, I do have to pay my bills, Vera. And when I wasn't working, I was out looking for my son, every chance I got. And I will say that it seemed like I was the only one. Unfortunately, my son's not a pretty little rich girl who plays the harp.

Vera: Where do you think Robert is right now?

Deb: I don't know.

Vera: Do you think he will attempt to steal another plane?

Deb: I hope not.

Vera: How did he learn to fly, Mom? That's not something I learned in high school!

Deb: Me neither, that's for sure! He's been playing these flying games on the computer for a long time. I guess he just figured it out. He's a bright boy.

Vera: Tell us about your son, Ms. MacPherson.

Deb: Like I said, Robert is a very bright boy. He's funny. He loves his dog. He loves the water. He keeps to himself mostly, and he wants to enlist in the army. That's why some of this talk about him being a terrorist is so shocking to me. It couldn't be further from the truth. He wants to fight *for* his country.

Vera: What do you say to reports that he was a troublemaker at school? Fighting, dealing drugs? He was eventually kicked out of school.

Deb: Vera, I'm sure this is going to come out sooner or later, but my son's father is in jail. He was never in Robert's life. He is not a good man. And I've had to raise him on my own, no help whatsoever, and I did the best I could. I can tell you Robert didn't use drugs. But I think not having a father in his life has really affected him.

Vera: What do you make of these lollipops, this

candy being left at the scene? Do you think your son is mocking the police?

Deb: (*laughs*) No. I think he just left behind some candy. And that's just hearsay. Some people are trying to make my son out to be this criminal mastermind, and it couldn't be further from the truth. He's just a kid who's in over his head.

Vera: Well, I have to tell you, Ms. MacPherson, I know some of our viewers at home just don't buy it. They're saying, "Teenage boys just don't wake up one day and steal a plane, Vera! There's some plotting that went on, and this mom's got her head in the sand!" So I have to ask, could you be blind when it comes to your son?

Deb: I'm as surprised by all this as anyone else. I could not be more shocked if a plane crashed into my own living room.

Vera: One still might! So you still maintain then, despite how unbelievable, how flat-out ludicrous it might seem, that one day your son just said to himself, 'You know, I think I'll steal that airplane over there,' and managed to do so without any training or forethought or help from anyone?

Deb: As crazy as it sounds, that seems pretty close to the truth.

Vera: Well, if my experience as a trial lawyer and investigative reporter has taught me anything, it's that the truth always comes out in these situations, and justice will be served. I'll ask my final question: if by some chance Robert can see you, hear you right now, wherever he is, whatever his state of mind might be, what would you like to say to him, Mom?

Deb: I love him and I want him to be safe. I want him to slow down and think about his safety. I'm always telling him to think before he acts, and he needs to do that now.

Vera: Would your son be safer if he turned himself in?

Deb: (long pause) I just can't answer that. I don't know. I just want him to be safe.

Vera: Thank you so much for being with us tonight, Ms. MacPherson. I'm going to go ahead and bring on Jonathan Richards, who has some new information just now coming to light in this developing story. We've already reported that Robert Jackson Kelley escaped from a "wilderness therapy center" mere days before his first hijacking, and we immediately questioned what a drug dealer with a record of fighting and violence was doing in such a place instead of in a locked-down juvenile facility. Well, tonight we have learned that it was none other than Yannatok's Sheriff James Holt who brokered the deal that allowed Robert Jackson Kelley to escape custody so easily and begin his airborne crime spree. Here's Jonathan Richards, who's on Yannatok Island tonight, to fill us in.

Jonathan: Thank you, Vera. What I hold in my hand is a copy of the diversion agreement that allowed Robert Jackson Kelley to avoid a drug charge when he was caught selling Adderall at Yannatok High School just last November. This agreement, as well as Kelley's stay at Sea Brook Youth Home, was arranged by Sheriff Holt—

Vera: I'm sorry, Johnathan, did I hear you correctly? A *diversion agreement*? Can we see that mug shot again? That smile is just frightening. A so-called diversion agreement, signed by none other than Sheriff James Holt. I can only imagine the fear in the hearts of the citizens of tiny Yannatok Island tonight, knowing that the man who swore to serve and protect them allowed Robert Jackson Kelley to sign one of these agreements and slip right back out into the community. Where was his concern for their well-being? Can you imagine sitting with your family around the dinner table, kids talking about their school days, and this hoodlum crashes through your ceiling in one of his stolen planes? What else did you find out, Jonathan?

Jonathan: According to a spokesperson from Sea Brook, Sheriff Holt himself recommended Kelley's placement at their school instead of a higher-security juvenile facility, like the one in Portland other teens from the area have been sent to.

Vera: So I have to ask: just what are they doing at this Sea Brook school? Training these wannabe thugs in the art of hiding out? Thank you, Jonathan. I'm going to go ahead and bring back our guest tonight, also coming to us via satellite from tiny Yannatok, Robert Jackson Kelley's mother, Debra, speaking exclusively with us. Ms. MacPherson, I know our viewers want to know: is your son armed?

Deb: Jesus, no. That boy wouldn't know what to do with a gun even if he could get his hands on one. I know my son, and he is probably more scared than anyone on Yannatok right now.

Vera: Well, that's where I have to disagree with you, Mom, because Robert Jackson Kelley doesn't seem scared *at all*. Would a scared little boy be leaving *candy* at the scenes of his crimes to taunt the police? I want to bring in Mr. Travis Tennant, the man who seems like perhaps the only person equipped to do something about this terrifying situation on the West Coast, also with us via satellite from Yannatok. Mr. Tennant, what do you make of tonight's bombshell regarding the sheriff's collusion with Robert Jackson Kelley?

Travis: Unfortunately, Vera, I'm not surprised at all. The sheriff has proven himself to be in over his head since the beginning of these events.

Deb: Vera, if I could go back to what you said about the lollipops—

Vera: Mr. Tennant, do you have any leads on where Robert Jackson Kelley is hiding out?

Travis: Yes, Vera, without saying too much and compromising our operations, we know Robert Jackson Kelley is still on Yannatok and that he will be caught.

Vera: Well, you've heard Robert Jackson Kelley's mother's claims. She says she hasn't seen him since before Christmas!

Travis: With all due respect to Ms. MacPherson, I believe she isn't harboring him, but I don't believe her son has left the island as she says.

Deb: Mr. Tennant, you haven't caught anybody yet. And if I could comment on these rumors about the lollipops, what is so threatening about a forgotten bag of candy? I can't believe the big deal being made out of it. And as far as I know, that's only a rumor. I doubt it's even true.

Travis: You seem to want to dismiss your son's actions as some kind of accident, or maybe a boyish prank, and what he's doing is about as dangerous as anything I've ever heard of.

Deb: And yet not a single person has been hurt! The only thing that's been hurt is a couple of pine trees!

Vera: Yet! No one has been hurt *yet*! And that is merely luck and God's watchful eye looking over the people of Yannatok! And certainly no thanks to the sheriff, who has botched this manhunt at every turn.

Travis: Well said, Vera. Why were there not armed guards at those airstrips? Why wasn't the FBI brought in immediately, given the possible links to terrorism? That's why the locals got anxious and contacted me.

Deb: The FBI? This is a kid who can't remember to bring a pencil to school, and now he's some kind of terrorist? If you could just understand, this is a kid whose best friend is his dog, who used to spend hours at the beach, just paddling around on a surfboard and keeping to himself, not getting in any kind of trouble.

Vera: How do you explain, then, the rap sheet from his school, the fights, the drug charge? Does this sound like a good kid, a kid who doesn't get in trouble?

Deb: He is just a boy. He never had a father.

Travis: All that being said, our focus now should be on finding him and bringing him to justice before his luck runs out and someone is killed. And I am going to do just that.

Vera: The people of Yannatok thank you, Mr. Tennant, and so do I, for being on our show tonight. Up next, outrage in the heartland! We update you on the trial of wife-killer Jack Benson.

FEBRUARY 14, 2010

Holt had received an invitation from a Vera Hunt *producer* to appear on the show, right next to Travis Tennant, and face Vera's screechy questions. He'd emphatically declined, figuring that the people of Yannatok would rather know he was at work, at the crime scene, poring over evidence, tromping through the woods himself if that's what it took to find Robert Jackson Kelley. They'd see him on TV and he knew what they'd say: *This guy needs to stop mugging for the camera and actually catch the kid! What, he thinks he's a big shot? A celebrity?*

He watched the show alone in his living room, kicking off his heavy shoes and pouring himself a whiskey. A blister bloomed over his big toe. He settled into his chair and pulled an old afghan over his legs. Bandit stretched out at his feet. His sips turned to gulps as the show unfolded, as he realized what a mistake he'd made. He grabbed his phone and frantically tried to reach the producer, clinging to the idea that they could patch him in over the phone, so he could defend himself, his job, his department. He had merely been giving a local boy a hand up, a second chance, the kind he'd luckily received himself. If they could have met that kid—not this Lollipop Bandit or whatever they were calling him, but the kid Holt had watched on the station's closed-circuit camera. Pacing around the cell, so squirrelly he couldn't sit still for two minutes at a time. If he didn't have the DNA results from the kid's own puke, Holt wouldn't believe he was the culprit.

The sheriff finished his drink and turned off the show before its conclusion. He stomped back into his shoes, his toe throbbing, and into his car, driving the streets of Yannatok in the dark, searching for a light, a shadow, a plume of smoke. His own personal bear, a kid who could not be caught.

Travis Tennant was probably kicking up his feet at the Pine Tavern, celebrating his TV debut. Holt cruised past the airstrips once, twice, three times. Somebody at Tomkins, probably Walt, had smartened up and set up floodlights, white orbs beaming over the runway. Holt banged once on the steering wheel, hung a sharp right, circled around the airport's parking lot. Thing was, those lights wouldn't give Kelley a minute's pause. The sun was peeking over the trees anyway, pink webbing the clouds.

He headed for the Yannatok Bridge, and there, lit up in the sunrise, was new graffiti, sprayed again in the same spot the Parks Department had power washed. *WWRF.* The *R* seemed larger this time, rising above the other letters' tips, its legs practically skimming the water. *R* for Robert, he was so sure of it. But then what about the *W*s, the *F*? Bright red paint again.

He was going to catch this kid, get that bridge cleaned up if he had to scale it his goddamn self, and then drive right over it and off this island.

His phone rang. A number he didn't know lit up the display.

What could it be, at this hour? Nothing good. He prayed he wasn't about to hear about a fourth wrecked plane. A teenage boy riddled with bullets.

He answered. "Sheriff."

"What do you think he'll get? If you catch him?"

That voice. Scratched as an old record. The only person who'd ask him that question, who'd even thought to ask about what would happen to Robert Jackson Kelley if he was still alive when they'd all moved on to the next story.

His mother, of course.

"In terms of a sentence?" Holt paused and pulled the car over, clicking on the hazards. "I can't say for sure. And I can't make you any promises. But I will tell you this. Right now, nobody's dead. Nobody's hurt." He weighed his words.

337

"With your job you know how quickly that can change. Without anybody truly meaning for it to."

"I do know."

Silence. What did she know? Whatever it was, she was close to telling, if he played his cards right.

"Ms. MacPherson? Deb? I saw you on television. I know you tried."

"Not enough." Silence again. "He's here. He's outside. I'll stall him if I have to." Her voice caught. "Don't hurt him. Please."

"I won't. I won't hurt him. I'm close by. I'll be there in—"

She hung up.

The cruiser's tires screeched as Holt hooked a left toward the trailer park.

The trailer rose before Robert like a mirage. He stumbled toward it, his feet so heavy he thought he must be leaving a trail of deep footprints.

Was anybody home? The shades were drawn, as always. He didn't know what time it was.

Deb's car was in the driveway.

Robert's head suddenly swam. He sank onto the porch step. Dark clouds eclipsed his vision.

Hulk bounded around the trailer's corner, trailing his leash. Why didn't his mom tie him up or bring him inside?

Robert didn't think Hulk would run away, but still. The scrappy dog would lose a fight with a bear or a pissed-off raccoon. What if he got picked up by the wrong person? Deb shouldn't let him run wild.

"Good boy," Robert murmured. He scratched the dog's back, behind his ears, under his collar. Hulk licked his chin appreciatively. Robert could already picture them on Tijuana's shore, Hulk's fur blowing in the salty spray, his ears alert as he tracked the swooping gulls. Robert would buy them each a soft pretzel.

"Stop! Put your hands up!"

Robert didn't turn around to see who it was. He started for the black thicket behind the trailer, but this time he was running through wet concrete, his clothes heavy as a suit of armor. Every breath a wound. He groaned, grunted as he pushed forward.

Hulk followed him to the trees, but wouldn't go any farther. The dog stood at the woods' edge, barking and scratching at the ground. His tags jingled. He might as well have been pointing right at his owner.

They caught him just past the tree line.

A dozen guys with masks and vests and guns, shades of black and gray from head to toe. A shield emblazoned with white letters. *Police*. Only one he recognized. The sheriff. Out of breath. Running.

"Holt!" Robert yelled. "What's good?"

The squad drew their guns. "Homeland Security! Put your hands up! Now!"

Robert spread his arms wide.

"Get down on the ground!"

Robert took a few steps back. "I don't have anything! Holt, I don't have anything!"

"He doesn't have anything," Holt told the other officers. "Let him surrender!"

Travis Tennant crashed through brush, trailed by a guy shouldering a camera. "Step back! He's a terrorist! He could have a bomb!"

"A terrorist?" Robert said. He laughed and choked, coughing. A bomb-wielding terrorist? He'd never been near a bomb in his life.

"Step back," one of the soldiers yelled, and Robert wasn't sure if he was ordering him or Tennant. One of the guys tried to pull Tennant back, and Robert instinctively leaned away and dropped his hands.

They charged him. A knee in Robert's back, blows raining on his neck, his shoulders. His chest ignited. His knees were hamburger. He couldn't tell if one guy was on him or twenty. He heard Holt repeat himself: "He doesn't have anything! He's not going to shoot!"

The biggest guy knelt on his chest, held his flailing arms. Robert struggled like a fish dropped on a boat's deck. Pine needles scratched his neck, his elbows. After all this, to be caught on the ground, pinned down like a wriggling insect. He wished he could have at least been shot down out of the sky.

Tennant's camera lens was only a few inches from his face. The footage might be on the news. CNN. The Internet. Embedded in a link Mira Wohl would click on, sparking to life on her pink phone. Beamed into his mom's living room, the bar his dad had hunkered down in so many nights so long ago. The waves carrying it would ride into the sky, out into space, where they'd bounce around forever.

He had one chance before they wrote the ending for him.

Robert grinned, his lip a fat, split worm. He winked at the camera, a bruise already shadowing his eye. "Want a lollipop?"

They yanked him up and walked him past the trailers. He wobbled, lurched.

"Mom!" Robert yelled out. His throat was shredded, his voice cracking. The handcuffs scraped his wrists raw as he struggled. Blood dribbled down his chin and onto his shirt. "Mom!"

"Shut up!" Tennant screamed.

"Mr. Tennant, one more outburst and I'm going to arrest you myself," Sheriff Holt yelled. He and Tennant lagged behind, arguing.

"Can I talk to my mom? Can I make sure my dog gets tied up? He's gonna run away!" Robert swung around, left and right, trying to see the sheriff. He stopped walking, dragging his feet as the men pushed him along. Had he just seen the curtains move? Was his mom home? "Shit! Dude, can I just talk to my mom for a minute?"

His shoe's sole split open. He dropped to his knees and refused to go any farther. "Mom! I'm sorry!"

The guys laughed as they pushed him toward the police car.

When Robert's father had vanished, Deb had looked away before he'd dived into the forest. This time she made herself watch. She told herself that a fraction of her penance would be to see her son in cuffs and hauled away.

Deb pulled back the curtain just in time to see Robert being marched through the yard. She crouched, peeking over the sill, not wanting to be seen herself. Not wanting to answer any questions. Not knowing if she could even speak through the stone in her throat.

She gasped at his bloody lip, his blackened eye, the scratches that vined up his forearms. The grime smeared all over his sweatshirt, his pants, his skin. The pine needles in his hair. She saw his shirt ride up as he struggled and caught a glimpse of his too-skinny chest, the ladder of his ribs.

He looked so small, the officers so enormous. Did they have to push him? Did they have to have grab his arms, his shoulders, so roughly? She could practically feel each new bruise. Holt had promised her they wouldn't hurt her son, but she couldn't find him through her narrow slice of window.

His gaping shoe. Deb's heart practically stopped. His dingy socks. They looked so exposed, so vulnerable. A tattered white flag, signaling Robert's surrender.

She saw him yelling, his mouth wide, but she couldn't make out the words. She pressed a hand to her own mouth, fearing he had howled in pain.

But when Deb realized he was saying he was sorry, that *he* was apologizing to *her*, that was when she finally had to turn away.

From the *Seattle Times*'s website, in the
comments section for the *Times*'s article
"'Lollipop Kid' Apprehended by Homeland
Security," February 15, 2010

Posted by AJ_Parton93 at 9:48 a.m., February 15, 2010
They can go ahead and put him in jail he'll get out anyway

Posted by AmericanIron2020 at 11:43 a.m., February 15,
2010
How's he ever gonna pay back all the people he's stolen from?
Vandalism, theft, destroying other people's property—it's
not a joke.

Posted by Nitro_Shootout at 4:14 p.m., February 15,
2010
He should run for sheriff of Yannatok. He'd win. And he'd
probably do a better job.

Three counts of piloting an aircraft without a valid airman's certificate. Three counts of aviation theft, a felony. Two counts of breaking and entering. Foreign transport of a stolen aircraft. Smashing that camera at Tomkins earned him destruction of property. The public defender had gotten any charges associated with violating his diversion agreement dropped.

The judge denied Robert bail, not that Deb would have been able to pay it. They were going to keep Robert in a Seattle prison until the trial. The judge didn't trust that the cell in Yannatok, or Sheriff Holt, could hold him. And he certainly couldn't go back to the trailer with Deb.

He was a flight risk.

Interview with Dalton White, Seattle Community College, October 15, 2010

From Flight Risk: The Robert Jackson Kelley Story

"So here's what really happened.

"He gave them total hell when they finally took him down. Took a whole bunch of cops and soldiers to get the job done, and Robert went down swingin'. He wasn't a fighter, everybody knew that, but they cornered him, and he wasn't gonna go easy. Gave Travis Tennant the business end of his own camera, right in the face. Pow! And the sheriff? He had scratches all over him, his ear half torn off, like a bear had ripped him up."

In prison Robert's goal was to not look at or speak to a single person. No Dalton in this bunch. The only person who didn't scare the shit out of him was his cellmate, Stan, an older guy and pretty quiet. Stan was in for assault and robbery. He'd been in and out of prison for decades.

"I got a son, too." He nodded at Robert. "Probably about your age now. Probably gettin' into all kinds of trouble, too. Hasn't been around to visit in a long time." He laughed, a veteran smoker's hoarse, phlegmy rumble. His teeth were yellow and sparse. "Next time I see him will probably be out there in the yard. We'll bump into each other."

Robert wished he had some tattoos.

He knew what happened in prison. He tried to plan for what he'd do if Stan came on to him, or if a bunch of guys jumped him in the cafeteria. His plans had always involved running before. Now he didn't know what to do.

The prison doctor who treated his two broken toes and his split lip and his sprained ankle and his bruised ribs and his burns and his concussion and his whiplash said there was an old Adderall prescription in his medical file, and asked him if he wanted it filled. Robert agreed. He tongued the pills for a week at a time, then sold them cheap to his cellmate, who in turn resold them to some younger guys. He used the money to buy paper and a pen. Robert sketched out potential tats, ones he thought he could give himself with the pen, but all his ideas seemed too goofy to permanently etch on his skin. Spider-Man. The Incredible Hulk. Wings.

He pled guilty. No other choice. The public defender's strategy was focused on proving Robert could be molded into an asset to society, and winning him the lightest sentence possible. The judge, she explained, would have a lot of leeway with his sentence. He might get away with time served, probation, and community service. After all, he was a nonviolent offender. She told Robert to work on a letter to the community, a statement about how sorry he was and the lessons he'd learned from his irresponsible behavior. About how he would make restitution and amends.

He spread out in his top bunk and tapped the pen against the paper. He scratched out opening after opening.

Dear everybody. Dear community. Dear island. To whoever ends up reading this stupid thing.

Dear Mom.

He pushed his pen into the wall's cinder-block crags and reminisced about his old high school ISS room's cardboard cubicles.

The. Hearings. Were. So. Slow.

He'd pled guilty, so he wasn't sure why this whole thing was dragging on and on. Not since school had Robert had to sit still in one room for so long and try to listen to someone talk. That he was the subject of the droning and lecturing did not make it any easier.

Robert tried to guess the judge's age. Sixty? Seventy? A hundred and thirty? His red bulbous nose matched his equally red and shiny bald head. His eyes bored into Robert if he so much as breathed loudly.

The public defender had to prod him to sit up, look at the witness, stop spinning in his chair, stop tapping the pen, stop cracking his knuckles, stop jiggling his knee. One day he was chewing a piece of gum, a prison commissary purchase, and his lawyer had demanded he spit the wad into her hand. She held it for a while, tucked under her fingers; right before recess, she stuck it under the table.

She leaned in and hissed, "You're annoying the judge."

Robert shrugged. "I'm pretty sure the judge hates me no matter what."

The public defender threw up her hands and walked away. Robert wasn't sure what to do, so he stayed in his chair, spinning back and forth, for the entire recess.

Photos from the crash sites were a highlight. Robert sat up for those. Holy shit, were those planes wrecked! And the fire! Action movie flames! These photos were the best look he'd ever had at it. He'd been there, of course, but as the sentencing went on and the witnesses paraded forward, Robert started to feel like they were talking about someone else entirely. There'd been a bandit on the loose, a menace stalking the streets and the beaches. Some dude who could cause all this destruction and walk away.

The Lollipop Kid.

He only wished someone had filmed it.

Holt came to visit him. He wore his uniform, his badge. His walkie-talkie crackled.

Robert hadn't been to the visiting area before. Holt was

the first person who'd come to see him. He approached an empty booth, his orange jumpsuit swishing as he walked.

In every cubicle, guys leaned forward, noses practically fogging the glass between them and their visitors. Some whispered. Some laughed. One cried.

On the other side, a little girl in a ponytail and tap shoes danced as her mother angled the phone toward the floor and the father stood so he could see her clacking feet.

Robert sat in the booth. He and Holt both picked up their phones.

Holt spoke first. "How are you? Health-wise?"

Robert decided to smile. "Good. Except for the brain damage. Who are you again?"

Holt didn't laugh, but Robert swore he was wrestling a grin. "Is there anything you need?"

Robert couldn't resist. "A saw. A shovel."

"I meant socks. Soap. Access to a shrink." Holt sighed. "I don't know if anyone has talked to you about this, but people get their GEDs in prison. Some leave with a college diploma. Some end up reading more books than I ever have." Holt leaned forward. "In a way, you're one of the smartest people I've ever come across. I bet you haven't heard that very often. Would you be interested in starting off with your GED?"

"I guess. Yes," Robert revised quickly. He paused. "But

don't you think I'm getting out? Not right away, obviously, but I mean, you don't think I'll have time to earn a whole college degree, do you?"

Holt dodged his eyes. They didn't speak. Across the room the kid in the tap shoes finished her dance, arms spread wide. Her father set down his phone to applaud. Then the girl started the routine all over again.

Robert's throat hurt when he asked, "Is my mom, like, not allowed to come see me or something?"

Holt leaned back in his seat. "She hasn't come?"

Robert shook his head. He couldn't answer. A boulder was lodged in his throat.

"I can only guess that she feels very badly about how everything's turned out, and she doesn't know what to say about it," Holt finally said. His gaze was on the girl as she jumped and twirled. "Maybe she needs more time."

Robert laughed. He wiped at his eyes and hoped Holt didn't notice. "Well, I guess I have that."

"I will look into getting you started in a GED program," Holt promised as he stood. "Maybe you should write her a letter."

"Maybe," Robert said. He thought of all the times he'd started and restarted the apology his lawyer wanted him to write and knew he probably wouldn't. Instead he asked the sheriff, "Do you think you'll ever catch that bear?"

"No. I don't believe I ever will," Holt answered, and then Robert was alone again.

For the sentencing, they made him wear a bulletproof vest, heavy over his orange jumpsuit, like the X-ray bib at the dentist. Robert didn't get it. He hadn't hurt anybody. Why would anyone want to hurt him?

The cuffs chafed his wrists as they led him into the courthouse. A crowd buzzed behind metal barricades. Someone was playing Gull Trouble's song, loud enough to be heard over the crowd. TV news vans were parked haphazardly by the courthouse steps, satellite dishes barnacled to their roofs.

It's Robert Kelley! The kid must be insane!

We represent the Lollipop Kid!

People shouted for his attention like carnival barkers.

"Robert, are you a terrorist?"

"Who taught you to fly?"

"Give us a smile, Lollipop Kid!"

Robert scanned the crowd: the guys who should have been at work but had been laid off, the guys who usually haunted the tavern but had ventured into the sunlight for a peek at the local celebrity; the kids on summer vacation, their eyes red from hours of TV and video games. A teenage girl held a sign, white cut-out letters on red posterboard.

Robert Kelley stole my heart and my plane! Were those actual lip prints, kissed onto the poster by an actual girl's lips? He tried to twist backward to see, hoping maybe he'd catch a glimpse of Mira Wohl, but the officer nudged him forward.

A white paper plane sliced through the air and bounced off the back of his neck. The crowd laughed.

Where was Holt? Why wouldn't Holt show for the sentencing? He'd been there when Robert had gotten expelled. He'd come to visit. A bunch of cops were gathered at the courthouse doors, and Robert wrenched and turned, searching. The grip on his elbow tightened. The sheriff wasn't there.

But his mom was, sobbing right in the front row. Her sniffles and cries were so loud that Robert was embarrassed for her. Just like when he'd gotten expelled. He tried to smile, but she didn't look up as he passed her and sat down.

"Mom!" He tried to get her attention, craning his head over his shoulder. He still had so much to say, but he couldn't do it here. Instead he just offered, "Mom, everything's okay."

She wouldn't look at him.

His shaking knees rattled the shackles that bound his feet.

The judge wasted no time in announcing his sentence. Ten years. Maximum security.

"We've heard some arguments for allowing you to serve your sentence in a less restrictive setting. But you have proven that you are a master of escape and evasion," the judge said. "So the maximum security setting is more than appropriate. Also, a message needs to be sent to the young people of this community and beyond that what you've done isn't funny or cool. Your actions were dangerous and criminal, and you must pay for them."

Cameras flashed. Robert kept smiling. He definitely wasn't crying, even though his throat tightened and his eyes stung. He'd have waved if he hadn't been cuffed. He remembered that mug shot, his wide smile on a T-shirt, and tried to be that kid. The public defender leaned in, gesturing, whispering in his ear, but the words bounced off him.

Holt never showed.

Interview with Mira Wohl, Willamette University cafeteria, October 2, 2010

From *Flight Risk: The Robert Jackson Kelley Story*

"I was outside the courthouse. I told my dad I was at Justine's house. Missed play practice and I found out they were workin' with only three angry men that day. Half the school skipped and went out there. They told us we'd all get a summons for truancy court, but of course that never happened.

"It was too weird. Like we were at some Hollywood premiere, with all those people and cameras. I started tweeting and then people were taking pictures of me, like I was someone important. I was half expecting someone to yell out, 'Mira, who are you wearing?'

"And then after, someone started this rumor that Robert had broken out of jail and was gonna fly again, over the beach. So we set a bunch of bonfires and got drunk on peppermint Schnapps while we waited. Somebody brought a metal detector and started looking for pieces of the planes, but we just found beer can after beer can. Kept looking up at the sky like a bunch of idiots. At first it was all funny. Then after a while, the whole thing started to feel like we'd been in on the joke, but the whole time the joke had been on us."

JUNE 2010

———————————————

Robert had heard a story once. Something for school. A myth or a legend, the teacher had said. He couldn't remember which. About a guy locked in a tower or a castle or something, and to escape he makes these wings. Only they're made of wax. So he jumps out of the tower and he's flapping his wings and he's flying and everything's going great. But he gets too close to the sun, and the wings melt, and he falls into the sea. The end.

In the story, the guy's dad warns him, but he doesn't listen.

EPILOGUE

From *The Beginning Pilot's Flight Guide* (p. 78):

Learning to fly is learning to land.

Mira Wohl's performance as Juror #8 was recognized by the *Yannatok Tide*: "Mira Wohl gave a convincing performance as Juror #8, the play's pivotal character. Ms. Wohl's powerful voice and commanding stage presence have this reviewer convinced she's got a future on the stage." She was awarded a theater scholarship to Willamette University in Oregon. Her father still calls her Meryl Streep, and she has kept her hair cropped. She is reconsidering a career in broadcast journalism.

Joey Kovach was arrested for petty theft after being caught on camera stealing a pair of boxing gloves from a Seattle Gold's Gym. After serving a sixty-day prison sentence, Joey relocated to Tacoma, Washington, where he is employed at a local gas station.

Dalton White was interviewed by the *Seattle Times*, *Outside* and *Rolling Stone* magazines, Nancy Grace, and

Geraldo Rivera, and finally appeared on an episode of *20/20* dedicated to the Lollipop Kid. He wouldn't admit it, but being interviewed made him nervous. He told nothing but the truth and still he sounded like a bad liar. He started carrying one of those tokens he'd jacked from Robert back when they were roommates, one with a wing on it, in his pocket. Steal a little bit of Kelley's nerve.

Each time Dalton appeared on television he wore one of his T-shirts, and each time sales spiked. He made enough money to buy a car and created his own Facebook page swarming with friends he'd never met. He loves the car so much he sometimes spends the whole afternoon just driving circles around the island, but sometimes he thinks longingly back to the one he stole, which, though it was duller and dented, for some reason seemed faster.

Sheriff James Holt resigned from his post on September 11, 2011. He moved with Bandit to San Diego, where he found work training police dogs. On the weekends, he boats.

Debra MacPherson passed her real estate license test on June 7, the same week as Robert's first court appearance, but the only thing she ever sold was her own trailer, before she left for Portland and her new apartment. She took Hulk with her.

Within a week of moving in, the trailer's new owners

called the sheriff's office to report a bear sniffing around the place.

And **Robert Jackson Kelley** is currently serving his sentence in a maximum-security prison. He has reread *Hatchet* and was shocked to learn Brian is rescued and reunited with his father and doesn't spend the winter surviving in the woods on his own. Robert was denied access to a flight manual, despite his claim that he only wanted to figure out where he'd gone wrong in his crash landings.

Robert still dreams about Kumaritashvili, airborne in his sled. Sometimes Robert is in the stands cheering, sometimes Robert is on the sled himself, and always, always, even after a month, three months, six months, Robert wakes up before the sled crashes and has three or four innocent seconds before he realizes he is in prison.

But then he sees the bars. Six march across his only window. Twelve make up the fourth wall of his cell.

Some guys read. Some guys do push-ups. Some guys write the parole board. Most of the guys pad around their cells in prison-issued flip-flops, looking out. Caught animals.

Robert looks up, squinting, straining to glimpse blue sky on gray wall. Shadows play on the ceiling, and Robert watches them like a movie.

Because how could it have gone down like this?

How could *Robert Jackson Kelley, the Lollipop Kid,* be stuck in this prison cell?

Robert spends days rewriting his ending, imagining another scene before the credits roll. Funny how now, without anything else to do, Robert can concentrate just fine, picturing every detail.

He careens down the runway, bullets flying, whizzing, missing him, of course. The engine roars, the cops dive out of his way. He pulls the throttle up, up, up. The plane's nose rises and he takes off, clearing the spruces and the Douglas firs, snapping off the tops neatly. The island shrinks, the vacation houses, the school, the tavern, the stables withering, dwindling into nothing.

There goes the trailer, a smudge out the window. Mr. Drew pauses with a ready arrow, a bow drawn tight, to stare skyward. "My best student!" Dalton White in a parking lot, hawking those T-shirts, thumbs dollar bills, and looks up. Mira Wohl pumps her BMW's brakes, gazes up at the sky, and blows the plane a kiss. Sheriff Holt steps out of his cruiser, his dog sniffing the air, and both squint into the sun, the sheriff offering a sharp salute. In the prison yard, his father points at the plane, a speck beyond the barbed wire. "There's my boy. They'll never catch him!" And his mom, riding on horseback, the horse her own finally, tugs on the reins to stop and smile at the sky.

The plane is his now. He yanks on the throttle, the flight deck needles leap, break through their glass, can't be held down. The windshield shatters, rains down on the beach. The glass flies past his popping ears, disintegrating.

He laughs and swallows the stars like round blue pills, the globe of the moon a lollipop.

AUTHOR'S NOTE

Colton Harris-Moore, also known as the "Barefoot Bandit," eluded the authorities for two years after a series of crimes, including the thefts of several small planes, two cars, and a boat, as well as over a hundred burglaries. A native of Camano Island, Washington, Harris-Moore was seventeen years old at the height of his notoriety and known for leaving barefoot prints at the scenes of some of his crimes, which stretched from Washington state to as far away as Illinois. In 2010, Harris-Moore was captured in a stolen speedboat off the coast of the Bahamas, and served six and a half years in prison. I became aware of Colton Harris-Moore's story while he was still on the run, and remember how even I, a middle school teacher and generally law-abiding citizen, hoped he would not be caught. And I wasn't alone. A Facebook fan club drew sixty thousand members;

T-shirts with Harris-Moore's face printed on them sold on-line. What was it about Harris-Moore's story that made so many people root for him, despite the dangerous nature of his crimes? This question initially inspired Robert Jackson Kelley's story.

ACKNOWLEDGMENTS

There are not enough thank-yous in the world for my mother and father, Linda Zebley-Stump and Joseph McDaniel, who taught me to value education, try new things, and do my best. Thank you for reading to me and always believing in me.

Siblings don't come cooler than my brother, Mike McDaniel. Thanks for your early feedback, sense of humor, friendship, and excellent tunes.

Utmost gratitude to my grandparents, Josephine and Thomas McDaniel, Thomas Zebley, and Sally and John Sitek, who have always cheered me on, broadened my horizons, and loved me no matter what.

Everyone should be so lucky as to have a best friend like Lauren-Alice Lamanna, my first and favorite co-author. Thank you for swapping notebooks and CDs, plotting bands and book series, and twenty-five years of friendship.

Much love to my favorite pen pal, Nathan Tatro, for over a decade of support and friendship.

I should have played the lottery the day Amy Tipton entered my life. Thank you for your positivity, feedback, and work on behalf of me and this manuscript, and for believing in this book.

The entire Roaring Brook team deserves a standing ovation, including Maya Packard, Nancy Elgin, Andrew Arnold, and especially Katherine Jacobs for her excellent editorial insight.

Thanks to all those who read and provided feedback on early versions of this book, particularly Abby Reed and Charles Holdefer.

Special thanks to the many supportive teachers I've been lucky enough to learn from, including Lycoming College's G.W. Hawkes and Rosemont College's Cyndi Reeves, whose input on this project was invaluable.

And last but most certainly not least, words fail to express all the love and gratitude I have for Brian and Zadie Fenn, who inspire me to be better every day. I wrote parts of this book while an infant slept on me, and now that baby is a funny, smart, curious, wonderful little girl. And everyone needs a co-pilot, a partner in adventuring and raising baby sea otters. I'm lucky beyond measure to have found that and more in my husband. Our story is my favorite.

Steve: You're listening to Steve and Mac on KRAW 91.3, and it's 6:45 in the a.m., bright and early here on beautiful Yannatok Island. It's a rainy one out there, gonna stay cloudy and get up to about 63. How's the traffic out there, Mac?

Mac: Backed up on the Yannatok Bridge toward Seattle, free and clear everywhere else.

Steve: Thanks, Mac. These next guys have the number-nine most-downloaded song this week on iTunes and we'll be seeing them next at none other than the Tacoma Dome, opening up at Monday's Dave Mathews Band show. Long way from the Pine Tavern. Wonder if they ever kick any money back to old Robert Jackson Kelley? Here's Yannatok's own Gull Trouble with "Ballad of the Lollipop Kid."